Chopping Block

Bobby Jaye Allen

Accolade Books
Southfield, Mi

This is a work of fiction.
The events described are imaginary.
The setting and characters are fictitious and are not intended to represent specific places or persons.

Library of Congress Control Number: 2003107129

ISBN 0-9712082-2-0

Quality Printing and Binding by
Morris Publishing Company
3212 East Highway 30
Kearney, NE 68847
800-650-7888

Published by
Accolade Books
Southfield, MI 48075-7626
888/318-4794

On the Chopping Block

also by Bobby Jaye Allen . . .

Every First Saturday

Early's Pride

1

Friday evening, June 23rd

"Hello, Penelope."

"You! What are you doing here? Is this a trick? Did you hire that poor, unfortunate person to lure me here?"

"Don't worry, pretty Penny, we're going to take good care of you."

Unwilling to put up with unexpected nonsense, she gathered her purse and books; and, in that final instant, Penelope Powder felt a sudden piercing, searing, blinding blow to the crown of her head—then nothing. She was dead.

A moment of silence was observed. Not out of respect, only the nanoseconds it took to pull an axe from Miss Powder's skull.

"What should I do with the axe?"

"Here. Hand it to me and stand back while I give her a couple of whacks myself."

Another spray of blood and brains followed the dull thud as Miss Powder's freshly styled ash-blonde hair was parted by the violent smashing thrust of the axe. A deep slice across the back of her head finished the job.

"All right, help me wrap up the body and the axe. We'll dump them after we've cleaned up this mess. And, for God's sake, keep your voice down. Your bellowing is enough to wake the dead, and Miss Powder wouldn't like that. You know how librarians are."

✦ ✦ ✦

Saturday morning, June 24th - 7:30 a.m.

Robert! There's a dead body in the shop! I think it's Miss Powder! Please! Come quickly!"

Carolyn Brickley hung up, praying her husband would drive to the bookstore immediately. She'd arrived early to greet the first customers in line for a book-signing session with best-selling author Holly LaFrance. She expected even more of the author's fans would visit her shop when the Founders Day Fair opened at ten across the street in Pride Park. This was supposed to be the biggest day of the year for Brickley's Books. Now what?

Saturday - 7:40 a.m – seven miles away

The soft June morning promised a lovely day. Six places had been set at the Fellmeyer breakfast table, coffee was perking, the griddle primed, and fresh egg bread was sliced and ready for toasting.

Joyce Fellmeyer was sleepy. She and her cousin Claudia had talked until two in the morning catching up and laughing over old times and new. Claudia Packer and her daughter Meggin had arrived in Early late Friday afternoon accompanied by Brady Kincaid.

Today everyone was going to the Early's Founders Day Fair. Then, on Sunday the family, along with Claudia, Meggin, and Brady, planned to drive to the Fellmeyer's lodge in northern Michigan for a week of fishing and relaxation.

Joyce glanced at the dewy grass outside her kitchen window, then across the lawn, where two hundred feet away the Fellmeyer Veterinary Clinic was already accepting patients.

The Fellmeyers moved to Early, Michigan, to launch Donovon's practice close to eighteen years before. Buying the farm on Bonnybridge Road on the outskirts of town had been a gamble. They loved the old two-story white frame farmhouse the moment they saw it, and Donovon was certain the barn could be converted to an animal clinic. It took time and a lot of money but he was right. Now, as Joyce watched, the sun rose over the roof of the clinic, making the newly painted white building shimmer in its light.

Donovon, first up and dressed, gave his wife a kiss. "Looks like a pretty day for the fair. Ought to be a big turnout."

Early's Founders Day Fair drew close to ten thousand people every year and ranked with the Fourth of July and Santa Claus parades in the little city's important events. Held on Pride Park grounds in the center of town, the surrounding buildings—City Hall to the west, the schools on South Park Avenue, the renovated Hotel Erin on the eastern end, and the shops lining North Park Avenue—were always decked with banners, streamers, and huge planters of summer flowers to celebrate Founders Day.

Donovon poured coffee and buttered a slice of toast. "Have to hustle. I want to set things up at the park before the crowd starts arriving." He'd volunteered to work in the Animal Rescue Society's pet adoption booth. They'd placed more than fifty homeless cats and dogs the year before—not bad for a town of fewer than forty thousand. The sad part for Donovon was taking the leftovers back to the shelter.

"Have you heard from Brady?" Donovon had spent only limited time with Brady Kincaid on two earlier occasions, both involving the one-time homicide detective's solving a murder. Yet, they'd formed a kinship, and Donovon looked forward to having Brady along on their fishing trip.

"Not yet. Claudia told me when they dropped Brady off at Lincoln Henderson's condo at the Erin, he didn't bother to say good-bye. I guess the drive from Lombardy was not an especially pleasant one."

"Why not? What happened?"

"Mostly Meggin. She's nearly fifteen and didn't want to come along. There's a boyfriend at home, and a week of fishing and listening to the crickets doesn't sound like fun at that age."

"Our girls don't seem to mind."

"Our girls know where there's a place for teens to hang, and they look forward to that part of the week. You know—maybe a new boy will be there. Stuff like that."

Donovon shook his head, glad that Joyce handled those details of their daughters' lives. The girls were growing up fast. Hannah was planning her Sweet Sixteen party and Steffie was already thirteen.

"Anyway," Joyce continued, "Claudia said that Meggin was just plain obnoxious during the entire four-hour drive. She even got going on Brady—I guess she's aware how he feels about Claudia. Meggin kept harping, without bothering to be subtle, that her dad is a rich and handsome guy; whereas Brady was hired by her mother and is only a glorified security guard for the college."

Donovon was appalled. "That's not fair. Brady is still a first-class homicide detective. What's wrong with Meggin?"

"Misplaced daddy loyalty."

"What does Claudia say about that?"

"Nothing. You know Claudia. She never clamped down on Meggin the way she had to with Rob before he left for college. I don't expect she will ever open up entirely about her marriage to Zack or how she really feels about Brady."

"Poor Brady. I wish he'd meet someone and get over her."

Donovon seldom expressed an opinion about Claudia's marriage to Zack Packer, a man who'd never met an attractive woman he wasn't ready to pleasure in his own personal way. Zack was a great guy to watch a football game with or knock down a couple of beers, and he and Donovon got along well together. But Zack was too restless to sit in a rowboat in the middle of a lake waiting for fish to bite and had begged off coming along on the fishing trip.

Swallowing the last of his coffee, Donovon was ready to leave. "I'll see you whenever you and Claudia stop by the booth, and I'll definitely be home by nine tonight. Love you."

"Love you, too."

Another kiss, and he was gone—first to check on patients at his veterinary clinic next door, then to drive downtown.

Less than twenty minutes later he was on the phone.

"Joyce! There are a half-dozen police cars in front of Brickley's Books. I don't know what's going on but thought you'd want to drive down here in case something happened to Carolyn."

Dear Lord! Her thoughts ran wild; she struggled to collect herself. "I'll phone the bookstore. Maybe it's another break-in."

"You can try, but I don't think you'll get much information that way. They've already strung crime scene tape across the front door."

He was right. Joyce hung up and hurried upstairs to wake her older daughter, Hannah, to tell her where she was going. Then, tapping on the guest bedroom door where Claudia slept, she poked her head inside.

"Sorry to wake you so early, but I have to drive downtown. Donovon just phoned and told me the police are investigating something at Brickley's Books. I must go and find out if anything's happened to Carolyn."

"Do you want me to come along?" Claudia remembered the bookstore from previous visits to Early, as well as its attractive owner, Carolyn Brickley, the lady with the perfect French braids pinned at the nape of her neck.

"You can if you want. But it's probably better if you stay here and bring the girls to the fair whenever all of you are ready. I'll phone you when I can. Maybe it isn't serious." Joyce shrugged and sighed. "Claudia, I'm really sorry. I know I should stay and make breakfast, but . . . "

"Never mind. We'll manage. Go."

During the fifteen-minute drive downtown, Joyce realized once again how lucky she'd been growing up with her cousin Claudia. Constant companions from birth through college in Lombardy, they were separated only after Joyce married Donovon Fellmeyer and moved to Early, two hundred miles away.

It was a great comfort having Claudia visit for a week. They still shared the same values, each worked to maintain her slender figure, and were flattered when someone asked if they were twins. Looking at Claudia was like looking in the mirror except Claudia's hair was dark blond and her eyes were hazel while Joyce had brown eyes and light-brown hair.

Joyce wondered how her cousin had really felt when she turned forty in April. She'd know soon enough. Her own birthday in September wasn't that far away.

Phone calls, e-mails, and visits at least twice a year kept them in close touch, but it wasn't the same as when they were the Carroway cousins of Lombardy, Ohio. *Oh, well,* she thought, *I have Donovon and the girls*, and knew she'd never trade her family for the past.

The broad one-way avenues surrounding Pride Park had been blocked off for the Founders Day Fair. Finding a spot to park behind City Hall, Joyce dashed the rest of the way on foot to Brickley's Books. Her heart leaped as she rounded the corner onto North Park Avenue and saw Carolyn in front of the bookstore being consoled by Donovon.

"Oh, Joyce, I'm so glad you're here." Carolyn left Donovon's arms for Joyce's.

Relieved she wasn't hurt, Joyce asked, "What happened? Did you have another break-in?"

Carolyn could only shake her head while Donovon answered, "Miss Powder, the librarian, was murdered, and Carolyn discovered her body in the bookstore when she opened up this morning. I guess it was pretty gruesome. Her skull was cracked open, and a bloody axe was found on the floor nearby."

"At first they thought I'd killed Miss Powder." Carolyn's voice wavered. "Then the police started questioning Robert."

"Why?"

"Because I phoned him before calling the police. The truth is, I wasn't thinking straight. Joyce, you must swear you'll never tell anyone. I wanted to hide the body until after the fair was over. I thought Robert would figure out where to put her."

Donovon already knew this secret and explained, "Carolyn thought by hiding Miss Powder's body and not reporting the murder immediately, the bookstore wouldn't automatically be shut down as a crime scene. It was important to Carolyn to keep the store open for the big-time author scheduled to show up today to autograph copies of her latest bestseller."

"That's right. Holly LaFrance is in town." Joyce knew how much the book signing meant to Carolyn. She turned to Donovon. "Why can't the autograph session be switched over to the park? I know the fair has a few empty booths left. All we have to do is post a sign on the front door of the bookstore directing everyone across the street. That, and carting a load of books over."

Donovon knew that meant *he* should immediately contact a member of the Founders Day committee about a booth for Brickley's Books. But seeing Robert Brickley coming out of the bookstore after being questioned by police, Donovon waited to hear what he had to report.

Robert Brickley was a handsome silver-haired man in his sixties who'd shared in a scandal that rocked his plastics factory years earlier. He and Carolyn became involved in a torrid love affair within weeks of her being employed in his office. Waiting a decent interval after the first Mrs. Brickley's divorce was granted and gossip had simmered down, the pair was married despite the thirty years difference in age; and Robert happily financed Carolyn's dream of operating a bookstore.

Robert put his arms around his wife. "I guess we're both off the hook for the time being. Detective Newkirk vouched for us and is trying to convince the new lady cop we're not good suspects."

"Who are you talking about? What new lady cop?" Joyce had been elected to city council and was supposed to be kept informed of all new hires for police, fire, or city hall staff.

"Bebout's on vacation, and an officer named Alice Drinker is filling in as Newkirk's partner."

Joyce didn't like the sound of that and, without thinking, blurted, "Brady Kincaid's in town. Should we tell Newkirk? I'll bet he'd like to have Brady's help."

Before the Brickleys had a chance to consider the idea, Donovon shook his head. "I don't know about that. Brady's here to relax and go fishing next week."

"I still think he should at least have a look at the crime scene. What's the harm?"

The Brickleys were in favor of calling on Brady. They remembered he had cracked the homicides of two city officials during his short visit to Early over the Christmas holidays. At the same time he'd solved the break-in at the bookstore, as well as discovering the person who'd been harassing the Brickleys with fax messages.

Donovon conceded half-heartedly. "I guess it won't hurt to tell Brady about Miss Powder. I'll try to get a fair booth on this side of the park so Carolyn's customers can find it."

"I'll help you, Donovon." Robert Brickley switched into executive mode and was ready to put the plan into action. "The bookstore is a member of the Downtown Merchants Association, and I know its director and the head of the fair committee."

Assured Carolyn would be all right without her, Joyce crossed the park to the remodeled Hotel Erin where Brady Kincaid had stayed overnight with his good friend, Lincoln Henderson.

Catching Miss Powder's killer by enlisting Brady to once again help Early's detective squad was high priority, and she couldn't wait to see him.

2

Saturday – 8:35 a.m.

Brady Kincaid seldom drank more than a couple beers at a time, but Friday night, visiting his pal Lincoln Henderson, the pair tied one on.

He faced the big five-oh in a month and wondered what he had to show for fifty years on earth. A wonderful daughter, of course, but his career as a homicide detective had been shot down literally forcing him into disability retirement.

Nowadays, Brady found he was embarrassed admitting to old buddies he'd taken the position of chief of campus security at a small teacher's college. The job lost its luster once he faced the fact that the passion he felt for Claudia Packer, Dean of Students for the college and his boss, was never ever going to be returned.

Lincoln Henderson, a seven-foot giant of a man, was equally distraught, having lost the love of his life, Geraldine Pozy, to the cable news network, CNN.

The pair killed a pint of Cutty Sark in less than six hours and both men, who ordinarily kept their personal problems to themselves, spilled everything to each other. The last thing Brady remembered before passing out was trying to help Lincoln come up with a new name for Hotel Erin. Lincoln had been in charge of remodeling the old building into sixteen luxury condominiums and remained on the premises as general manager. He insisted the opulent new development deserved a name befitting its present grandeur. So far, *Erin on the Park* was the name tossed about most often.

"How about the *Error on the Park*?" Brady had giggled, but seeing his inebriated friend begin to weep at the suggestion, said, "Sorry, I was only trying to help."

The moment the door to Lincoln's suite opened, Joyce knew the men were drunk. The living room was a mess and reeked of cigars. An empty pint bottle of Scotch was on the floor, a half-eaten pizza rested on the coffee table, and Brady was sound asleep on the couch, snoring loudly and still wearing yesterday's shirt and slacks.

Lincoln was nearly sober and thought he fooled Joyce, saying in his deep, resonant voice, "How charming to have you drop by this lovely morning, Mrs. Fellmeyer. To what do I owe the pleasure?"

"Save it, Lincoln. I can tell you both had too much to drink last night, and I wish you hadn't. We need Brady sober. There's been a murder—the town's head librarian—and right now the police are looking at Carolyn Brickley and her husband as possible suspects."

"Why? Mr. and Mrs. Brickley are both decent, law-abiding citizens. Neither would ever kill anyone."

"I know, and that's why we need Brady. Do you mind? Can we wake him up?"

Waking Brady wasn't going to be a breeze, and Lincoln tapped the man's shoulder gingerly. Who knew if Brady was the kind of guy who woke up swinging?

There was no response.

"Honestly, Lincoln, let me try." Joyce was peeved Brady had gotten drunk, and she had no intention of being gentle.

The sleeping Brady Kincaid's cherubic appearance bore no resemblance to the Brady Joyce fondly admired. The tall, lean man with flashing gray eyes and weathered complexion was an appealingly masculine individual who kept himself under control—not this guy who'd ignored his limits.

She was out of patience and grabbed his shoulders, shaking them roughly. "Come on, Brady, wake up. Wake up."

"Huh? What time is it?" Brady looked around. "Where am I?" He saw Joyce and smiled. "Hiya, Joyce. What are you doing here?"

"Make a pot of extra-strong coffee," Joyce barked at Lincoln. "And find some tomato juice and Tabasco sauce. This silly jackass is going to sober up if we have to drain every last ounce of alcohol from his body with a penknife and a long tube."

She had a notion both men had drowned their sorrows over the women in their lives. She felt it was time for Brady to realize Claudia would probably never have an affair with him, and the sooner he got on with his life the better.

Lincoln Henderson was a different story. He'd poured his heart and soul into helping the woman he loved transform her appearance by losing forty pounds. New wardrobe, new hairdo, and lessons in the art of applying makeup further changed Geraldine, the *Early Eagle's* star reporter, forever.

Now, Pozy was gone, leaving Lincoln with bittersweet memories of their first date in February and their moments together every day and every night—until black Tuesday in May, exactly thirty-nine days earlier. She'd left a message on his answering machine that she'd accepted a job with CNN and was about to board a flight to Rome. Pozy's last words were, "I really had a lot of fun with you, Lincoln. Thanks for everything. See ya."

The phone rang. It was Donovon. "Joyce, the police just took the Brickleys to the station to make their statements. Carolyn asked me to ask you if you'd mind overseeing the book-signing, which is supposed to start in less than an hour. I tried to get you off the hook and told her I didn't see how you could possibly manage."

"That's all right. I'll call Claudia. Between the two of us we should be able to handle an autograph session. Did Carolyn say when Holly LaFrance is supposed to show up?"

"Any minute now." He added, "Robert asked me to contact Dyanne Dove. He thinks they'll need an attorney before this is resolved. Of course, suspecting the Brickleys is nonsense."

"I agree. Meanwhile, our ace detective and Lincoln got themselves smashed here in Lincoln's condo last night. So, it'll be a while before Brady shows up at headquarters. By the way, did you get a fair booth?"

"I'm still working on that. Carolyn gave me the keys to her store so you can get in and load up books."

Joyce lined up Claudia for duty, and on her way out of the condo told Lincoln, "Have Brady completely sobered up and delivered to the police station in a half-hour. Then, Lincoln, after you've tended to this lump, will you kindly haul yourself and someone from your staff over to the bookstore to pitch in and help us out. We need a dolly and a couple strong backs to load up several hundred books and have them delivered to a fair booth across the street."

Lincoln knew that wasn't a simple request and he swung into action immediately. He'd been able to sober up faster than Brady, as he hadn't put away as much Scotch and he outweighed his drinking buddy by nearly a hundred pounds.

Brady was still wobbly entering police headquarters a half-hour later. He was full of strong black coffee, tomato juice, oatmeal, and mouthwash, and worked to keep a grip on his balance.

He felt like kicking himself for letting go last night and wondered how big a fool he'd made of himself. He knew he'd blabbed to Lincoln how he felt about Claudia Packer and how, now that she'd been promoted to Dean of Students from her former position as Dean of Women, she'd become totally unattainable.

Maybe Lincoln wouldn't remember. He'd had a lot to drink, too, and had blubbered endlessly about losing his Geraldine.

Early's police headquarters hadn't changed since Brady's visit in late December. It was clean and orderly, but soap and fresh paint didn't make it into an ordinary office workplace. It was a police station, with cells, iron bars, interrogation rooms, old desks, hundreds of file cabinets, and hard wooden benches.

Brady remembered Joyce mentioned Detective Bebout was on vacation and Newkirk's temporary partner was someone named Alice Drinker. He cringed wondering why he'd giggled and asked, "Another Drinker? The more, the merrier."

Regretting Joyce had to see him hung over, Brady hoped he wouldn't bump into Claudia until much later in the day.

After waiting fifteen minutes in the lobby to see Newkirk, he began to feel uneasy. He'd walked through the security metal detector without raising an alarm, registered at the desk, and knew he didn't fit anyone's profile of a terrorist. Nevertheless, it was a relief to see Detective Newkirk bounding out to greet him with hand extended.

"God Almighty, Brady, it's great to see you. When did you get into town? Bebout will be sorry he missed you. He's on vacation."

It was the first time Brady had ever seen Newkirk without his partner, Detective Bebout. The two were like twins—both in their early thirties, both six feet tall, both weighing a trim one hundred-eighty pounds. They had dark hair, hazel eyes, and always wore dark suits, white shirts, and conservative ties.

"I know," Brady answered. "Joyce Fellmeyer filled me in. She wants me to nose around on behalf of her friends, the Brickleys."

Newkirk's face changed. "Oh, you heard, huh?"

Brady nodded. "How bad is it? Do you honestly think either of the Brickleys could have killed this woman? I understand she was the town's head librarian."

"Look, I have complete trust that the Brickleys had absolutely nothing to do with the homicide. It's my temporary partner, Alice Drinker, who's gung-ho and insists on going by the book, not by instinct. She wants to impress the chief with her thoroughness."

"I get it. Should I back off? Maybe the chief wouldn't want me interfering."

"Don't worry about Chief Rygard. He's still asks Bebout and me about you. Like, do we think you'll ever want to move to Early and work in homicide again."

That was encouraging. It was nice to know if his job in Lombardy with Claudia became intolerably uncomfortable, he had a place to land.

"Okay. If you think I can help on this case, why don't you fill me in."

"Great! Come on back to the bullpen and I'll show you what we have. Not much, so far. But that's only because Drinker keeps insisting we concentrate on the Brickleys. Once you and I start moving around, we'll get somewhere."

Brady recognized a few faces that lit up seeing him; and before he sat down, Chief Rygard strode from his office, a big smile on his face. "Are you ready to accept my offer to join Early's force?"

Rygard was anxious to bring Brady into the detective squad. Experience like Brady's would be needed if Early's population continued to grow at a rate of just under ten percent annually, with the unfortunate and predictable increase in crime.

"Not yet, sir. But your offer is still tempting."

"Glad to hear that. Maybe the homicide Newkirk's on right now will persuade you to stick around. It looks juicy. In fact, from what I've learned, it's downright grisly. This'll be a case you'll find interesting. Has to be a lot more stimulating than policing the campus to break up panty raids, eh?" Rygard laughed and walked back to his office.

"What'd he mean *grisly*?" Brady asked Newkirk.

"The librarian's skull was split open with an axe and some of her brains are missing."

"Didn't you find any splattered about in the bookstore?"

"No, and there wasn't any blood on the carpet."

So, she was moved. Aloud Brady asked, "You said *axed.* Did you find the murder weapon? Was it an axe?"

"Yeah. Dried blood was easy to spot, and the county crime scene investigation team is already testing to make certain it's Miss Powder's blood. There was so much blood on the axe, the crime scene boys said it appeared someone smeared it around just for the hell of it."

The chief was right. This case already intrigued Brady. He asked, "What else have you found? Anything close to a motive? And, by the way, how old was this woman? Was she married? I understand Carolyn Brickley found the body when she opened her shop this morning."

"Here's what I learned. Miss Powder grew up here in Early and went to college at Bayside U over by Lake Huron. She came back to Early and started working at the library down on Bank Street. I don't know how long she was on the job before she was promoted to head librarian. The city recently honored her for twenty-five years service in charge of the city's library, so she's about fifty-three or four. She never married, as far as anyone knows, and Drinker's supposed to be trying to locate next of kin." Newkirk glanced across the bullpen. "Uh-oh. Here comes trouble."

He stood and tried to smile as Attorney Dyanne Dove approached.

"Good morning, Newkirk." She greeted the detective, then turned to Brady. "Donovon told me you were in town and that you've been asked to look into Miss Powder's death."

Brady acknowledged that was right. Before he could add more, the gorgeous young attorney turned back to Newkirk.

"All right, let's end this absurdity and cut the Brickleys loose. We both know that young wannabe detective, Officer Drinker, is spinning her wheels trying to interrogate my clients, and it has become very annoying."

Without a word, Newkirk walked into the interview room and announced, "Mr. and Mrs. Brickley, you are free to go. Sorry we inconvenienced you. We'll wrap up our investigation in your shop as quickly as possible, and you should have it back by Monday morning at the latest."

Alice Drinker remained seated and speechless, her mouth open, as Carolyn and Robert left the station with as much dignity as they could manage. The Brickleys had given statements and answered questions that bordered on a nasty interrogation. Carolyn repeatedly explained to a suspicious Officer Drinker why she had no regular full or part-time employees. Her bookstore was seldom busy enough, and she'd never given extra keys to anyone who'd ever helped out.

Carolyn had emphasized, "The cleaning crew shows up every morning at nine, an hour before the store opens. I let them in and catch up with inventory and other paperwork while they vacuum, mop and dust. They're in and out in thirty or forty minutes and have never been given a key."

"Tell me, Mrs. Brickley," Officer Drinker had asked, "what did you do between the time you phoned your husband and his arrival?"

Carolyn tried hard to remember. "I know I paced around a lot and I remember taking another look at poor Miss Powder. That's when I noticed three books on the floor near the bloody axe."

"What did you do then?"

"First, I had the crazy notion Miss Powder had broken into my shop and tried to steal the books. But the books weren't mine. They were all stamped *Property of Early Public Library*."

"Are you saying you handled the books before police arrived?"

"Not exactly. I left them on the floor where I found them and used a tissue to open the covers to see if the books had been stamped library property. Later, when I was able to focus better, I realized none of the three titles were in my inventory."

Officer Drinker appeared skeptical but by the time Carolyn and Robert left police headquarters, they hardly cared what she did or did not believe.

"Thanks, Newkirk." Dyanne Dove smiled after the Brickleys left, then turned to Brady. "I hope to see you again before you leave town. I understand you're planning to go fishing at the Fellmeyer's lodge next week."

"Maybe. Maybe not. This Powder case looks interesting, and I might stick around to see how it turns out."

That was music to Newkirk's ears, but not to Alice Drinker's. She had returned to her desk fuming, ready to have it out with Newkirk. How dare he interrupt her interview and let the Brickleys leave without at least privately telling her in advance what he was going to do? And what about this Kincaid guy? Where'd he come from?

Brady didn't have to be told Alice Drinker was upset and needed time alone with Newkirk to square things. He made an excuse to take a walk. He sympathized with Officer Drinker—it was tough trying to break into homicide without experience. Maybe even harder if you were a woman, and a very attractive one, at that.

Choosing to wear his brand-new light-blue knit shirt and tan chinos this morning seemed like an excellent idea now. Brady couldn't remember the last time he'd taken a second look at a woman. Yes, he could. It happened the first time he met Claudia Packer.

But Alice Drinker was probably too young. She appeared to be in her late twenties, and Brady was practically fifty. Maybe it worked for the Brickleys, but they were the exception. Nevertheless, Brady was drawn to this person with eyes as green as a cat's, a soft olive complexion, shiny black hair, and a long, slender torso. He guessed her to be about five-eight and maybe a hundred-twenty pounds. Other than that, he told himself, nothing special.

Another voice asked, *Who do you think you're kidding? That lady's got you wanting her, and you haven't even been properly introduced.*

3

Saturday – 9:15 a.m.

Brady tried to pay attention to what Newkirk was telling him during the short walk from police headquarters to Brickley's Books; but his mind was on Alice Drinker, who chose to walk ahead of them. He liked her style—her well-cut regulation slacks, crisp blue shirt; her long, lustrous hair pulled back out of the way. He wondered if she was married or seeing someone and how he'd find out.

It had been more than a dozen years since Brady's ex-wife pulled the plug on their stormy marriage. Having dated a number of women since then, he found he used his former wife as the standard against which he judged all women. If they showed signs of being even half as nasty-tempered, sarcastic, or demanding, he dove for cover.

They reached the bookstore, where yellow crime scene tape stretched across the front door. A hand-written note was taped to the show window for customers who showed up at the store to read. *Brickley's Books is still open for business but has temporarily moved into a fair booth across the street. Miss Holly LaFrance will be signing her latest book as promised and you can meet her at ten o'clock in the booth. See you then and there!!*

The gray silence inside was creepy in contrast to the sunny day and the noise from the fair across the street. Newkirk flipped on lights and showed Brady where Miss Powder had been found slumped over the coffee bar.

Brady flashed back to the first time he walked into the bookstore six months earlier. It was his first visit to Early, and he'd bought a street map from Carolyn. He remembered thinking how cozy and well-arranged the shop was.

It hadn't changed. Easy-to-read section signs were still posted, browsing benches between stacks were still available, and the counter was skillfully cluttered with reading suggestions. Brady noted the lounge section, with couches and coffee tables that invited customers to sit awhile and chat, was undisturbed. However, the coffee bar and stools, where Miss Powder had been dumped, looked untidy, obviously from the county coroner's men hauling the body away. The county's criminologists had also come and gone having gathered all the evidence they needed for processing.

"Whoever killed Miss Powder placed her on that bar stool and laid what was left of her head on the bar." Newkirk had to control his gag reflex, remembering the condition of the split-open skull.

"Were photographs taken before the body was carried away?" Brady wanted to see exactly what Carolyn Brickley found.

"Yes, sir," Alice Drinker replied. "I took a full set of Polaroids. They're back in the department to look over when you're ready."

Officer Drinker had been informed Brady Kincaid was formally consulting for Early's Police Department and she could like it or lump it. She was still undecided.

"Thanks, Alice. That'll be a big help." Brady felt the chilly attitude and hoped Officer Drinker would thaw out soon.

Walking around the bookstore looking for anything that appeared out of line, he inhaled deeply. "Do either of you notice the distinct aroma of perfume? Was it the victim's?"

Alice replied, "That's one of the first items we picked up on. We established this scent does not belong to either Brickley."

"Good work. What about the corpse? Is it possible her perfume was so strong it still lingers?"

Newkirk shrugged. "Hard to determine. The odor was stronger away from the body, especially in the storeroom."

"Excuse me." Alice heard a thump coming from the rear of the store and left to investigate. In a moment she was back, dragging seven-foot Lincoln Henderson by the ear.

"*Ouch*," Lincoln complained, "you're pinching too hard." Seeing his friends, he grinned. "Good morning, Newk. Well, Brady, I guess you met another Drinker, huh?" He was still a little tipsy.

Alice saw no humor in the question. "Just what were you doing in the Brickley's storeroom That's part of a crime scene and you're forbidden to cross crime scene tape." She told Newkirk, "I caught him loading books onto a Hummer parked in the alley."

"He wasn't stealing. Mrs. Brickley wants those books hauled to her booth at the fair, and Lincoln's helping her out." Newkirk turned to Lincoln. "Good to see you, man. What do you hear from Pozy?"

Lincoln's face fell. He hung his head. "Another time. Okay?" He collected himself. "May I go now? I'd like to finish loading these books and get this job over."

Newkirk nodded. "Sure. Talk to you later when you feel better."

Walking to the storeroom with Lincoln, Brady noticed the scent was decidedly stronger and asked, "Can you identify that brand of perfume?"

"Not especially. Geraldine sent me some after shave from Italy that's similar."

Mentioning *her* name was still difficult for Lincoln, and Brady changed the subject. "I don't know how long I'll be working on this case, but I'm certain now I'm not going fishing with the Fellmeyers next week."

Lincoln understood. "You'll need a place to sleep and a car to drive. That's no problem. You can stay in the extra bedroom at my place, and the condo association has courtesy cars just sitting around waiting to be driven."

After Lincoln and his helper finished loading books and drove away, Alice joined Brady in the storeroom. Examining the back door lock, he asked her, "What about the doors and locks?"

"That's the odd part. Mrs. Brickley said when she opened the back door from the alley this morning she was surprised the key turned so easily, as though the door wasn't locked. Of course, she forgot all about that when she discovered Miss Powder. But later, she found the front door's thumbturn in vertical position. In other words, the front door wasn't locked either, and Mrs. Brickley is positive she locked both doors and turned on the alarm system when she left last night."

Alice checked her notepad. "I called the alarm company. They recorded Brickley's alarm system was activated at 9:07 p.m. last night, which jibes with Mrs. Brickley closing for the night. The alarm was deactivated at 7:27 a.m. this morning when Mrs. Brickley entered the back door and flipped the alarm switch off."

Newkirk had joined them. He pointed to a well-concealed switch close to the rear door and mentioned a second switch was installed near the front door. "This alarm system is the simplest made. You don't have to punch in a code; just flipping the switch sends a signal to the alarm company. Mrs. Brickley said she chose that system because between all her bank and credit card PIN numbers she didn't want to have to remember another one."

Brady learned the alarm would have been triggered if either door had been opened during the period between 9:07 Friday night and 7:27 Saturday morning.

"Is there a chance the alarm company missed a signal? Maybe the person watching the monitor took a break?"

Alice didn't think so. "Besides an employee who watches the monitor, there's a computer readout much like an electrocardiogram that records the slightest quiver of either door. The readout for Brickley's Books was negative for the entire period."

Brady shook his head as if to clear it. "We're fairly certain Miss Powder wasn't murdered here in the store. However, you're telling me there's no record of anyone trying to break into the store, turning a doorknob, or even rattling either door between the time Mrs. Brickley left last night and arrived this morning. So, tell me, how did someone gain access to the bookstore, dump Miss Powder's body, then exit without opening a door?"

Newkirk reminded Brady, "You once said you loved puzzles. Well, this one's a whopper."

Obtaining fair booth space for Brickley's Books meant dealing with the Founders Day Fair committee co-chairperson, Marva Greeves.

Marva took the rules and regulations for booth registration seriously and told Joyce and Donovon, "There are no exceptions. The instructions clearly state you must be registered twenty-four hours in advance of the start of the Founders Day Fair to receive and occupy booth space."

The Fellmeyers argued that since Brickley's Books had been closed by emergency police order an exception must be made. After wasting time in fruitless sparring with Marva, they'd gone in search of the executive director of the organization sponsoring the fair, Clement Codd.

Codd had been on the job with the Downtown Merchants Association close to four years and feared he'd never find another position. His predecessors always moved on within two years, but Clement Codd, try as he might, could not find another job.

Now, asked to tangle with Mrs. Greeves, Codd felt his ulcer start grinding. He wanted to go home, stick his head in the oven, and never again have to deal with that little troublemaker. Unfortunately, the stove in his apartment was electric.

Instead, he followed Councilwoman Fellmeyer's suggestion that he poll the other members of the fair committee. With the exception of Marva Greeves, the rest of the committee agreed, in light of the circumstances, an exception should be made for Brickley's Books. Booth space was instantly granted.

The next hurdle was finding a location easy for Holly LaFrance's fans to find. Nursing her newest grudge, Marva took delight in assigning the bookstore to Booth 54 in the southwest corner of Pride Park, as far from Brickley's Books on North Park Avenue as she could find.

Joyce told Carolyn, as they made their way through the park, "Just wait till Marva Greeves appears before city council to renew her appointment to the board of the Downtown Merchants Association. I will make very certain that nasty never-was regrets the way she handled this situation."

Joyce felt guilty wondering if the trouncing she'd given Marva Greeves when they both ran for city council had played a big role in her trying to deny booth space for Carolyn's bookshop.

"Joyce, it's not you and the rivalry with Mrs. Greeves. It's not the booth at all. And it's not finding Miss Powder's body that's jinxed the day."

Joyce didn't understand. "What are you talking about?"

"I'm talking about yesterday's *Early Eagle.* I didn't get a chance to read the review section until someone gave Robert a copy this morning. Here, see for yourself."

Joyce took the clipping of *On the Chopping Block.* The syndicated column, created by a critic who called her or himself *Chanuary*, was devoted to what the columnist delighted in stating were reviews of the worst books ever published.

"Read the underlined parts. You'll get the idea."

Joyce cleared her throat and read, "'*The latest garbage from Holly LaFrance . . .*'" She stopped and remarked, "Her books aren't garbage. I've read several and thoroughly enjoyed each one."

Carolyn shook her head. "Read on, please. It only gets worse."

> "'*Ms. Holly LaFrance has once again rewritten her first so-called epic. In this re-hash, the setting is the early nineteenth century in the Upper Peninsula of Michigan, where a family settles following a hectic voyage from a village in Norway. After two hundred thousand words of toil and trouble, accidents, diseases, deaths, marriages, births, and, oh yes, a murder or two, the author finally succeeds in putting this reeking, rambling wreck to rest.*
>
> "'*The Upper Peninsula of Michigan is famous for its year-round beauty, and I trust someone will write a book worthy of the region. In the meantime, I have to say this story about the area affectionately known as the U.P. is strictly a Pee-U.*
>
> "'*A record low rating of Five Chops for* Farewell, Fjords.'"

Joyce didn't know what to say and wondered why the *Early Eagle* printed the nasty review on the eve of the author's personal appearance. She'd have a word with the editor, Bob Oden, at her earliest opportunity. Meanwhile, it seemed important to give as little credence to the review as possible.

"Carolyn, I don't think Holly LaFrance's fans will pay attention to this column. It isn't Chanuary's opinions that make the *Chopping Block* so popular. We only read it for the bizarre and occasional witty comments like 'reeking, rambling wreck to rest.'" Chuckling in spite of herself, Joyce asked, "Come on, Carolyn, when was the last time a grownup wrote 'Pee-U?'"

Carolyn could not be consoled. "It's not just the newspaper. Chanuary is quoted all over the Internet. This is going to ruin the day. I ordered five hundred extra copies of *Farewell, Fjords* for this event along with what I hope are enough of Miss LaFrance's earlier novels for fans who want autographed copies." She sighed. "What am I going to tell her when no one shows up?"

"It's not your fault. You're not responsible for this review, though I'd like to know why this Chanuary came down so hard on *Farewell, Fjords.* It just wasn't that bad."

They reached the booth and were surprised nearly two dozen women were already lined up waiting for Holly LaFrance to appear. Twenty-four women meant the sale of twenty-four copies of *Farewell, Fjords*, barely a dent in the five hundred on hand. Carolyn hoped she wouldn't start crying.

4

Saturday – 9:40 a.m.

Early's public library occupied the southeast corner of the municipal complex that had been built nearly a century earlier. Completely renovated within the last decade, the library appeared brand-new. With its entire basement devoted to children's books, the two-story brick library was conveniently located only a street's-width west of Early's schools. Every student had visited the library at one time or another, and every student, past and present, knew Miss Powder.

The library's small staff—Miss Powder's assistant, two part-time staff members, and two summer interns, Becka and Tony—had been summoned to the library's main desk by the detectives.

The news of Miss Powder's death brought identical shocked reactions. Penelope Powder had been an institution in Early, a staunch enforcer of good behavior and respect for property, especially books. She insisted on everyone having clean hands before they could touch her library books. Students, and an occasional adult, were sent to the restroom to wash and thoroughly dry their hands if they appeared soiled under Miss Powder's close scrutiny.

Brady got the impression no one loved Miss Powder; that their respect was mingled with fear. "Did anyone have an argument with Miss Powder lately? Did she have an enemy you think could have committed murder?"

All shook their heads. It was obvious the regular library employees weren't going to tell anyone anything about Miss Powder. But Brady had a notion the intern might spill a few beans and asked,

"Tony, would you mind showing me around the library?"

Wandering about the lower level away from the rest of the staff, Brady said, "Okay, Tony. I know you have something to say. Let's hear it."

He hesitated. "It isn't that Miss Powder had enemies. She was super-strict, but no one really minded. She had her rules and only a few jokers played tricks on her. But you have to believe none of that stuff was meant to kill her."

At last, something interesting. "All right, Tony, you've opened the door. Now you'll have to give me the details of these so-called tricks."

Tony was clearly sorry he'd said anything. "I hate getting anyone in trouble. Even Miss Powder didn't report those guys."

"If that's so, then there's no problem and it won't go past me. Deal?"

The young man muttered an unconvincing, "Deal." He took a breath and said, "Sometimes a guy would turn in a hollowed-out book that held a snake or a toad. It was supposed to scare Miss Powder when she opened the book to stamp it *Returned.*"

"That's it?"

"Someone might bring a bag of marbles to the library and spill them on the floor to make a racket. Miss Powder hated loud noise."

Brady remembered the dumb pranks he and his pals thought were clever back in high school. "How'd Miss Powder get along with you and the rest of the staff?"

"Okay, I guess. She was nice to let me intern at the library for the summer. I'm an education major at Michigan State, and Miss Powder knew it. She said I might want to reconsider when the summer was over." Tony stared into space and added, "She could be right. I really like working around books."

Alice Drinker came halfway downstairs. "Kincaid! Where are you? Newkirk and I are leaving. Do you want to come along?"

He guessed so and shook Tony's hand. "Thanks for your time, and good luck with your career, whatever you choose."

✦ ✦ ✦

Newkirk led the way to the library's parking lot to check Miss Powder's 1956 Austin Healey roadster. He told Brady, "Miss Powder's employees remembered her car wasn't in the parking lot when they closed the library last night at nine o'clock. However, when they reported for work this morning, it was parked there where you see it. They assumed Miss Powder had arrived at the library early."

"Weren't they surprised she wasn't around even though her car was in the lot?"

"They said it wasn't unusual for Miss Powder to arrive early and walk over to Brickley's Books. Sometimes she stopped at the bakery near Brickley's and brought back cinnamon buns for the staff."

That accounted for why the staff was so completely surprised when they learned she was dead.

Newkirk added, "Those librarians are extremely closemouthed not only in *what* they say but *how* they say it. You know, *very, very* quietly. Were you able to understand everything they said, Alice?"

"Most of it. Did you notice it didn't take them long to decide not to shut the library down in honor of Miss Powder's memory?"

Newkirk nodded. "They might have been shocked she was murdered, but not one showed any sign of mourning."

"Exactly," Alice agreed. "My impression was Miss Powder kept her relationships with the rest of the staff on a professional level. Her personal life was completely separate, and no one had any idea how she spent her leisure time or where she went on vacation. They all said Miss Powder *devoured*—that's the word they used—books and believed she read at least two books a day."

"During library hours?" Brady thought that was stretching the job description a bit.

"I guess so. Miss Powder told them she evaluated each book, whether to make it a part of the library's inventory."

"So, we now have a tiny window into the victim's personality. What about her desk? What'd you find in the drawers?"

Newkirk deferred to Alice again. "First, Miss Powder kept her desk locked—maybe to prevent anyone messing up her system. The drawers were rigidly neat but we found nothing helpful. They held only supplies, like blank library cards, blank computer disks, book mending tape. That sort of thing."

Alice opened her notepad. "The staff mentioned Miss Powder checked out four books yesterday and that's a problem. Mrs. Brickley said she found only three books with the body. I'm going to check with the crime lab again for their exact count." She paused then added, "Miss Powder's assistant asked when we thought the books could be returned from the evidence room at headquarters."

"Is there a hurry?"

She shrugged. "They wrote down the names of the books and said one, *Street Monkeys,* was a current bestseller and certain to be a popular request at the library."

"Don't forget the appointment book," Newkirk reminded Alice.

"That's right. There was a notation for seven-thirty last night. It said *Pic at Z's Studio. Take coupon.*"

Newkirk explained, "We think that means she had an appointment with the new portrait photographer, Randall Zebner. He handed out a bunch of $10-off coupons to try to drum up business. Coincidentally, his studio is next to Brickley's Books, where the antiques shop used to be. Remember?"

Newkirk was referring to the store on North Park Avenue once owned by the woman whose murder Brady helped solve during his first visit to Early.

Alice turned her back, and Brady knew she felt left out whenever Newkirk referred to past cases. *Too bad. I hope she'll get used to me.*

Newkirk broke into Brady's thoughts. "I think we ought to interview the store owners and employees on North Park Avenue now. I'd like to know if they noticed anything funny last night."

He asked Alice to take the beauty shop next to the bookstore and keep checking the photographer's studio on the other side in case he opened up.

"I'll take the drugstore on the corner and the hardware store if you'll take the other end, Brady." He meant the grocery store, the bakery, and the little variety shop.

Brady's first stop was the variety store, whose owner said he'd closed his shop at eight Friday night in order to carry goods over to the park to his Founders Day Fair booth. He'd seen nothing.

No one at the grocery store remembered seeing anything unusual in front of the bookstore or in the alley behind it. The manager told Brady, "We put a box of day-old bread in the alley about ten o'clock for the charity kitchen to pick up. Ten minutes later I heard someone pawing through the box and went out to chase her away."

"You know who it was?"

"Sure. It happens all the time, and we've warned the woman we're going to call the police if she doesn't stop." Watching Brady make notes, the manager told him, "I don't think that had anything to do with Miss Powder's death."

Brady put his notepad away and stopped at the bakery. The baker's wife remembered him from his first visit to Early and insisted on giving him a box of fresh cupcakes. She also gave him some interesting information.

"We expect to sell a lot of pastries to people attending the fair, so we worked extra late Friday to get a jump on Saturday's business. Around nine last night I tossed the trash into our dumpster in the alley, and I saw a little cream-colored convertible parked with a traffic ticket stuck under the windshield wiper."

She explained alley parking was restricted to sixty minutes.

"I didn't think much about it, since the street in front had been blocked off to traffic because of the fair. When my husband and I left about a half-hour later, the little car was still there and my husband said it belonged to the lady who runs the library.

"We went home for a few hours sleep then came back to the bakery. When we pulled into the alley around five this morning, the little car was gone. I remembered the ticket and wondered if the librarian's car had been towed away. You can imagine how surprised and shocked we were when we heard she'd been murdered and her body found in Carolyn's bookstore."

Brady thanked the woman and hooked up with Newkirk and Alice to return to police headquarters, where the cupcakes disappeared in minutes.

Newkirk's interviews had yielded nothing; and Alice, after checking Zebner's Studio front entrance as well as the alley door, decided she'd have to try to find him at the fair.

She reported the beauty parlor had stayed open later than usual Friday night and opened early Saturday morning. The owner had explained, "Everyone wants to look good for the fair. In case it makes any difference, I personally shampooed and styled Miss Powder's hair during her lunch hour Friday."

Interviewing the hair stylists separately, Alice found two who'd seen Miss Powder's roadster parked in the alley when they left the shop at nine-thirty the night before.

The third operator, Sally, told Alice, "My appointments got backed up so I didn't leave the shop until after ten last night. As I walked down the alley to the public parking lot on High Street, I saw Marva Greeves running through the alley. She'd probably been snooping through the market's charity box again."

"Whatever for?" Alice wondered.

"If you knew Marva Greeves, you'd understand. She's been called eccentric, but she's more than odd. Marva is financially comfortable, yet she helps herself to whatever she can get away with. She has a grudge against nearly everyone—the entire city council, Miss Powder and the rest of the library board, and even Carolyn Brickley, because she and Miss Powder got along so well with each other."

"Did you know Miss Powder very well?"

"Not really, but neither did anyone else. Miss Powder was sort of a town character. She didn't have close friends and didn't seem to want any. That's why her stopping at the bookstore and visiting with Carolyn Brickley regularly was surprising."

That completed her report and Alice closed her notepad.

With this new information, Newkirk decided to make a flow chart of events according to time as reports came in. Something was off, and he thought the chart could help them spot it. He also made a note to check exactly what time the parking ticket had been written for Miss Powder's car.

After reviewing his messages, Newkirk phoned the county medical examiner's office. "Okay if we come by now to catch up with your preliminary exam?" He nodded, then asked Brady and Alice if they wanted more coffee before heading over to the county offices in Dover.

Brady shook his head and Alice answered, "You guys go ahead. I've already seen the victim and don't want to be around if Newkirk starts gagging again when he sees what's left of Miss Powder's brains. I'd rather visit her home to see what I can scare up there. Is that all right with you, Mr. Kincaid?"

She's not going to cut me any slack at all. Aloud, Brady said, "Fine with me, but Newkirk's the one you have to check with."

Newkirk didn't care and, in fact, was happy she wasn't tagging along. Drinker's attitude rubbed him the wrong way, and he wished his regular partner would miraculously return from vacation early.

Traffic was light on the eight mile drive to Dover. The cities of Early, Dover, and Solo formed an inverted triangle with Early at the southern tip. Solo was nearly eight miles to the northeast and Dover was located directly west of Solo at the northwestern point.

Less than twenty minutes later, their footsteps echoing through the nearly empty county office building, Brady and Newkirk entered the morgue and greeted the medical examiner.

"Here she is."

Penelope Powder had been autopsied; and, not surprisingly, the fifty-four-year-old woman died of massive brain injuries caused by the blow of an axe.

"The first blow killed her instantly. The second and third cuts, made from different angles, were superfluous and definitely examples of overkill."

"What do you mean, second and third cuts?"

"The killing blow, which came from behind the victim, landed on top of her skull. The lady was only five-foot-one, so anyone five or more inches taller than Miss Powder could have struck that blow from behind very easily. The second cut was dealt by someone standing in front of her and slicing a straight line down the middle of the top of her head, starting at her hairline. The third cut was delivered to the back of her skull in line with her ears."

The medical examiner paused, sorry to have to report, "The second and third blows were both driven two inches deeper into Miss

Powder's skull than the initial blow and were delivered post-mortem. My best guess is they were struck by a second person standing close to the body—first in front, then behind—taking big, vicious, deliberate swings both times."

He respectfully covered Miss Powder's face with a sheet. "You fellows probably already know she wasn't killed in the bookstore. She was moved from the killing scene and was dropped along the way. Both ankles were fractured post-mortem. I'd guess she was dropped from a fairly steep height. The crime scene boys will figure that out for you."

"What about drugs in her system?" Newkirk asked.

The medical examiner shook his head. "I'll run a tox screen, but I'm positive we won't find anything in this lady. Her general health was excellent. Look at her fingernails. She didn't wear press-ons—only clear nail polish. Notice how strong and healthy her nails appear."

Newkirk remembered, "When I was a kid and had to go to the library, I always avoided Miss Powder. She was the kind of lady you knew disapproved of boys, and I never really looked at her until now. She was a pretty lady and kept herself in good shape. This is a damn shame." He turned to Brady. "I'm glad you're here. Miss Powder deserves to have her killer caught and strung up for doing this to her."

Brady interrupted before Newkirk became more emotional. He asked the M.E., "What about her clothes and other personal effects?"

"Crime lab's got them. They came across some other business you fellows will be interested to hear. You better hustle. They try to close their office early on Saturday."

They thanked him and hurried upstairs to the crime scene investigators' office.

Newkirk was greeted at the door by Jeffrow Heepe.

"Look who's finally here."

There were handshakes all around and Brady was introduced to the criminologist.

"Well, Newk, you're going to thank us. As usual, we probably cut two weeks off your investigation." The smiling, tousle-haired criminologist wore thick glasses and resembled a movie-version mad scientist.

"The M.E. said you found something interesting."

"It won't solve your case, but it's fairly conclusive your killers planned this murder in advance and knew a bit about forensic evidence."

"*Killers?* As in more than one?"

"Yep. First, regarding fingerprints—the storeroom and sales area were wiped clean on and around the doors and at the coffee bar where the victim was found. Only the owner's fingerprints were found where she touched the doorknob and light switches when she entered the shop early this morning. Her office wasn't wiped clean, indicating the killers didn't enter that room."

Neither Brady nor Newkirk interrupted, knowing Jeffrow would relate his findings in his own way.

"As far as the weapon—the axe—goes, it's a standard four-pounder with a twenty-four inch handle and six-and-a-quarter inch head. Take a look."

Jeffrow laid the murder weapon across his desk. "See, you can tell by the weathering of the handle and all the nicks on the head, it's probably fifty or sixty years old. There's a bit of distortion on the back of the handle where someone whittled away, then tried to sand down the rough edges. This tool saw plenty of service once but has accumulated a lot of rust since. Even the brand label is partially worn away, though I was able to determine it was made by Niter Tools, a company that went out of business about twenty years back."

Brady ran a finger along the blade. "This blade is dull."

"That's right, and that means the blows were struck with a great deal of force."

Newkirk wondered aloud why the blade hadn't been sharpened.

"The killers were cautious," Brady responded. "First, they used an old axe instead of buying a new one that could be traced back to the manufacturer and to the store where it was sold which might identify the buyers. Not using an axe grinder's services to sharpen the blade, no matter how far away from Early, makes a simple nationwide police query useless."

"Here's a tidbit for you," Jeffrow announced. "Both persons handling the axe wore latex gloves and we're certain the person striking the first blow held the axe handle at the end to deliver the blow to the top of Miss Powder's head. That person has sweaty palms. A trace of talcum powder was found near the end of the handle. The second person held the axe like a tomahawk, closer to the head and, lucky for us, did not obliterate the trace of talcum."

The crime lab investigator looked at his notes. "It appears the killer who delivered the first and deadly blow tested the blade with his index finger just as you did, sir." He nodded to Brady. "He didn't leave a fingerprint behind since he wore gloves. Testing the blade's sharpness was his first and worst mistake. The blade, dull as it is, cut a tiny tear in the glove's index fingertip. When he gripped the end of the handle for leverage and swung, a trace of talcum powder, along with a minute gram of his sweat, oozed through the glove's tear."

"Did you collect enough sweat for a DNA test?"

"Maybe. The real question is if the evidence became compromised at any point before or during transfer, making a DNA test invalid." Jeffrow paused, then asked, "Are you aware the victim's body was dropped post-mortem?"

They were, and he continued. "My calculations indicate the victim was dropped feet-first from a height of no less than twelve feet, meaning that she may have been dropped from the roof of a commercial building."

"This is weird." Newkirk asked, "Do you think she was killed in someone's office and, instead of being carried downstairs or using an elevator, Miss Powder was simply dropped out a window or off a roof? Then, did they gather her up from wherever she landed and take her to Brickley's Books?"

Jeffrow laughed. "That's what you boys are paid to find out—and good luck with that one. By the way, here's what I meant by the killers knowing something about forensic evidence. We picked up white cotton fibers from the carpeting in the bookstore's sales area.

There were two sets, indicating two people, and we've determined the fibers come from athletic socks. In other words, your killers wore white socks over their shoes when they entered the bookshop and walked around."

He didn't have to explain by wearing socks over shoes prevented trace evidence from their shoes being left behind.

"This case just gets better and better. What other good news do you have for us?" Newkirk was beginning to feel bowled over.

"One of the persons, whom we believe to be a man, carried Miss Powder slung over his left shoulder, because his left foot made a deeper impression in the carpet than his right foot. His shoe size is ten and a half. "

"How about the second killer?"

"We found nothing useful in the way of shoe or fingerprints."

"Any shoeprints in the storeroom?"

"That has a tile floor, and no useful shoeprints were found."

That seemed to be the extent of Jeffrow Heepe's report until he asked, "By the way, did either of you notice the strong scent left behind in the storeroom and sales area? We established the perfume doesn't belong to the bookshop owner or her husband, and it didn't come from the victim, either."

Brady asked, "What are you driving at?"

"There's a specialized occupation known as a *Vrai Nez,* which translated means *true nose.* They're especially valuable in the perfume industry, as they can tell just by smelling what ingredients make up a particular fragrance. A *Vrai Nez* could identify that brand of perfume or cologne, narrowing down your list of suspects."

"That's news. Where would we find such a person?"

"I'd get on the Internet, and fast, before the scent in the bookstore fades away completely."

5

Saturday – 10:45 a.m.

Joyce hurried across the park from Booth 54 to Brickley's, where Claudia stood watch. It was her third trip to see if anyone else had stopped at the store to buy an autographed book, and she told Claudia, "It's written all over Carolyn's face how badly she feels about the low turnout so far. I wish we could do something."

"How's the author taking it?"

Joyce shrugged. "Hard to measure. She's very animated, and if she's disappointed, it doesn't show."

"Good for her. What about that famous agent of hers? What's his name? Worthington something. I believe he was an English lit professor once."

"I know who you mean. Worthington Smitterly. Miss LaFrance said he attended a book fair in Muskegon yesterday and didn't reach their hotel until the middle of last night. She said he's sleeping in and will join us later."

"Great. I've heard so much about him and his wonderful lectures. I'd like to invite him to guest lecture at Lombardy if his fee isn't too steep."

Joyce smiled. "That must be one of the nicer perks of being promoted to dean of students. You don't have to go though Dan Dunne anymore."

"Nope. I just do what I darn please when I darn please."

"What about Mary? What's she going to do?" Joyce was referring to Mary Canova, Claudia's assistant during her two years as dean of women.

"I don't know. She'd set her heart on becoming dean of women when I stepped up to full dean. When someone from outside was picked over her, she was devastated."

"Couldn't you have helped her?"

"I tried. But, Joyce, the truth is Mary has only two years work experience and that was as my assistant. She was fresh out of Ohio State when I hired her, and she's never taught a class in any subject. That's important at a teachers college. The trustees felt two other candidates were better qualified. They had teaching credentials, experience in school management, and both were pleasant, decent, intelligent individuals."

"What will Mary do now?"

"I offered her the job of assistant in my new office if she'll take it. She thanked me and said she'd let me know when she came back from June break. I know she won't work for the new dean of women. There's a good chance we'll lose her, and I'll be very sorry to see her go."

"Plus you'll have to go through the wringer of looking for a new assistant again."

Claudia groaned. "Don't even think about that."

A close friend and Brickley's Books regular, Mandy Morning, approached. "I just came from Carolyn's booth, and everything appears to be running smoothly considering the terrible circumstances."

She exchanged more chitchat then excused herself. "I'm going to spend the rest of the day with the cast of the founder's family play. There are a few new cast members, and I want to run their lines with them again before the curtain goes up at seven."

Mandy was the fifth generation of the founding Early family, and it was important to her that her ancestors be portrayed as professionally as amateurs could.

"By the way," she added as she left, "Holly LaFrance's agent showed up. I'm certain the word *pontificate* was invented just for him."

As they returned to Booth 54, Joyce whispered to Claudia, "Mandy's right about Smitterly, and I'll add *bombastic* to the list. Listen to that man speak."

Claudia watched Worthington Smitterly hold forth to a group of nearly fifty enthralled women. "I think *grandiloquent* describes the professor better, and I can't wait to corner him to see if he has an opening this fall to guest lecture at LTC."

The cousins stepped closer to the circle of women surrounding Smitterly. An interview was being conducted by a local radio announcer, who'd asked him, "What effect do all those negative book reviews written by Chanuary have on Miss LaFrance and the sales of her books?"

Smitterly, elegant in cream-colored suit with shirt, tie, shoes and socks to match, pulled himself taller than his usual five-foot-ten-inch height and beamed broadly at the admiring circle around him.

"First, let me tell you I look forward to Chanuary's reviews. I enjoy them from a literary point of view. I know he or she has dug deeply into a well-worn thesaurus to come up with all the dark and nasty adjectives spewed out in those crudely constructed, badly written reviews."

He stroked his precisely trimmed mustache. "Miss LaFrance's publisher has sales figures showing that every time one of Chanuary's vitriolic reviews of Miss Holly's books appears, sales go through the roof. An *On The Chopping Block* article guarantees the sale of an additional five thousand copies that month alone."

The agent spoke directly into the microphone. "To all radio listeners, I invite you to come to Early's Founders Day Fair. We're in Booth 54 located next to the bandstand in the southwest corner. Just follow the sound of the wonderful music of the Early High School marching band and you'll find us. Miss Holly will autograph copies of *Farewell, Fjords* until four this afternoon or until Brickley's Books' supply is exhausted. Mrs. Brickley was wise enough to also have a goodly supply of Miss Holly's former bestsellers on hand to be autographed as well."

Joyce caught Carolyn's eye and winked. Both knew the radio interview would be re-broadcast hourly and could well generate the five hundred sales Carolyn had counted on.

Claudia waited until the crowd around Smitterly worked its way to the autograph table to speak to the man. She introduced herself and handed him her business card.

"Lombardy Teachers College!" he boomed. "A proud institution known for turning out some of the finest teachers in the country."

Claudia beamed. "Thank you, Professor Smitterly."

"It's *Doctor* Smitterly now. I don't often mention having received a doctorate in the literary arts, but I know a person with your academic background appreciates the honor. I'm not ashamed to admit I was near tears I felt so proud when the degree was bestowed."

Claudia congratulated the new doctor. "I hope that doesn't mean you're going to give up your lecture tour."

"Not at all, my dear."

Studying the handsome face before her, Claudia thought he looked far younger than his reported sixty-seven years. Looking closely, she detected carefully applied cosmetic concealer. It also appeared Smitterly was vain enough to have had extensive cosmetic surgery, with a good many nips here and tucks there.

"Wonderful," she replied. "It would mean so much, if your schedule permits, to have you guest lecture at Lombardy any time during the coming school year. That is, if our budget can meet your fee."

"My dear, my fee is whatever your budget will allow."

Claudia laughed and shook Smitterly's hand. "Fair enough. Who do I call to set this up?"

Smitterly pulled a card from an inside pocket. "Here's my booking agent's name and numbers. Just tell him you and I reached an agreement on fee at the Early Founders Day Fair, and you and he can schedule a date from there."

Wow! She'd never expected he would be so agreeable.

He lowered his voice. "Don't look now, but Miss Holly is staring daggers at you. She cannot abide seeing me with a woman as beautiful as you. You must excuse me. The temperamental *artiste* awaits."

Claudia believed Smitterly would have exited doffing his hat if he'd worn one.

"My, don't you look like the cat who lapped up all the cream," Joyce commented when Claudia rejoined her.

"Joyce, that man is so subtle. He doesn't flirt but makes you feel that you're the most desirable woman on earth and he would like to spend all his days with only you."

"Did you happen to ask about his relationship to Holly LaFrance? They travel everywhere together, and one of the gossip rags said they are secretly married."

Claudia smiled, knowing Joyce was trying to dash any romantic hopes she had about Smitterly. Joyce could save her breath. Claudia knew better. The man was a perpetual charmer, and she was already married to one of those guys, Zack Packer. That mistake was clearly one too many.

"Oh-oh, Claudia. Don't look now, but Brady and one of our detectives are heading this way."

Rats! "I don't want to talk with Brady yet. The way he left yesterday was inexcusable."

"Too late." Joyce's voice went up a notch. "Hi, Brady. Hi, Newkirk. How's the investigation going?"

"That's what we want to talk to you and Claudia about." Brady looked to Newkirk. "What were those two words Jeffrow told us? You know, those two French words."

"Pardon my French, ladies." Newkirk grinned. "The words sound like *very nay*. He said they mean *true nose* and have something to do with the perfume industry."

Claudia understood. "He's right. Master perfumers are known as *nez* or 'noses' after they've trained for seven years, learning to recognize at least six thousand different scents. Then they apprentice for a number of years, and before they become a master perfumer, they must create an original scent."

The men were impressed, and Brady asked, "Where would we find one in a big hurry?" He glanced at Newkirk to try to judge if it was all right to confide in Joyce and Claudia why they needed a master perfumer. He hoped so. "The bookshop has a very distinct floral scent in it, obviously left behind by one of the killers. If we could find a master nose to identify the fragrance, maybe we could find the killer, or at least narrow the field down a bit. But we have to hurry before the scent fades away entirely."

The cousins glanced at each other. They'd never been acquainted with anyone who'd wanted to become a master perfumer, much less someone who had studied for it.

Newkirk asked Joyce, "What about the couple at Triangle Plaza with that little kiosk at the north entrance?"

"They only sell knockoffs—fragrances that are identical to famous, expensive brands but sell for far less."

"I know and I heard the owner creates all the different perfume copycats, and he and his wife bottle them. So, instead of paying fifty dollars an ounce, they charge maybe ten bucks for something most of us can't tell apart from the real stuff."

He'd made his point, and Brady thought it was worth a shot. "Come on, Newk. Let's visit that kiosk. See if we can get some help there or if they can point us in the right direction to find one of those noses."

The men thanked Claudia and Joyce and hurried away.

"Wish everything were that simple, don't you?" Joyce commented.

"Um-hmm. I'm ready for lunch How about you?"

"Fine with me. What about the girls? Should we look for them?"

Claudia shook her head. "From what I gathered, our daughters planned to hang around the booth where the high school athletes have a dunking tank to raise money for the Special Olympics."

"Do you remember how thrilled you and I were hanging out with the jocks? I would have died if my mom showed up to take me to lunch."

"Same here. Do you want to find Donovon?"

"No. He'll find us when he's ready. I'm sure he's busy persuading everyone who stops by the pet adoption booth to just stroke this kitty—just hold this puppy for a moment. Donovon thinks once a person makes contact with an animal, they're hooked."

"I hope he's right."

"Me, too. Let's check with Carolyn and Robert that everything is under control and then we'll eat. I want to try the booth manned by the head chef for the Erin. He promised to serve kebobs marinated in his special out-of-this-world sauce. You'll appreciate what heaven is like when you taste them."

6

Saturday – 11:30 a.m.

Alice Drinker's Jeep was in the station's parking lot when Newkirk and Brady returned from the county building and the fair. Anxious to see what Alice could report after inspecting Miss Powder's home, they hurried inside.

"Just in time," she greeted the pair as they entered the bullpen. "Chief wants us in his office." Seeing Brady about to sit down, she added, "You, too, Kincaid."

Chief Rygard nodded as they filed in. "Officer Drinker brought me up to date on her inspection of the victim's house. I'll let her tell you what she found."

"First," she told them, "Miss Powder's house is immaculate. I found two laptop computers downstairs—one was hidden under a pillow in her bedroom and the other in a smaller bedroom she'd turned into an office. Both are password protected."

She took a breath. "At the top of the stairs to the second floor there are two doors, both padlocked. I think whatever is behind those doors could be the solution to this murder."

Rygard agreed. "The department's locksmith has been contacted. He's wild about puzzles and says he wants to try to unravel the combinations first. He promised to use bolt cutters if that takes too long. The truth is, we know he hates to destroy perfectly good padlocks with a bolt cutter if he can help it."

The chief paused and directed his attention to Newkirk. "Now, what have you and Kincaid been up to since interviewing the library staff?"

"Well, sir . . ." Newkirk shifted his weight from one foot to the other as he ticked off the interviews with the medical examiner and the crime scene investigator. "We're on our way to interview a couple who may have the ability to analyze the overpowering perfume scent left behind in the bookstore. We're making this a priority before the smell disappears."

Chief Rygard was familiar with the term *vrai nez* and suggested, "Take Drinker with you. Women are born with an awareness of odors. She'll be a big help to you." Noting Alice's frown, the chief told her, "After that, Newkirk and Brady will help you open the locked doors at the Powder house. I know you're anxious, but whatever's inside those rooms won't disappear. The perfume's scent will."

Rygard stood. "That's it. Keep me informed."

Brady's attempt to make small talk with Officer Drinker during the drive to Triangle Plaza in Solo failed. He wondered why the women he found attractive wouldn't give him a tumble. He didn't think he was that bad-looking. In fact, he'd even been told he was "rakishly handsome," whatever that meant. He knew he was tall enough, at six foot even, and still had all his sandy-brown hair.

Aloud he asked, "How are we going to approach this once we reach the perfume counter?"

Newkirk replied, "I'll identify myself and explain we're looking for a Nose who can identify a strong, sweet-smelling scent for the police that would help solve a murder."

"What if the so-called Nose says he's too busy running his business and can't get away until tomorrow?" Alice wondered.

Brady smiled and leaned close to the back of her seat. "That's where you come in and charm the Nose that this is an emergency and you'd take it as a personal favor."

Alice turned around slowly and stared directly into his eyes. "You jerk! Of all the dumb sexist remarks I've ever been hounded with, that's the worst! Kincaid, you're lucky you're not on the force because I'd have your badge for sexual harassment."

"Huh! What'd I do? What'd I say?" Brady's head spun.

Newkirk stepped in. "All right, boys and girls. First, Brady didn't mean to imply your only value in this instance is as a sexual inducement, and I know he's sorry if you took it that way."

He glanced in the rearview mirror. "Second, Brady, I think you were only trying to be friendly, but you're going to have to watch what comes out of your mouth, especially around *Miz* Drinker."

The rest of the drive to the shopping center was totally and completely silent.

The Empress Perfumery, located in a kiosk at the northern point of the Triangle Plaza, was a wonderland of tiny ornate bottles on gleaming glass shelves. Each exquisitely detailed flacon was adorned with an elaborate stopper of unique design. The popular perfumery was the Yee family's business, with Peter Yee, the master perfumer, in charge and his wife, son, and daughter-in-law handling sales.

Their Saturday morning rush was over and the Yees were chatting easily with each other in Chinese. Seeing Brady, Newkirk, and Drinker heading into the plaza, the son, Kenneth, remarked, "Wonder who the cops are after." Imagine his surprise when the trio stopped at the kiosk, and two showed their badges.

Newkirk spoke first. "Don't be alarmed. We only want some professional help with a perfume problem."

The Yees smiled.

"We've learned there's a person known as a *nez*, or nose, who can smell a scent and can tell what flowers or other ingredients made up that odor." He glanced from one Yee to the other. "Am I making sense?"

Kenneth Yee nodded. "Yes, you are. My father is a nose. He studied many years and apprenticed another ten with one of the great houses of Paris."

"Good!" Newkirk was relieved and quickly told the Yees exactly why he was there. "Would your father be willing to drive over to the bookstore in Early now while the scent is still strong?"

From the middle of the kiosk, concealed behind the stacks of shelving and bottles, came a short, round, beaming man. Peter Yee, the *nez*, had overheard every word from his tiny laboratory and was intrigued with the challenge of identifying a mystery scent. Buttoning his jacket and kissing his wife on the cheek, he announced, "I am proud to serve the City of Early and its police force. Who's driving?"

Brickley's dark and stuffy storeroom made no difference to Mr. Yee. When the alley door was closed, the *nez* sniffed long and deeply.

"Is there another area in the bookstore where this scent is also noticeable?" he asked, and was led to the coffee bar in the sales area where Miss Powder had been discovered.

Peter Yee nodded. "The fragrance is less intense here, but is more refined. Perhaps because this area is not as dusty."

Three faces fell expecting Mr. Yee to say he would not be able to help.

He smiled. "Not to be concerned. My nose is true, and if I may borrow a scrap of paper, I shall begin listing all the wonderful ingredients that have gone into this magnificent original blend."

Peering over Yee's shoulder Brady read *sandalwood, cedar, Mediterranean cypress, grapefruit, honeysuckle, violet,* along with a few Chinese symbols. Mr. Yee visited the storeroom again, found a chair, and sat down. He checked his list and added several more items.

"There. I believe I've identified every one of the ingredients. Of course, knowing the ratios is another matter and will only be determined through trial and error, not to mention a bit of intuition."

"Are you telling us that you cannot give us the brand name of this fragrance?" Alice asked.

Yee nodded. "That is correct. I can tell you it is a man's fragrance and it is a custom blend. That is, this scent is not one that's sold to the public. No. This one was specially created for the wearer."

He studied the faces around him. "You think you'll never find the person who wears this scent, but you might. First, find someone who visited Europe long enough to have spent a bit of time at a perfumery. Not many are open to the public, so that narrows it down. Next, using my list of ingredients, inquire of perfumeries if such a man's cologne was assembled. Be cautious admitting this is a police matter, as a perfumer might fear placing a client in trouble with the law."

"You've been very helpful, Mr. Yee. Is there a chance you could duplicate this fragrance and sell us a little bottle?"

"With pleasure, Mr. Kincaid, and I shall commence when I return to my modest laboratory."

Brady hoped Yee wouldn't take offense. "Your son mentioned the many years you spent in France studying and apprenticing to become a true nose. I'm curious how you and Mrs. Yee ended up here in America, since so many perfumeries are in Europe."

"Our lives together started when we met in China on our wedding day. It was an arranged marriage, and we were both most apprehensive becoming married and immediately traveling together to Europe to begin my studies."

Yee smiled, remembering. "We were twice-blessed. We quickly learned to love each other, and soon our Kenneth was born. But, during the long years of my apprenticeship in France, my wife became desperately lonely for her family, many of whom had fled to America. I understood her sadness and promised my wife we would move to America after I became a Master Perfumer, which wasn't easy. You see, one of the final tests is to create and successfully market a new fragrance. Mine is called Empress of the Orient and is still available."

Returning to the Triangle Plaza, Mr. Yee remarked, "When you contact a perfumery with these known ingredients, you might also ask if they made up a special order soap with the same fragrance. If I'm any judge of the type of personality who would have a perfumery create a one-of-a-kind scent, I'd guess he carries himself like royalty and perhaps, in his field, he is."

7

Saturday – 1:00 p.m.

Newkirk asked Alice to take the wheel driving back to the station. This was the first time he'd been put in charge of a case, and he had serious thinking to do. His partner Bebout always took the lead and he followed orders. If he wanted to look good in front of the chief and Brady—Alice didn't count—he had to get his ducks in line.

"There are a couple matters I want to handle next. Do you two want to divide up or work together taking one at a time?" he asked.

Alice took her eyes off the road to glare at Newkirk. "I hope one of those *matters* is finding a way through the locked doors at Miss Powder's house."

"It is. The other is finding the photographer, Zebner, who was supposed to have had a photo session with Miss Powder last evening at seven-thirty. We know Miss Powder was killed between eight and nine o'clock last night so Zebner may have been the last person to see her alive."

"Aside from the killers." She couldn't resist sticking in the final word.

Brady wondered if she was always so prickly or was she only trying to assert herself. She might be hungry, too. It was almost one o'clock, and he asked if there was any chance of grabbing lunch.

"I have a coupon for chili dogs." Newkirk dug through his wallet.

"Honestly, Newkirk, there are at least a dozen food booths at the fair today run by the best restaurants around." Alice glanced in the rearview mirror and asked Brady, "Wouldn't you like to visit the fair and taste something different than the usual fast food we eat every day for lunch?"

"Sounds good to me," he replied and wondered if that'd soften her up a little.

"Okay, okay." Newkirk gave in. "We can look around for Zebner at the same time. If his studio next to Brickley's is still closed, he's probably taking photos in one of the fair booths. I know the guy's trying hard to get his business up and running, and he's promoting every way he can."

Clement Codd, as director of the Early Downtown Merchants Association, was responsible for the Founders Day Fair and was overjoyed at the way the event was going. The weather was perfect—clear and seventy-two degrees with low humidity—and the crowd was large and spending money.

He'd hired an aerial photographer to snap shots of the fair from aloft and to take video footage to provide to Tri-Cities Television. This was the perfect time of year to photograph Pride Park, with its trees fully leafed out and its lush grass carefully edged along the pathways. The bandstand, the picnic table area, and sixty-four gaily-striped tents covering the booths completed the picture of a perfect community fair.

Codd had spent months preparing and promoting the event, and so far, everything was flawless. His biggest concern every year was the food booths—that no one became sick from food poisoning, that no one started a food fight, and that none of the restaurateurs got into a scuffle with each other or, worse, with a customer.

His heart skipped a beat seeing Detective Newkirk with Officer Drinker and another man. He'd heard about the librarian's murder and fervently hoped the police weren't at the fair to arrest someone.

The Codd family fortune had been made in men's underwear, the featured garment being an athletic supporter, appropriately named the Codd Piece. Thus, for Codd, having grown up in an environment of privilege and civility, the thought of a murderer mingling among the crowd at the fair was unacceptable.

Clement had a notion to speak to the detectives to ask them to kindly make their arrest off the grounds. But his ulcer began barking, and he rushed to a private spot behind the food tents to gulp another swig of antacid.

Brady spotted the Erin tent by its sign *Erin on the Park*. Deciding the new name would never fly, he thought of suggesting a contest to change the name. Lincoln's condominium association could award a prize of dinner every month for a year at the new restaurant on the building's first floor. He'd sampled the chef's food during his earlier visit and knew it was superb.

While Newkirk and Alice bickered over which food booth was best, Brady took his double order of the Erin's marinated kebobs to a nearby picnic table. With show tunes from the Early High band in the background and perfect weather, he chowed down and enjoyed every bite. Lincoln Henderson soon joined him, asking in his deep booming voice, "How are the kebobs?"

"Absolutely the best I've ever tasted."

"How do you feel?"

"Pretty good, considering how much we drank last night. How about you?"

"I'm good," Lincoln nodded. "Brady, about last night, I hope you don't think I'm a complete fool the way I sometimes carry on about Geraldine."

"Heck, no. You had a good thing going, and she up and left town. I guarantee one of two things. You'll get over her and find a new lady. *Or* Miss Pozy will return and you'll be back together like nothing ever happened."

Lincoln didn't look convinced.

Brady asked, "By the way, has the editor hired anyone to replace Geraldine at the *Eagle*? Too bad she's not around to report on this new case. If she were still in town, she'd have been all over the librarian's murder interviewing everyone in sight and saving Newkirk and the rest of us a lot of time and shoe leather."

Lincoln moped. "Oden hired some guy he knew from college named Eldon something. He's not much of a writer. In fact, I heard he's a boozer."

Brady and his drinking buddy had a good laugh over that.

Still squabbling, Newkirk and Alice sat down next to Brady.

"Newkirk, you have a world of choices yet you buy a fried fish sandwich with tartar sauce, something you can have for lunch any day of the week. What's wrong with you?"

"Do you mind letting me eat my lunch in peace?"

Brady interrupted. "Officer Drinker, I'm certain you remember your encounter with Mr. Henderson this morning at the bookstore. Now I'd like to formally introduce the two of you. Lincoln's responsible for remodeling the old Hotel Erin into luxury condominiums."

Both seemed delighted to be properly introduced, and Brady wondered if Alice might not be the one to fill the void for Lincoln. It could work. Geraldine Pozy was difficult and Lincoln had handled it. Perhaps Alice Drinker's nature was exactly what Lincoln needed to divert his mind from his lost love. Then Brady wondered how *he* was going to feel if someone he'd been instantly attracted to fell into the arms of a good friend.

He heard Alice ask Lincoln, "Where's the closest fair map? We're trying to locate the photographer named Zebner and think he has a booth. He might be the last person, aside from the murderers, to have seen Miss Powder alive, and we want to talk to him."

Newkirk appeared ready to blow his stack. Instead, he told himself he'd have a word with Chief Rygard. Alice was blabbing too much about the case, and while he trusted Lincoln Henderson's discretion, he didn't trust hers.

"A map of the fair is posted right over there." Lincoln pointed to a signboard a hundred feet away.

When Alice walked over to check the site map, Brady asked, "Why didn't you go with her? She's tall and very attractive."

"No thanks, pal. Ms. Drinker's reputation has gotten around. She's combative as hell. She's only thirty-five and has already been married and divorced three times." Lincoln thought for a moment. "How about you, Brady? You have police work in common, and as you said, she's attractive and, by the way, available."

Brady shrugged wondering if Newkirk, a placid, easygoing individual, had a tough time getting along with Alice, could he?

She returned. "Zebner has Booth 18 in the northeast corner of the park. If either of you are ready, let's go." Alice smiled up at Lincoln. "It was nice meeting you, Lincoln. If your food booth is still open at dinnertime, I'm coming back to try the marinated kebobs. According to the schedule over there, you'll be serving pilaf as well. I can't wait. Bye now."

Brady and Newkirk quietly echoed her words—*bye now*—then snickered like schoolboys.

Randall Zebner's high school yearbook nicknamed the chunky, nondescript fellow student, *Smiley*, for lack of any memorable trait. He'd held nearly fifty jobs in the twenty-four years since graduation, and became a portrait photographer after inheriting camera equipment from an uncle. Why Uncle Douglas left such gear to Randall was a mystery and he'd resented the bequest. Why not cash? Randall always needed money.

He'd stumbled into photography after visiting a studio to try to sell his uncle's equipment. Watching the photographer work, Randall decided he could do that. He could click the shutter when the subject smiled. All he needed was a studio and a little advertising. The space on North Park Avenue in Early was his fifth choice, but the rent was right and his closest competition was at the shopping center eight miles away.

Zebner was having a fine time at the fair. His booth was busy, and he'd taken in nearly two hundred dollars in deposits.

Writing a receipt for a couple of teenagers, Zebner looked up to see detectives waiting to talk with him. He knew they were cops. He'd never been in real trouble but was aware he'd been tagged as a fellow on the fringes. It wasn't a compliment and Zebner hoped thc label hadn't followed him to Early.

He smiled pleasantly. "Are you folks here to have your pictures taken?"

Newkirk shook his head. "We're investigating the murder of Miss Penelope Powder."

"I heard about that. I could hardly believe it. She came to my studio just last night. Supposed to have her photograph taken for a library magazine, I think. She was being honored or something."

"What happened? "

"Miss Powder showed up at the back door of my studio about seven last night."

"I thought her appointment was for seven-thirty."

"It was. She showed up early to ask me to postpone the appointment until next week, which was all right with me. In fact, I was glad she cancelled last night so I could get a jump on fixing up my fair booth."

Alice asked, "You said she *showed up* at the back door. Did she just walk in? And why did she enter your studio from the alley?"

"Miss Powder said she used the back door because she had to park in the alley. North Park Avenue was already blocked off for the fair."

"Don't you keep your back door locked?"

"Yes, it's always locked."

"How'd you know she was there?"

"There's a doorbell next to the back door for deliveries. Miss Powder used it, and I let her in."

"Did she say why she was postponing the appointment?"

"No. I didn't know her very well, and she seemed like a private person. You know, the kind you don't ask personal questions."

Alice nodded. "What about library books? How many was she carrying?"

Zebner shook his head. "I don't know. I don't remember seeing any books. I do recall her pink dress and thinking it was a very pretty choice for the lady."

Brady stepped closer to Zebner. "Miss Powder's appointment book mentioned a coupon. Was there an expiration date on it?"

Zebner smiled. "I think so, but I never pay attention to that. I'm new in town and I'm happy just to have someone want to have their picture taken. If a ten-dollars-off coupon brings them in, that's fine, and I don't care when they show up. Anything else?"

"Yes. When Miss Powder left your studio last night did she leave through the back door into the alley?"

Zebner nodded.

"Which direction did she turn?"

"I don't know."

"Didn't you walk her to the door to let her out?"

"Yeah, I think so."

"So when Miss Powder stepped into the alley didn't you see which way she went?"

Zebner appeared stumped by the question. He shrugged and said, "I guess I closed the door before she moved one way or the other."

Brady nodded and let it go. But he wasn't satisfied, and both Newkirk and Alice knew it.

Brady had taken a dislike to the photographer and didn't mind sharing his distaste with Newkirk and Alice as they returned to the station.

"Refresh my memory, please. Didn't that bozo say earlier he knew Miss Powder parked her car in the alley because the streets around the park were already blocked off for the fair? What kind of a guy wouldn't at least keep an eye on a woman walking down an alley alone?"

Newkirk had lived all his life in Early and, like all Earlyites, knew Miss Powder's classic roadster on sight. "I wondered about him, too. Her Austin Healey convertible is a real eye-catcher, and Zebner was sure to have noticed it if Miss Powder parked anywhere near his studio's back door."

"Don't forget the girls from the beauty shop." Alice reached for her notepad. "The two who left the shop at nine-thirty Friday night both said Miss Powder's Austin Healey was parked in the alley."

She started to read aloud her notes from Sally, the third hair stylist, who left the shop after ten o'clock, but stopped. She knew she hadn't asked Sally enough questions. She'd have to return to find out if Sally remembered seeing the little roadster when she left after ten. Alice also wanted to know how Sally was able to identify Marva Greeves running down the alley in the dark.

Newkirk turned to her. "Didn't the women at the library say they were certain Miss Powder's car was not parked in the library's lot when the library closed at nine last night?"

She nodded and told Brady, "We figure after Miss Powder left the library at five-thirty, she drove home to eat, change clothes, and prepare her rose exhibit entries. When she drove back to Zebner's to cancel her seven-thirty appointment, she parked her car in the alley behind the photography studio. We don't know where she went after leaving Zebner's but her car wasn't moved until at least ten o'clock, an hour or more after Miss Powder's time of death."

Brady recalled the staff also stated they thought Miss Powder had arrived at the library early Saturday morning because her car was already parked in the library's lot when they pulled in.

"Did either of you call the crime scene lab to process Miss Powder's car?" Brady knew by the look Newkirk and Alice gave each other, they hadn't. "Okay, that's next. Newk, if you have Jef-frow's home number, I suggest you phone him immediately to have the car towed to the police garage for processing before it's stolen or contaminated by vandals or classic car buffs."

The Austin Healey hadn't driven itself to the library's parking lot, and reaching the station, Newkirk decided, "I'll handle getting the car processed myself while you two go on to Miss Powder's house. I'd like Brady to take a look at the locked doors before the locksmith shows up."

The scowl on Alice's face was Newkirk's reward as she handed over the keys to the Austin Healey from Miss Powder's key ring. Well aware she wanted to be the lead investigator at the house, he'd very subtly given Brady that honor.

During the cold and silent drive to Miss Powder's house in north central Early, Alice spoke only to ask Brady to pull a couple pairs of latex gloves from the glove compartment. With any other woman Brady might have joked "Frost Warning." He'd been in her presence most of the day and wondered how he could make her laugh or at least smile. He had a hunch Alice thought he was her competition for a spot on the detective squad, a concern he could easily overcome.

"This is it," she announced, pulling her Jeep into the driveway of a story-and-a-half light-gray shingled bungalow, complemented perfectly by sparkling white trim and black roof. The landscaping was impeccable, from the emerald-green grass and trimmed shrubs to the healthy flowers growing in pots on the porch, exploding with blooms.

It was more of the same inside Miss Powder's home. Brady understood a tidy woman living alone might well have a spotless home, but every room was flawless. More than that, the furniture was expensive, and Brady wondered how the woman afforded luxury tables and chairs on a typical librarian's salary.

Remembering the medical examiner's remark that Miss Powder had eaten baked chicken with mashed potatoes for dinner, Brady headed for the kitchen. By now he knew there would be no dishes soaking in the sink, and he wasn't surprised the dishwasher had been unloaded and the kitchen wastebasket emptied. He had to satisfy his curiosity. Sure enough, pawing through a trash barrel in the garage he found a bright-red frozen chicken dinner box neatly disposed of in a paper bag sealed with tape.

Alice stuck her head into the garage. "What are you doing? I thought we were supposed to be checking out the secret bedroom upstairs."

"Sure. I was seeing if the M.E. was right about what the victim ate for dinner last night."

"Well?"

"He was right. There's an empty frozen chicken dinner box at the top of the trash. The M.E. puts her dinner at six o'clock, which jibes with her leaving the library at five-thirty."

Climbing the stairs to the second floor, Brady asked, "Is it me, because I'm pretty casual about keeping my place in order, or do you notice how extraordinarily neat this house is?"

"It's not you, sir. I haven't been able to find so much as a thread out of place. That's why I'm anxious to see what's behind the locked doors. Someone keeping such a rigid house has to let loose in some way, and I'm betting we find something wild and crazy locked up."

While the uncomplicated layout for the first floor was typical for a story-and-a-half home, Brady expected the second floor to consist of a single large room at the top of the stairs, a bathroom, and closets.

Instead, he found a short hallway partitioned from the rest of the second floor, and two solid wooden doors with combination locks installed that appeared to be top-of-the-line double-cylinders. Brady wondered if an inmate doing time in Early's jail or at county would know how to crack the locks.

Wait a minute! He noticed the hinges on one of the doors were on the hall side, meaning the door swung into the hall, not into the room as a door normally would.

"All we need is a screwdriver and a hammer to open this sucker." He asked, "Did you come across a tool chest anywhere?"

Without a word, Alice hurried downstairs to a closet in the pantry, returning with a toolbox that not surprisingly held a complete line of household tools laid out in perfect alignment so each could be easily seen and grasped.

"Thanks." Brady drove the screwdriver into the top hinge and tunked gently with the hammer until the long pin inside was raised and removed. He tackled the bottom hinge next, and when the pin of the middle hinge came loose, he said, "Cross your fingers, Alice. With luck this side of the door will swing open."

It did. But to their surprise, they found another door—a regular in-swinging bedroom door that, too, was locked. After studying Miss Powder's key ring, Alice opened the door on the third try.

She'd expected a bordello room with long red-velvet drapes and matching bedspread, a fur covered floor, and mirrored ceiling. Brady had no expectations; he'd concentrated on opening the door.

They found a library, complete with rows of floor-to-ceiling shelves crammed with books. Glancing at the ceiling, Brady noted slight irregularities in the center and felt certain this huge room was once two bedrooms overlooking the street. By removing the wall between them, Miss Powder had created her own library.

"There must be a thousand books here."

"More like ten thousand," Alice guessed.

"Wonder why she kept these books under lock and key."

She shrugged and found a double-door closet. "Hey, Kincaid, over here!"

The closet held a safe five feet high, three feet wide and two feet deep, making Brady wonder how someone was able to hoist it upstairs and if the floor had been reinforced for the weight of the safe as well as all the books and shelving. The safe alone had to weigh a thousand pounds.

"*Shoot!*" Alice was discouraged. "I was hoping to find out what all the secrecy was about."

She opened the door to a second closet, where Miss Powder had stacked more books on a three-shelf trolley. "Kincaid, give me a hand, will you? There's something behind these books."

Wheeling the heavy trolley out of the closet into the room and finding a light switch inside the closet, they flipped it on to find another door and another combination lock.

"This is breaking my heart, Kincaid. We're so close, but we're still locked out."

Brady agreed, happily noting she'd addressed him by name. Last name, to be sure, but at least she'd dropped the *sir*. He hated working with an angry partner and knew they'd accomplish a lot more once she relaxed and accepted him as just another detective.

"If you have your cell phone handy, Alice, I wish you'd call Newkirk and tell him what we've found. If Jeffrow has started processing the roadster for prints and blood, ask Newk when the locksmith is expected. When you mention the safe, tell him someone will have to contact the manufacturer to learn how to open it."

As she dialed, he added, "Also, ask Newkirk to check if Miss Powder has a silent alarm system that goes directly to the station or a security company. I don't want to trip an alarm and have some officer or guard poking a gun in my back thinking I'm robbing the place."

Alice reached Newkirk, still with Jeffrow getting ready to process the Austin Healey. She covered the mouthpiece and whispered to Brady, "I think those two are gaga over Miss Powder's roadster."

She listened to Newkirk a moment and asked, "Are you certain about that? This Jeffrow guy really knows his stuff."

Brady grew impatient. "Remind him we need the locksmith over here whenever he can get around to it."

The sarcasm wasn't lost on Alice and she relayed the message, adding, "Don't forget, if Miss Powder's alarm system has a direct line to headquarters or a security service, to alert them we're here investigating her murder."

Hanging up, Alice told Brady, "Newkirk said he'll take care of everything right away, and he's going to ask Chief Rygard to personally get involved in this case."

Brady nodded with satisfaction.

"So, what do we do now?"

"We wait, I guess. Unless . . ." Brady had a brainstorm. "Come on, let's go outside and figure out which of the upstairs windows leads into the second secret room. If we can scare up an extension ladder from the garage, I think we're back in business."

8

Saturday – 2:00 p.m.

Making the rounds at the fair and singing along with the music of the Early high school band, Joyce and Claudia felt like schoolgirls again. Poking fun at the booth offering battery-operated toothpicks was irresistible. Another booth had drawn a crowd for a demonstration of a miracle cream for every known skin blemish. Remembering their disappointment in similar products when they were teenagers, the cousins hurried past.

They'd bumped into their daughters several times, only nodding and waving. They were determined not to interfere in the girls' world that day and burst with pride what attractive young ladies their daughters had become.

Claudia asked, "Do you remember when we got fed up with our not-quite-blond hair and bleached it as yellow as possible?"

"Do I? My dad still calls me Blondie."

"I wonder when one of ours will break the mold. I hope they appreciate their good looks."

"Everyone says the girls look just like us."

"We should be so lucky." Claudia mused, "It gives me such joy seeing Meggin having a wonderful time with Hannah and Steffie, giggling and sharing secrets like we did. Joyce, your girls are so sweet letting her tag along."

"Tag along, nothing. Hannah knows the boys show up when there's a new face around. Meggin is a magnet drawing the bees to the flowers."

"Perhaps, but Hannah has her own set of admirers. She doesn't need Meggin's help." Claudia's thoughts drifted. "Your Hannah is a truly generous young lady. She has her own circle of friends yet she cheerfully buddies up not only with Meggin but with her little sister as well. You and I were only five months apart, so running around together was natural. Steffie is nearly three years younger than Hannah, and that's a big gap when you're in your teens."

Joyce nodded. "True, and I can't explain Hannah. She's simply a good-hearted, unselfish soul. I wish you could have seen how she helped transform an *Eagle* reporter from dumpy to glamorous enough to land a job on television. I wonder if Lincoln Henderson will ever completely forgive her. That reporter meant everything to him and now she's gone."

"I've been meaning to ask you about Lincoln. I met him briefly when he and his girlfriend stopped in Lombardy on their way to a Florida vacation. What's his story?"

"He came to town representing a consortium who bought the old Hotel Erin. Lincoln took charge of remodeling the Erin into sixteen luxury condominiums with a five-star restaurant on the main floor. While Brady was in Early over the holidays solving murders and working closely with Pozy, the reporter, he introduced her to Lincoln. It was love at first sight for Lincoln. It took Pozy awhile to warm up to him, but apparently not that long to cool down. It was right after their Florida vacation that Pozy took the new job, and Lincoln found Brady's shoulder a place to cry on."

Claudia got the picture. "Brady's a nice guy. He doesn't smile much but he knows how to listen, and he only gives advice after he's thought a problem through. He knew I was going crazy while LTC's trustees were deciding whether to promote me to dean of students. He said all the right things and made waiting it out a lot easier."

"Have you written your speech for Freshmen Orientation Day?"

"Not yet. That's where Mary was so valuable. I could ask her to write a first draft of anything I needed—whatever popped into her mind. From there, I always found enough material to get going. If she decides to leave LTC, I'll have a dickens of a time coming up with that first speech."

"You can always borrow Dean Dan Dunne's famous phrase, 'Shall we conjugate together?'"

"Sure, Joyce. Perhaps I'll find a pun for *Packer*."

"How about *Packer Up and Kiss Me?*"

"Oh, please, that's terrible." Claudia changed the subject. "Do you know if the fair has a scrimshaw booth this year? I remember last year there was a huge commotion at the exhibit. A group showed up claiming illegal ivory and whalebone had been carved and was being offered for sale."

Joyce recalled the incident. "Poor Clement Codd. The brunt of the protest fell on him so you can be certain this year's scrimshaw exhibit is one-hundred-percent legal. The carver wasn't allowed to register for a booth until he produced evidence the products used are legal—not from protected whales, elephants, walrus, or hippos."

"That's a relief. The scrimshaw displays are always extraordinary and I'd like to pick up something for Mary. She has a collection of tiny animal figurines, and I think she'd adore the carvings, especially of polar bears."

"What if she leaves Lombardy for good?"

"Then the scrimshaw will be a going-away present; otherwise, it's a gift for her birthday in November."

Joyce consulted her fair map and found the scrimshaw tent. "This way, Claudia. Remind me to check out the rose exhibit not far from the scrimshaw booth. In years past, it was always filled with tension between Miss Powder and other rose growers. A shootout would not have been a surprise. Once an exhibitor actually accused Miss Powder of lacing his rose garden with slugs. He said it happened when she and the rose exhibit committee met at his house."

"What happened?"

"Nothing. Without a witness, his claims were considered circumstantial. The *Eagle* quoted the president of the Rose Society that the slug infestation occurring immediately after Miss Powder's visit was simply a coincidence. The brouhaha went away."

Passing the fudge counter, Joyce couldn't resist buying a pound—half for her family and the rest to share with Claudia.

The scrimshaw exhibit was breathtaking in its delicate beauty and the tiny intricate detailed artistry that went into every piece. Claudia found a mother polar bear and two cubs on mirror glass that she knew her assistant would adore and had it carefully packed in double bubble wrap. It occurred to her that if Mary quit her job at LTC, she might keep the exquisite piece for herself.

"While we're here, I want to place my order with the artist who made your holiday greeting cards." Claudia meant the Fellmeyer's lovely Christmas card of their farmhouse in winter detailing the trees and decorated evergreens with the veterinary clinic in the background. "I took a snapshot of LTC's Administration Building last December and I hope your artist will be able to paint a holiday scene from it."

Joyce was flattered that her cousin thought her holiday cards were so special. "Did you know there's a five-hundred-card minimum for special orders? That's why Donovon and I keep sending the same card every year. We haven't used up our minimum yet."

"No problem. I expect to send out bushels of cards as dean of students."

Joyce wondered who was going to address all the envelopes if Mary Canova didn't accept Claudia's offer to be assistant in the dean of students office.

While Claudia made arrangements with the artist, Joyce wandered over to the rose exhibit. A red-and-white-striped triple tent housed the exhibit with fans gently blowing from all directions. The tent's side flaps had been tied back to provide further ventilation to avoid premature wilting.

"I wonder if paradise smells this heavenly." Claudia inhaled the scent of nearly two hundred rose arrangements when she rejoined Joyce.

"Oh, look! Here are Miss Powder's roses. She must have delivered them in time last night. I think the deadline was eight o'clock. The judges want all roses delivered by eight so they can see which hold their beauty for twenty-two hours. The judging begins at six this afternoon, and the winners will be announced on the bandstand when the Founders play is over."

Claudia bent close to sniff a black rose named *Gun Powder*. Its card said the rose had been bred and grown by Penelope Powder. Next to the black rose, she found another rose bred by the late Miss Powder. Named *Powder Puff*, the flower's huge, double ruffled creamy white petals were tinted with a hint of pink at their edges.

"Early's head librarian certainly had an impressive hobby."

Joyce agreed. "She's entered in the Best New Rose competition this year, too. Her entry is this gorgeous fiery orange one she named *Chili Powder*, and it ought to win. I wonder who'll accept the awards on her behalf. I never heard if Miss Powder had any family."

Leaving the rose exhibit, both women brooded over Miss Powder and her efforts breeding those splendid roses but not being around to accept her blue ribbons and the honor of once again winning Best New Rose.

They perked up arriving at the Animal Rescue Society's booth, where Donovon was busy convincing a young couple the mature cat in the husband's arms was perfect for the baby they were expecting. The pet booth was located only two tents away from the photographer's booth. A deal had been struck that, for only a dollar, Zebner would snap an instant photo of all new pet owners with their newly adopted cat or dog. Zebner didn't know if he'd break even but thought the goodwill was worth it.

As cat and couple left to be photographed, Donovon greeted his wife and Claudia. "We're having a great day. In fact, we're running out of pets to adopt." He glanced toward Zebner's booth. "The girls were just here, and I think they're having their pictures taken, if you want to talk to them."

The cousins shrugged, and Claudia said, "As long as they're having a good time, I don't want to interfere."

"Me neither. Maybe we should disappear so the girls won't think we're following them."

"You're both wrong. In fact," Donovon added, "Hannah said she'd like to have a picture taken of all six of us."

"She did? How'd the other two react?"

"Meggin said it was a 'cool idea' and Steffie agreed."

"Huh." Joyce was surprised. "Well, what should we do? Should we look for them?"

Donovon peered over her shoulder. "You don't have to. Here they come now."

"Hi, Mom. Hi, Claudia." Hannah had a broad smile. "We just had our picture taken by the funniest guy." She asked Meggin and Steffie,

"Did he ever stop talking?"

Meggin shook her head. "I don't think he's been a photographer very long. He kept telling us to 'look up.' I thought he meant to look up at the top of the tent. I was holding my head back, still looking up, when I heard the shutter click."

"What about when he put his hands on us?" Steffie piped up.

The adults were immediately outraged.

Hannah assured them. "It was nothing. He was just arranging us for our standup photo. He touched our backs, and we all noticed how sweaty his hands are. But he didn't seem particularly nervous. He just talked and talked."

"What'd he talk about?" Donovon wondered.

The girls looked at each other and laughed. They didn't remember—they weren't listening.

"I can take a break now if this is a good time for the six of us to have a group photo taken. Okay with everyone?" Donovon asked.

It was, and the girls skipped ahead to Zebner's booth to be next in line.

Forty minutes later, their photographs taken and the girls off to visit the dunking booth again, Claudia remarked, "He has to be the world's clumsiest photographer. I can't wait to see what we look like in his shots."

The Fellmeyers laughed, remembering Zebner getting tangled in cords, knocking his floodlights over, then backing up too far and taking a header onto the grass outside his tent.

Making certain Donovon didn't want a snack delivered, Joyce and Claudia left to take in more of the fair. Passing a fortune-teller's booth, they asked each other, "Why not?"

Claudia said, "Maybe we'll find out if you're going to run for city council again next year and miss another homecoming."

"I've told you I was sorry I missed last fall's homecoming. You know we had a political debate that Saturday. If I hadn't shown up it would have looked to the voters like I wasn't interested in being elected to council."

"I'm only kidding, Joyce, as long as you promise to show up this October. My first homecoming as dean of students is important to me, and I really want you and Donovon to be there."

They'd entered the fortuneteller's tent and found a woman with black hair several feet long that hid most of her face. Covered in a billowing red-and-pink satin gown, she spoke with a bogus gypsy accent in a voice much like a creaking door.

"Who's future shall I look at first?"

Joyce pointed to Claudia. "My friend is from out of town. She'd like to know where she'll end up next."

Claudia kept a straight face, knowing Joyce was trying to mislead the would-be gypsy.

The fortuneteller did not look directly at Claudia. Instead, she lifted a purple veil from a crystal ball, polished the ball, and said, "I see your future and it is troubled. If you still want to know what I see, you may want to ask your friend to step outside while I tell you everything."

Joyce left the tent quickly, a trifle disturbed by the words.

A few minutes later, Claudia appeared outside. She tried to smile, but Joyce knew she was shaken. She said only, "It's your turn."

"Ah," the fortuneteller welcomed Joyce to her table. "You are the fortunate one. Your life is smooth with few bumps in the road ahead except for one. You must keep close watch on a child of yours. That child is inquisitive and will come to harm unless you take steps now to curb her curiosity in certain dangerous situations."

Joyce was floored. The woman had to be speaking of Steffanie, her younger and sometimes reckless daughter. People were supposed to have fun at the fair, not be scared witless by predictions of dreadful family events. She gathered her purse, laid down a ten-dollar bill to cover both Claudia's and her fortunes, and hurried outside. She had to find Clement Codd.

"Come on, Claudia. That fortuneteller has to go. This fair is no place for her kind of nonsense."

Joyce turned her head to look back at the fortuneteller's booth and saw the woman standing outside her entrance curtain lighting a cigarette, a nasty smile on her face.

9

Saturday – 2:45 p.m.

While Brady rummaged through Miss Powder's garage searching for an extension ladder, Alice walked around outside looking for the most likely upstairs window to open. The pair of twin gables in front led to the room they'd already entered. Neither side of the house had windows upstairs, only louvered vents—not an inviting way to try to break in.

When Brady appeared in the backyard carrying a light-duty aluminum extension ladder, Alice pointed up to the second floor. "I think we're looking at a full-width second floor addition onto the back of the house. Take a look at that ledge up there with the flower box. That seems to be a small balcony with a door leading inside."

Propping the ladder against the rain gutters, Brady climbed up and easily mounted the wrought iron railing across the narrow balcony. The locked screen door was no obstacle; he slit the screen with a pocketknife. Opening the solid wooden door was another matter, and none of the keys from Miss Powder's key ring turned the cylinder of the deadbolt.

From the grass below, Alice asked, "What about that little window to the left of the door?"

"Looks like a bathroom window that's been left open a few inches." Brady slit the screen and, with effort, raised the bottom of the double-hung window as far as it would go. The opening appeared to be fourteen inches wide by sixteen inches high, and he knew his shoulders would never make it though.

"Alice, this window opening is too small for me to crawl inside. Do you want to give it a try? Maybe you can wiggle through."

She was on the third rung of the ladder when a stranger pushed through the precisely trimmed hedge at the rear property line. "May I ask what you two think you're doing. You're on private property and you'd better get out of here or my wife will call the police."

Alice, dressed in police blues, complete with service revolver, gun belt and holster, wondered how dumb could anyone be. "We *are* the police, sir, and we're here on official business. Who are you?"

"I'm Penny Powder's neighbor. I live back there." He pointed to a house partially screened from view by the tall hedge. "Did something happen to Penny?"

"You could say that. She was murdered last night, and we're investigating her death." Alice had climbed down from the ladder and whipped out her notebook. "What's your name and address?"

Tom Shroeder gave his name and address then yelled, "Hey, Marge! It's okay! They're the cops! Penny Powder was murdered last night!"

Seven more neighbors appeared through the hedge. Alice looked up to Brady on the balcony, her palms held upward, asking *now what?*

Brady climbed down immediately and quietly told her, "I'll take this group to the front and ask questions while you try to climb through that window. I don't think they should see you entering the house that way."

Leading the neighbors to the front yard, Brady asked them to be seated on the porch steps. By that time, four more had joined the group. All were genuinely shocked to hear that Penny Powder had been killed, and Brady began asking routine questions. Did Miss Powder have any uninvited or unwanted visitors lately? Did anyone notice she seemed nervous or scared? Had she altered her usual routine in any way?

The neighbors only shook their heads. She was seen coming home early Friday evening and was observed cutting roses from her prized bushes in the backyard. It was assumed she was entering her prize roses in the Founders Day Fair competition. Before seven o'clock, one of the neighbors saw Miss Powder leave and thought she was probably driving downtown to deliver her entries before the eight o'clock contest deadline.

One neighbor summed it up for him. "She was what you'd call the perfect neighbor. Never threw loud parties, kept her music to herself, her yard was flawlessly manicured, and her house, as you can see, always looked beautiful."

For a private person, the neighbors kept an interested eye on Miss Powder's business. Brady wondered what they'd thought when a thousand-pound safe was delivered or when the second floor addition was constructed. Would the secret rooms be a surprise? Unwilling to risk hampering the investigation by mentioning what had been discovered inside the house, he only asked them to report anyone suspicious lurking about the premises.

As the neighbors drifted away, Brady circled around to the backyard. Alice was nowhere in sight and he wondered what she'd found inside and if he should climb the ladder to poke his head in the bathroom window and call her.

He was half way up when Alice's head appeared through the window. She'd been able to crawl through the narrow opening and gain access to the second secret room. But the doors from the new secret room to the rest of the house were locked on the inside and the windows were nailed shut as well.

"I need help raising this blankin' window. It's stuck and I can't get out." She'd lowered the bathroom window after she entered, but, bad luck, when she raised it to crawl back out, it jammed halfway up.

Brady pulled, shoved, and pounded on the stubborn window. Penetrating oil didn't help. It wouldn't budge. "Do you want me to break the glass?"

"Not yet. If the locksmith hasn't shown up in an hour, give me a hammer and I'll smash my way out."

The new secret room with three additional computers, each with password protection, had lost its fascination. Alice Drinker was stuck inside, forced to sit and wait to be released. Though highly amused by her predicament, Brady was wise enough not to show it.

✦ ✦ ✦

Criminologist Jeffrow Heepe and his assistant were ecstatic examining Penelope Powder's 1956 Austin Healey Model 100-6 two-seater convertible. The beautiful roadster's custom paint had been blended to Miss Powder's specifications, flesh-tone with a hint of pink and, coincidentally, a color to match her favorite rose, *Powder Puff.* The pair considered the car a thing of beauty and deserving of tender, loving crime lab processing.

The roadster had been towed to the police garage, where the criminologists walked around studying it before starting their tests. Neither believed they'd find much evidence on the exterior of the car that hadn't been degraded by sunshine or compromised by a touch from a passer-by. Dusting for fingerprints proved futile. The exterior of the car had been wiped clean.

Jeffrow had hopes for a nearly invisible smudge on the inside of the driver's-side window. "My guess is the person who drove the car back to the library parking lot wore a short-sleeved shirt. It was probably warm inside the car last night, and instead of wiping sweat from his forehead with a handkerchief, he rubbed his brow with his lower left arm. Before it dried, I think he accidentally bumped his bare forearm against the window and left behind a smudge of perspiration for us to process."

Watching Jeffrow carefully scrape the dried sweat into a plastic vial, Newkirk hoped the new specimen would match the perspiration taken from the axe handle.

Jeffrow remarked, "I think we're going to get lucky with the results of DNA testing of this specimen. The driver's side of the roadster was parked facing north, away from the sun. Should be no degradation here."

The garage lights were turned off while Luminol was sprayed around the roadster's interior. The lack of a blue glow from the Luminol's spray made it apparent there were no traces of blood inside the car. No dirt had been tracked onto the carpet. Wearing a mask, Jeffrow's assistant fumed the entire interior of the roadster for fingerprints and found none, not even Miss Powder's. The door handles, steering wheel, dashboard control levers—everything had been wiped clean.

"What about the radio?" Newkirk asked, and learned it was tuned to the local Tri-Cities Broadcasting station, a probable listening choice for Miss Powder. "Whoever we're looking for seems to have thought of everything, including moving the seat forward to Miss Powder's position."

Leaving to return to the crime lab to process the window scrapings, the assistant voiced what Newkirk and Jeffrow had been thinking. "I guess a little joyriding in the Austin Healey is out of the question now that Miss Powder's roadster has become crucial evidence in her murder."

Too bad. A spin around town in the little convertible would have been sheer joy for everyone.

Jeffrow decided to stay awhile in Early, stroll around the fair, and grab something to eat. He invited Newkirk to join him. Begging off, Newkirk explained that Alice Drinker had phoned to say *interesting stuff* had been uncovered at Miss Powder's house.

"Is Alice Drinker your partner?" Jeffrow asked.

"Temporarily. Do you know her?"

"Only by reputation. She's the one who shot her second husband in the butt when she caught him in bed with some other babe."

"Yeah, I heard about that. I guess that's when she resigned from Solo's force and hooked on over in Dover."

"Did you know when she joined the force in Dover, she turned around and married one of their cops? That didn't work out either, because that time she was the one who got caught with a young rookie, no less. So, Newkirk, who do you suppose Alice will boink here in Early?"

Newkirk grimaced. "Not me, for sure. She and I don't get along at all."

Jeffrow laughed. "That's what the other guys said, so look out."

As he watched Jeffrow make his way into the fair, Newkirk wondered if he'd have time to slip over to Brickley's Books' tent. His new girlfriend, a dispatcher for 911, was on duty until six. She'd mentioned she was a fan of Holly LaFrance and was disappointed she wouldn't have a chance to visit Brickley's to have the latest book personally autographed by the author. Newkirk thought he'd score points with Beth if he showed up for their date later with a signed copy.

Making a dash for the bookstore's booth, Newkirk ran into Joyce and Claudia. "Mrs. Fellmeyer, could you do me the large favor of buying a copy of that book and having it autographed?" Newkirk peeled off a twenty and a five. "Will that cover it?"

Joyce nodded, accepting the cash. "I didn't know you were a Holly LaFrance fan."

"I'm not. I'm buying it for Beth, a 911 dispatcher. She's on duty too late to meet Miss LaFrance, and I want to surprise her."

"Good for you. By the way, how's the murder investigation coming? What's Brady doing?"

"That's why I can't take the time to stand in line. Brady and Drinker are at Miss Powder's house right now, and according to Drinker, they've found a lot of interesting evidence. I'm on my way there right now."

Joyce wished Newkirk good luck and turned to Claudia. "Guess I'll have to stand in line myself. Want to join me?"

"No, thanks. I'm going to look around the crafts booth across the way. See you later."

Carolyn Brickley spotted Joyce in line. "Joyce, you don't have to buy a book to help me out."

"I'm not. This is for Newkirk's girlfriend." Joyce didn't mention she'd been hanging around to keep tabs on how sales were going in light of Chanuary's deplorable review and Worthington Smitterly's radio rebuttal.

"I admit every copy helps. So far, only two hundred-fifty *Farewell, Fjords* and a dozen of Holly's older books have been sold."

"That sounds pretty good. It's only three o'clock. You still have plenty of time."

Carolyn stared at Joyce. Her friend didn't understand that fans eager to buy autographed copies often swamped a bookstore early in the morning, sometimes lining up at dawn. If she had to return a couple hundred unsold books to the distributor, Carolyn estimated she'd lose over two dollars a copy, plus shipping, both ways.

"Before I forget, Robert and I are hosting a little dinner party at the Erin's new restaurant for Holly and Worthington. Please say you and Donovon will attend. Your cousin is invited as well, and I know the chef won't have a problem making room for anyone else you'd like to invite."

"Gee, Carolyn, you've spent all day with Holly and Worthington. Won't you be sick and tired of them by the time you close the booth?"

"The truth? I already am. The professor is a total gasbag, and he has the nerve to ask to be called *Doctor*. His honorary doctorate is nothing more than a mail order degree that probably cost him less than a thousand dollars."

Joyce wondered if Claudia was aware of the honorary doctorate deception. She'd seemed quite impressed with Worthington Smitterly, doctor or not.

Carolyn quickly added, "I hope you didn't get the impression I meant I was tired of Holly. Isn't she a terrific person?"

"I agree. I was surprised how much she resembles the photographs on the back covers of her books. Any idea how many books she's had published?"

"Fourteen, so far. What do you think of Holly's personal style?"

"Miss Holly LaFrance certainly knows how to make a lasting impression in her beautiful white garden party dress with gobs of those gorgeous sapphires."

Privately, the ladies hoped their own outfits—Carolyn wearing a two-piece blue linen dress and Joyce in cream-colored top and cropped pants—were appropriate for the occasion. Neither would ask the other's opinion, not wanting to appear to be fishing for a compliment.

Carolyn commented, "I guess image is what it's all about for a best-selling author on tour. Holly is probably accustomed to being recognized. I love the way her dark hair has been frosted with strands of silver. It's so dramatic and highlights her blue eyes."

"*Doctor* Smitterly's hair could use a bit of frosting, as well."

Carolyn shook her head. "Isn't his hair awful? You would think someone would tell him, at his age, hair dyed jet-black is unbecoming and doesn't help him look any younger."

"By the way, how old do you suppose Holly is?"

"My guess is somewhere in her forties with plenty of energy left to maintain a hectic pace signing books all over the country."

Carolyn changed the subject. "You know who I miss today?"

She didn't wait for an answer. "Miss Powder."

"Was she a Holly LaFrance fan?"

"I couldn't say. I don't remember Miss Powder ever commenting on Holly's books one way or the other. What I recall best about Miss Powder are the times I held autograph sessions for lesser-known authors. She always showed up and waited in line along with everyone else. She told me it was important to support all writers, as it was so very difficult to become published."

Carolyn paused a moment. "Holly's been a real trooper throughout this rotten day. She never complained that I should have been able to turn out more fans. It would be so much fun if all the books sell, but who knew that Chanuary person would come out with such an unfair, stinking review just in time for this particular stop on the book tour. It's not like Holly hasn't signed *Farewell, Fjords* in other cities. She just spent three days in Chicago and a couple days each in Indianapolis, St. Paul, and Milwaukee. Why Chanuary picked the very weekend when Holly is autographing books in little Early is a mystery."

"Remember the Bible, Carolyn. '*This, too, shall pass.*'"

Carolyn hoped the image of Miss Powder's split-open bloody skull would pass as well.

10

Saturday – 3:15 p.m.

Chief Everett Rygard had already arrived at Miss Powder's house and taken charge by the time Newkirk showed up. The chief had risen through the ranks and spent three years on Early's detective squad, though no murders had occurred during his days as an investigator. This was the first homicide Rygard was personally involved with, and he looked forward to the challenge.

The chief, a champion weightlifter in college and still a man of substantial girth, surveyed what they were facing. He asked Brady, "What's your take on the contents of this house?"

"It's not just the contents that are out of the ordinary, Chief. The second floor is a maze of locked closets and passages to a secret room. We've discovered five computers so far, and I have the strange notion the librarian's job was a cover. Powder could have been working for the FBI or the CIA or even been an undercover espionage agent."

Rygard agreed. "We're going to have to proceed very cautiously. Who knows what booby traps have been set."

He and Brady hovered over Ted, a young computer expert employed by the city. Working on one of the laptops found downstairs, the technician had no trouble finding the computer's password: *librarian*. Opening *My Documents*, he asked, "Where do you want me to begin?"

"Start looking for a file that contains the combinations to the safe upstairs as well as the locks on every door." Rygard added, "Be sure to make a printout of anything you come across that points to the lady being connected to some undercover organization."

Ted stared in surprise.

The chief elaborated. "I'm talking about a government or law enforcement agency—the FBI or CIA—or something that smells like foreign spies."

It was soon obvious each computer file contained a short synopsis of a book Miss Powder had read and considered ordering for the library. The technician told the chief and Brady, "I think this computer is linked to the library's computer down on Bank Street, and Miss Powder used this laptop when she was at home to catch up on library orders."

Brady asked, "How about personal business? Maybe a letter to a friend or relative out of town. Anything that isn't connected to books and the library."

Ted scrolled through the list of files. "Here's something—*My Roses*." He found nearly fifty pages of Miss Powder's notes outlining her step-by-step procedure for producing new breeds of roses.

Brady asked, "What do you think, Chief?"

"Unless her rose bush file is some elaborate cover for funny business, we're not going to find anything there." He directed the technician to see what Miss Powder's e-mail contained and then be ready to work on computers upstairs when the door to the second secret room was unlocked.

Chief smiled and asked Brady, "How's Drinker doing?"

"Still stuck. I offered to hand coffee or soda through the window. If looks could kill, Alice wouldn't need her police revolver."

Rygard was amused. He liked Alice and thought this was good experience. Maybe the next time she'd consider how to get herself out of a jam before she actually jumped in.

The master locksmith had arrived and concluded that contacting the safe manufacturer was the quickest way to unlock the fifteen-cubic-foot safe. In minutes an encrypted e-mail message arrived detailing exactly how to open the mammoth safe without triggering the forced entry attempt alarm. Seven minutes later, the safe's four-inch-thick door swung open.

The locksmith didn't take time to see what his work revealed. He had two more tricky combination locks to deal with.

"I'm for disassembling these babies," he said after studying the catalog from Early's police department. He'd found the manufacturer's ten-step procedure to follow. When the lock's combination was unknown, it had to be cleared by removing the combination chamber from the lock housing. With tool kit and a diagram, the first closet door was soon unlocked. Applying the same method to the lock on the secret room in back, Alice Drinker became a free woman.

The next decision was where to start. Rygard assigned Ted to tackle finding the passwords into the three computers upstairs. He asked Alice to poke around the closet that had just been unlocked while he, Newkirk, and Brady unloaded everything that had been stored in the safe.

An armload of ledgers was carried from the safe to a nearby table, along with three desk-set checkbooks. They found letters tied with black ribbon, a videocassette labeled *Library Honor Dinner*, and a family photo album. A metal box held photocopies of stock certificates, savings passbooks, a birth certificate, high school and college diplomas, and the deed to Miss Powder's home, as well as a cancelled mortgage.

If the men were amazed by the contents of the safe at that point, an even bigger surprise was finding photocopies of Certificates of Incorporation for *Critical Bypath, Inc.* and *Bibliophiles United*, companies with Miss Powder's home address and listing her as president and treasurer of each. The vice president and secretary of the corporations appeared to be attorneys with offices in Lansing.

Quickly examining the materials from the safe, Rygard decided Penny Powder's secret life had nothing to do with undercover work. Instead, her secret seemed to revolve around the accumulation of money, and he wondered if the source of the funds wasn't the mystery that led to her murder.

"Listen up, people," he announced. "It appears we can relax. No terrorist booby traps have been set."

Speaking directly to Newkirk he said, "You're going to need help with all this financial data. So, if you can find them on Saturday, call in the city's auditors now."

Rygard turned to Brady who'd been examining the contents of a small metal trinket box.

"Here's something, Chief. Looks like the key for a safe deposit box at the Bank of Early."

"God knows what's been stashed there." Rygard asked, "Who wants to find the bank's manager and open the safe deposit box?"

Neither Brady nor Newkirk seemed anxious, and Rygard decided, "All right, I'll do it myself. I suppose I'm going to have to get a court order." His parting words were "Keep pushing Jeffrow and his crew. This case is top priority, and they should come up with conclusive DNA on Hot Paws in a few hours."

After the chief left, Brady asked what *Hot Paws* meant.

"That's the chief's way of pinning a name on whoever we're after and haven't identified yet. Remember *Big Boots* last winter? That was one of the chief's brainstorms. The chief chose *Hot Paws* when he learned Miss Powder's murderer had sweaty hands."

"Clever. All right, Newk, where do you want to start?"

Newkirk shrugged, and Brady offered, "I'll look at the ledgers, if you don't mind going through those checkbooks."

"Okay with me. I have to tell you I don't know a darn thing about bookkeeping. I barely keep my own checking account balanced."

Both men took deep breaths and opened the books. In minutes, Brady admitted, "I don't have a clue what I'm looking at, do you?"

"Nope. I think these check stubs are in Miss Powder's handwriting, and they're mostly disbursing money to stockbrokers or buying CD's and fixed annuities. But there's no way I can tell where the money's coming from."

"Why waste our time and energy? Let's wait and let the city auditor breeze through this stuff. It'll be a piece of pie for him."

The thought of pie made Newkirk ask, "Are you as hungry as I am?"

"I wouldn't mind taking a break."

"Me, too. Let's duck out now before Drinker knows we're gone."

✦ ✦ ✦

Like schoolboys, Brady and Newkirk enjoyed playing hooky from the grind for an hour. For Newkirk the pleasure of ordering food without Drinker's comments was enormous. He'd been thinking about the kebobs Brady had enjoyed earlier and, reaching the fair, walked directly to the Erin's food booth where Lincoln was filling in at the counter. He took Newkirk's order and gave Brady a message.

"Joyce wants to know when you're going to get around to say hello to Donovon."

Brady groaned. He knew he should drop by the Animal Rescue booth. Donovon was a pal, and it was wrong dodging him. "Okay. I'll stop by and say hello."

"Joyce also said to tell you that you're expected at the Erin's new restaurant by nine tonight. Carolyn Brickley and her husband are hosting a dinner party for Holly LaFrance and her agent before they leave town."

Why can't they leave me alone? It was Claudia's fault he hadn't looked up Donovon. Claudia should have put her foot down when her little brat, Meggin, started harping how much greater her daddy was than Brady, the stupid ex-cop. At least, that's how he heard it.

"You can tell Joyce I'll try to make it. Newkirk and I still have a lot of ground to cover on the homicide, so I may be late."

"Tell her yourself. Joyce and her cousin are heading this way."

There was no place to hide, and Brady toughed it out. "Hi, Joyce. Hi, Claudia. Having a good time?"

Both nodded, and Joyce handed Newkirk a copy of *Farewell, Fjords*. "Tell your friend it's been autographed with the best wishes of the author. I'm sure she'll enjoy reading it. I know I did."

"Thanks, Mrs. Fellmeyer." An awkward silence followed. Newkirk took another bite of kebobs and told Lincoln, "These kebobs are really terrific." He glanced at the ladies. "If you haven't tasted them, you ought to."

That did it for small talk. Joyce came right to the point, "Have you found anything yet to solve Miss Powder's murder?"

"We have a lot of evidence to sift through. Miss Powder was much more than a librarian, and we're calling in experts from various fields to interpret our findings."

"Like what?"

Newkirk shook his head. "Sorry, can't say yet—and please don't repeat what I just said."

Brady looked around. "Is Carolyn still at her booth? I'd like to talk with her again. See if she has any notion why Miss Powder was dumped in the bookstore."

Newkirk liked the idea, wiped his mouth, threw his napkin in a waste can, and led the way across the park to Brickley's booth.

He remarked to Brady, "Hope you didn't mind the quick way I got us out of there. I have a feeling you're sore about something, and take it from me, most things are better left unsaid."

Newkirk was at least fifteen years younger than Brady, but at that moment he was a Dutch uncle with good advice.

Seeing Brady and Newkirk approaching her booth, Carolyn asked Robert to take over again. The line of book buyers was down to a trickle, and even Worthington Smitterly left, deciding the audience was too small for his profundity.

"I see Joyce delivered the book to you."

Newkirk nodded. "We want to talk with you again about this morning."

"I don't know what I can add. I entered through the back door from the alley, turned on lights as I walked to the front door, and before I unlocked the front door, there she was at the coffee bar. I don't remember if I screamed. All I do recall is phoning Robert." She glanced from Brady to Newkirk. "I know that sounds bad. I should have called the police first, but honestly, Robert is my rock. He knows exactly what to do in every situation, good or bad."

"Sure, Carolyn, we understand." Brady hoped she trusted him. "What we haven't been able to figure out is why Miss Powder was left in your bookstore. Did you and she have some sort of connection?"

"You could say that. Miss Powder sometimes ordered books for herself or for the library through me. Bookstores get a bigger discount from distributors than libraries do. When she wanted to buy a book, I'd order it through the store and sell it to her personally or to the library with a small markup to cover expenses."

Hearing that the librarian took advantage of discounts whenever possible explained why the affluent Miss Powder was careful with a $10-off coupon for Zebner's Studio. Brady decided it was the woman's nature to be thrifty.

He tuned back in to hear Carolyn say, "In return, Miss Powder wrote short synopses, giving me some knowledge what the books in my inventory were about. Then I could recommend and talk intelligently whenever someone asked about one book or another." Carolyn added she didn't have time to read every book in stock, and Miss Powder's thumbnail accounts were invaluable.

"So, you became good friends?" Newkirk asked.

"Not exactly. Miss Powder was too reserved. I learned early on not to ask personal questions except about her roses. That was the only subject she seemed happy and relaxed talking about."

Brady asked, "Do you know who her close friends might be?"

Carolyn shook her head. "I never heard her speak of anyone. I think everyone in town feels as I do. She was a very intelligent and well-mannered lady, but not at all sociable. I can't imagine what her funeral will be like. Of course, Robert and I will attend, and I'm sure the library staff will, too. But as far as the rest of the town—her neighbors, people who used the library—well, I guess we'll see who shows up and who doesn't."

Brady wandered to the counter to say hello to Robert and stopped in his tracks. "Newk! Mind stepping over here." When Newkirk was close enough, Brady asked him to sniff the air. "Smell anything?"

Nose high, Newkirk breathed deeply. "Maybe." He stepped closer to the booth and inhaled again. Peering at Robert, Newkirk asked quietly, "Don't get the wrong idea, Mr. Brickley, but may I smell your neck?"

"Geez, Newkirk, it's not Robert! It's coming from the counter. The person wearing the perfume you and I remember was here and might have bought a book." He turned to Carolyn. "I know some customers are paying cash, but are there any charges?"

"A few. What are you looking for?"

Brady shook his head. "Just a hunch. I want to check names from credit cards and anyone you can remember paying cash."

"Newkirk paid cash."

"Yes, and the author inscribed Beth's name. Could I speak with Miss LaFrance for a moment?"

Carolyn approached Holly, saying the police had a question to ask if she didn't mind.

Brady told the author, "Someone is passing counterfeit money. It would be a big help if you could remember the names you inscribed inside your books along with your autograph."

"Let's see." Holly LaFrance found a scrap of paper and started writing. Newkirk made a list of the people who'd used credit cards, and in a few minutes, both lists were completed.

Holly's list contained only first names, and Brady commented it was remarkable how many people she remembered.

"I always remember the people who buy and read my books," she said quietly.

Ready to leave, Brady thought of something he should have asked Carolyn earlier. "When you locked up and left your shop a few minutes after nine last night, did you notice Miss Powder's little roadster parked in the alley?"

"Yes, it was parked right across from the beauty shop's back door."

"Didn't you wonder why it was still there at nine o'clock?"

Carolyn shook her head. "I assumed she'd parked in the alley because the streets around the park were barricaded for the fair. It was no surprise that Miss Powder was still downtown. She might have been talking with folks at the rose exhibit, or perhaps she was visiting one of the fair booths being set up. After all, Miss Powder was a big girl and allowed to stay out past nine o'clock."

Carolyn was out of patience, and Brady had to be satisfied with her answer. He thanked her and walked quickly away, saying quietly to Newkirk, "Come on, slow poke. I don't want Carolyn to catch up and beg me to attend her dinner tonight. I'm only sorry I won't see Donovon. He and I are always on the same page."

11

Saturday – 4:00 p.m.

Alice Drinker was sore Brady and Newkirk had ducked out without telling her where they were going; but the laugh was on the boys. Searching through the just-unlocked upstairs closet, she found old manuscripts, all written by Miss Powder.

Using the pen name Anna Powell, Miss Powder started, more than thirty years earlier, writing a novel calling it *My Own, My Muse.* It was the story of a college girl in love with her professor, who inspired her to great and wonderful fame and fortune.

The original dog-eared manuscript, now yellowed with age, had been submitted to dozens of publishers and Miss Powder had kept their replies. Alice was surprised how many different ways *Not interested* could be stated. Penelope Powder did not give up and, with a fresh batch of pen names, re-titled and rewrote her novel over and over. Every version had the same plot and every rejection letter carried the same message: *no thanks.*

Alice noted the manuscripts' appearance. The original copy came from a manual typewriter in need of a fresh ribbon, followed by submissions typed on an electric typewriter with film ribbon. If Miss Powder were still sending manuscripts to publishers, her computer printouts would look decidedly superior.

Poor Miss Powder, she thought after reading the opening chapters of the latest version, *the story is pretty good. She should have sent it to a publisher who specialized in romance novels.*

Alice interrupted Ted still trying to crack Miss Powder's passwords for the computers in the secret room. "I have an idea for the password for the computer I found under Miss Powder's pillow.

If Miss Powder stored a copy of her novel on that computer, maybe the password is connected to her writing. Perhaps *writer, author, romance, fiction,* or even one of her pen names."

"Worth a try." Ted was frustrated and any fresh idea was welcome. He hit it on the fifth try—*Penny Wise*—words that bore no connection to Miss Powder's writing, but encouraging nonetheless. Maybe he was on the right track to crack the remaining passwords.

The city's auditor stepped into the room. "Is Newkirk coming back this afternoon?"

Alice shrugged. "Can I do something for you?"

"Well, you might want to take a look at what I've pulled together from Miss Powder's accounts."

Spreading sheets across a table, the auditor explained each represented one of Miss Powder's checking accounts. He'd followed the money by tracing a deposit from one account to another, finally winding up at the Bank of Early in Miss Powder's personal checking account.

"The mystery starts at the source," the auditor explained. "A company called Americus Syndication made a direct deposit on the fifth of every month to an account titled *Critical Bypath.* The amount varies from month to month but ranges from a high of twenty-five thousand dollars to a low of twelve thousand. The *Critical Bypath* account is with a branch of Circle National Bank. Every month, exactly five days after the direct deposit to the Circle National account, Miss Powder wrote a check for ninety percent of that deposit and mailed it to an Internet bank at a post office box in Los Angeles. The name of the second checking account is *Bibliophiles United.* She always allowed ten days for the deposit to clear in her Internet account, then she'd write a check to herself, Penelope Powder, for random amounts she'd deposit with Bank of Early."

He paused and asked Alice, "Does this make sense to you?"

Alice nodded. "She was hiding the source of some kind of income, wasn't she?"

"Yes, and doing it very cleverly and very precisely. She was most careful not to overdraft and always left a cushion of a couple thousand dollars in each account."

Alice asked, "Do you suppose Miss Powder was getting set to spring a giant check-kiting scheme to bilk the banks out of thousands of dollars?"

"I doubt that. The local Bank of Early account has been active all of Miss Powder's adult life. The account with Circle National replaced one with Grant Savings after it merged with Circle National five or six years ago. The Internet account was set up about a year ago. I found documentation in the safe that each institution was aware they were dealing with Penelope Powder, who claimed to be the treasurer for an organization of bibliophiles."

He explained, "She represented that she was the head librarian for the City of Early and part of an organization of book collectors. Because of Miss Powder's unblemished record—no arrests, no convictions—and the fact that each account was opened with a sizeable deposit, the banks required only certification of incorporation and letters of authorization from the secretary of the company. The accounts were opened, and she was in business, whatever that was."

Alice heard the front door open, and Brady's and Newkirk's voices. *Darn.* She was having such a good time without them.

The auditor greeted Newkirk. "Glad you're back. Miss Powder was quite the financier, quietly moving money around. All of her actions appear legal—Officer Drinker can explain that. The only question left is exactly what Americus Syndication is. When we learn that, we'll understand what those monthly payments cover. Also, I'd like to see more paperwork for the *Critical Bypath* account. We ought to know what kind of organization Miss Powder represented it to be."

Packing his briefcase, the auditor said, "The Internet may give you information about Americus Syndication. When Miss Powder's other computer passwords are discovered, I have a hunch you'll find all the answers you need. Sorry I have to leave now. My wife's family is in town for the fair, and she'll raise the roof if I'm absent too much longer."

At the door, the auditor advised, "Locating Miss Powder's personal and corporate tax returns ought to be your next priority. You'll find the name of her accountant on the returns, and he'll save you lots of time."

The auditor left, and Alice was ready to leave as well.

"Where are you going?" Newkirk asked.

"I'm hungry. I'm going to get something to eat. Is that all right with you?" Alice was ready for a fight.

"No, it's not. You should stay long enough to fill us in with what the auditor found. Is that asking too much?"

"Considering you two took off without a word, I'd say *Yes,* you're asking too much. I'll be back in no more than half an hour, and you can do what I did while you were gone—start searching through Miss Powder's desks and closets. I'm certain two of you can come up with *something.*" She opened the front door, slammed it, climbed into her Jeep, and drove away.

Brady knew Newkirk was seething. "Let it go. She'll be back, and then she'll tell us everything the auditor learned. Meanwhile, let's see if Ted can do anything with *Critical Bypath* or *Americus Syndication.*"

Alice was pleased with herself. She'd stood up to Newkirk. At the same time, by hiding them under her shirt, she'd smuggled out fifty pages of one version of *Purity's Passion*, written under the pen name, April Daye.

Arriving at the fair, Alice walked directly to Carolyn Brickley's booth to see what the bookstore owner thought of the romance novel. She knew it had nothing to do with the case, but it seemed a terrible waste if the love story were good and would die with Miss Powder.

Approaching Booth 54 Alice was relieved she wouldn't have to wait. Mrs. Brickley wasn't busy and only the photographer, Zebner, was at the counter. She overheard him asking if Mrs. Brickley would like to have her picture taken with Holly LaFrance.

Carolyn thought that was a good idea. "Perhaps you could take the photo with Holly signing a book." She glanced around and saw Alice. "This officer could be standing nearby as though it's her book being autographed."

Zebner looked up in surprise. "Oh, hello, officer. Would you care to pose for a photograph with Miss LaFrance signing a book?"

"I'd be happy to." Alice smiled willingly for the camera.

Not satisfied, Zebner said, "Mrs. Brickley, I think if you stood looking over Miss LaFrance's shoulder, that would help balance the shot." He fussed about studying different angles then asked, "Miss LaFrance, are any members of your entourage close by? They might make this scene even better."

Holly smiled. "My entourage? I'd hardly call my agent my *entourage*. And, no, dear Worthy is resting at our hotel and I don't expect to see him until dinner this evening. You'll have to make do with just the three of us."

Zebner took two shots and left.

"What was that all about?" Alice asked.

Carolyn shrugged. "I think he's taking photos for the *Eagle*. I've seen Oden, the newspaper's editor, around the fair taking notes. It appears he's avoiding Holly and me, and with good reason."

Carolyn was still angry that Bob Oden had allowed Chanuary's review of *Farewell, Fjords* to be included in Friday's *Eagle* on the eve of Holly's appearance in Early.

Robert had spotted Oden as well and quietly excused himself. Carolyn was certain her husband was going to have a chat with the editor and would no doubt insist Oden write an article or editorial denouncing the bad-tempered, uncalled-for criticism of the LaFrance epic.

Alice still wanted to ask Mrs. Brickley's opinion of Miss Powder's book but not in front of Miss LaFrance. Stalling for time, she bought the autographed copy of *Farewell, Fjords*. As she paid she whispered, "Could I talk to you alone for just a minute, Mrs. Brickley?"

Carolyn guessed it had something to do with the murder and stepped outside the tent. "Have you found something new in Miss Powder's murder case?"

"No, I mean, yes. We're finding new evidence all the time but that's not why I'm here. You see, in searching Miss Powder's house, I came across manuscripts of a book Miss Powder wrote that was never published. She kept all of the rejection letters from publishers.

Every time she was turned down, Miss Powder re-wrote her story and submitted her newest version to another publisher."

Carolyn encouraged her to continue.

"I wonder, Mrs. Brickley, if you'd read the first fifty pages to see what you think of Miss Powder's love story. It seemed pretty good to me, and I think she tried to sell her book to the wrong publishers. She should have sent her work to one of those paper-back romance places."

Holly LaFrance joined them. "You're speaking of the bodice-buster houses, and you're probably right. Some love stories are most exciting to read, but, in years gone by, were too steamy for main-stream publishers."

Embarrassed the famous writer had overheard, Alice stammered, "What I've read so far isn't that racy. In fact, since Miss Powder wrote it, you have to know most of the parts where you'd expect it to become juicy, are just . . . ah . . . "

"Delicate?" Holly understood. She, too, had no ability to write graphic love scenes and was proud she gave her readers a glimpse of passion without opening the bedroom door completely.

Carolyn took the partial manuscript, telling Holly, "As long as we're not busy, I'll read ten pages then pass them to you. The manuscript is double-spaced so it shouldn't take long. All right?"

It was fine with Holly, though Alice was uneasy. She'd broken a strict regulation about removing a victim's property for personal use. If she were caught, this could well be her first and last homicide case.

With serious misgivings about having filched part of the manuscript, Alice said, "I have to get back to Miss Powder's house. Would you please not tell anyone about me sneaking the story out and would you be careful with those pages? They're the only copies."

Holly asked, "What about the writer's computer? Surely she saved all her work."

That was a possibility and Alice hoped the meticulous Miss Powder had stored *Purity's Passion* on her *Penny Wise* computer and backed it up on disk. Glancing at her watch she decided she had just enough time to grab a frozen custard.

"Officer Drinker, you forgot your book." Carolyn ran after Alice on her way to the nearby custard stand.

"Thanks." Alice reached into her pocket and realized she didn't have enough money for the snack. She'd spent all her cash paying for the book. "Mrs. Brickley, I'm embarrassed to ask but could you lend me a couple dollars? I'll pay you back. I seem to have spent everything I was carrying."

"Of course. Come on back to the booth. My purse is under the counter."

Carolyn wondered about this attractive officer, who appeared to have everything under control, yet was walking around the fair without enough cash for even a frozen custard.

12

Saturday – 4:20 p.m.

Brady joined Ted who was still trying to find passwords for the three remaining computers. The words *Critical Bypath* and *Bibliophiles United* were no help.

"What about numbers?" Brady asked. "Maybe a birthday or street address."

"I'm open for suggestions. Do you know the lady's birth date? Even her driver's license number."

Brady almost shivered. He hollered to Newkirk, "Do you remember the license plate numbers on the Austin Healey?" He turned back to Ted. "In fact, try Austin or Healey or its model number 100-6 from the year 1956."

He had a second flash involving the prize-winning roses and hurried to the computer downstairs with the data covering Miss Powder's roses. He returned with *Powder Keg, Powder Puff, Powder Blue, Powder Burn, Gun Powder,* and *Powdered Sugar,* all names of her prize winners.

AH100-6, Powder Keg, and Powder Puff worked. All of Miss Powder's computers had been unlocked and were open for browsing.

Ted thought his work was done until Newkirk discovered another hitch. "I think there's a web site on this computer, but I can't get in."

The young man had another go at it. This time *Lucky Penny* was the password, and he was bowled over by the beautiful, skillfully designed web site he'd entered.

Its tag was simply *www.chanuary.com.*

Unaware who Chanuary was and how her words affected so many

authors, the technician tapped into the latest entries.

He called over to Brady, "You ought to read this stuff. I can't tell yet if Miss Powder was the webmaster or this was her own site, but these book reviews are mean. Listen to this '*This travesty wouldn't even make decent chum to attract fish.*' '*This story fell on the floor, was scraped up, and is being passed off as fresh.*' '*. . . a minced-meat pie of a tale and it's not even Christmas.*' '*Woof-woof—this one's a real dawg.*' '*This stew has been warmed over once too often and has lost its flavor.*' '*This puny plot completely disappeared by page ten.*'"

Ted wasn't through. "Here's my favorite—'*A real hangnail of a story—annoying as hell!*'"

"Hold on to those pages, Ted. I found something on this computer that's about the same, except I seem to be outside another Internet connection. Can you help me over here?"

The techie traded seats. "Here we go—*Pretty Penny* is the password for this connection." He turned to Brady "Okay, I'm in and there are a few incoming e-mails to read. Do you want to see them?"

"Print them out for me, will you?" Brady was fascinated with the Chanuary web site on the *Lucky Penny* computer. If Miss Powder was the critic who'd written those mean-spirited reviews, that would explain all the books and her hand-written comments on the inside covers—*Good* or *So-So* or *Material for the Chopper.* It appeared if she didn't like the book she posted a caustic piece criticizing the book or the author, sometimes both.

Ted became excited. "I think we've broken into the *Critical Bypath* connection. It looks like those reviews not only made the web but Miss Powder, using the name *Chanuary*, was writing a syndicated column for newspapers all over the country. I heard the city auditor talking about Americus Syndication. It appears they bought and paid for Miss Powder's *On the Chopping Block* column."

Brady watched over Ted's shoulder as he tracked the last transmission to Americus. "She wrote a short note saying 'Here comes this week's column by Chanuary to be released on Thursday, June 22nd.' That's the day before yesterday. Then she adds an attachment that she'd written earlier, and that's it."

The young man was impressed. "Do you have any idea what she

was paid for her columns?"

"Americus paid monthly amounts between twelve thousand and twenty-five thousand dollars. I don't know if we'll ever find out exactly what each payment represented."

"She had one helluva good income, plus whatever the city pays a head librarian. No wonder everything in this house is so expensive. She could afford it."

"Ted, do you mind tapping into the last attachment sent to Americus. I'd like to see what book or writer she dug into this week."

In less than thirty seconds Ted found the offering for June 22nd. "There are four books listed. *Farewell, Fjords, Sweet Death, Shuffles,* and *The Bedside.*"

Farewell, Fjords sounded familiar. "Who's the author of the first book?"

"Holly LaFrance." Ted was surprised. "That's the lady who's signing books for Mrs. Brickley today. I wonder if she knows about this review." He read to the bottom and quoted " . . . *strictly a Pee-U.* Boy, that's just plain ugly. I hope no one saw it."

Brady was certain Holly LaFrance had read it. Probably Carolyn Brickley as well. He had to talk with both of them again and asked Newkirk to go along.

"Can't right now, Brady. Just got a call from Jeffrow. They were able to get a good analysis of sweat from Hot Paws. The scrapings from the axe handle and from the roadster's driver's side window are a ten-point DNA match!"

Watching Newkirk drive off to the county crime lab to pick up a copy of the DNA results, Brady knew a moment of abandonment. He was stranded without wheels. A quick call to Lincoln to take him up on the offer of a loaner solved the problem. An automobile would be waiting for him in the Erin's parking lot, and all Brady had to do was identify himself to the attendant.

In minutes, Alice pulled into Miss Powder's driveway. Perhaps Brady could cover two bases with one trip. Bringing her up to speed on everything they'd learned while she was gone, he asked if she wanted to return to Pride Park with him to talk with Carolyn and Holly LaFrance again. He'd mention picking up the loaner auto when the timing was right.

Alice remarked, "I just met Miss LaFrance and I have a hard time believing she'd become violent under any circumstances. Plus, I don't think she's tall enough or strong enough to have driven that axe so deep into Miss Powder's skull."

"She could have hired someone. Those were devastating words in yesterday's *Eagle*. If LaFrance discovered Powder was Chanuary, who knows?"

Alice halfway agreed. "The problem with that idea is how did Holly LaFrance discover Miss Powder was Chanuary. No one in town, not even the librarians who worked with her every day, knew about Chanuary. Or how about the editor of the *Early Eagle*? The paper prints Chanuary's column, *On the Chopping Block*, every week. Would he have kept Miss Powder's secret if he'd had any inkling?"

Brady didn't know and remembered something else. "There's a scent at Booth 54 that's a good match for the perfume at the crime scene. It could have come from LaFrance but Newk and I didn't catch it then."

"That's interesting. I was just there but didn't notice anything. Too bad the *Nez* isn't around. He'd know."

Brady wondered how Mr. Yee was coming along. "Do you suppose we ought to call him?"

Alice pulled out her car keys and headed for the door to drive back to the fair. "I don't like to hurry a talent like his."

Brady agreed and decided to let it go for the moment.

"Mrs. Fellmeyer! Oh, Councilwoman Fellmeyer!" Clement Codd called Joyce, who by coincidence had been looking around the fair for him. "Glad I caught up with you. There's a problem with the Founders Day pageant this evening. Miss Powder was going to play a role but . . . "

"Darn it, Clement, are you asking me to take her place?"

"If you wouldn't mind too much."

"I mind a lot, but I'll do it." She turned to Claudia. "I hope you understand I'm only doing this as a favor to Mandy Morning. She's in charge of the pageant, and I know the lines for Miss Powder's part. It's the same role I played with Donovon a couple years ago."

Claudia snickered. "That's the scene where old Danny Early, to make sure the town's named after him, passes around a hat with a false bottom. After everyone else votes for their favorite name for the town, he shakes the hat and the false bottom falls into place covering all previously cast ballots. Then fifteen members of the Early family cast their votes for the name *Early*. Their ballots are on top of the false bottom and the only votes available for the town priest to pull from the hat, explaining why the town is named *Early*."

Joyce smiled. "I love that story, whether it's true or not. My part is just before that where everyone attending the town meeting gets a chance to nominate a name for the town. The husband stands up and says 'In honor of my wife, I say we call our town *Battle Axe, Michigan*.' Then I as the wife stand up and say, 'I return the compliment and suggest *Drunk and Disorderly, Michigan*.'"

Clement Codd beamed. "Good, Mrs. Fellmeyer. You remember. I'll tell Mrs. Morning she has nothing to worry about. You'll play the part perfectly. She'd like you to be in makeup and costume at six-thirty, please." Codd turned to leave.

"Just a minute, Clement. Have you bothered to check the fortuneteller's booth?"

"No. Why?"

"Because this fair is supposed to be fun. Instead, the fortuneteller is trying to scare us. At least, that's what she pulled on my cousin and me. She told me one of my daughters was going to get in trouble because of her curiosity." She turned to Claudia. "Care to say what she told you that made you so upset?"

Claudia was surprised Joyce noticed. *Oh, well,* she thought, *it's all mumbo-jumbo; not at all scientific.* "The fortuneteller said I was about to lose one of my closest friends. I asked if she meant someone was going to die and she said, 'No, but they'll soon move away and you will no longer see them.'"

Joyce understood. That could apply to Mary, Claudia's assistant, or Brady Kincaid, LTC's security chief. Both were near and dear to

Claudia, and it would devastate her to lose either.

Codd's ulcer barked. The fortuneteller was Marva Greeves and asking her to tone down her predictions was like asking a dictator to follow the rules of the Geneva Convention. He knew Marva would forever harbor a grudge against Mrs. Fellmeyer for beating her in the race for city council. He was also positive Mrs. Fellmeyer had no idea Mrs. Greeves was the fortuneteller.

"Yours is the first complaint I've had about any vendor," he replied without conviction. "But I'll check around and speak to the fortuneteller."

"Clement," Joyce's tone was low and, from Codd's viewpoint, threatening. "When city council meets to review the successes and failures of this year's Founders Day Fair, I hope I don't have to mention the fortuneteller's uncalled-for dire predictions or that you didn't bother to correct the problem."

He nodded and scurried away.

Joyce apologized to Claudia. "I don't usually throw my weight as councilwoman around."

"He deserved a little shaking up. But, honestly, Joyce, I didn't know you could be so menacing. That poor kid looked like he was ready to run away and hide somewhere."

"Matter of fact, he is. Codd's applied for so many jobs so many times, it's almost funny."

"How'd you find out?"

"Reference checks. He works for the Downtown Merchants Association, which is funded by taxpayer dollars. City council has oversight on all its activities, including Clement's salary. When a query comes in regarding employment, council is notified."

"Any second thoughts now that you're on city council?"

"Not really. Recent issues before council haven't been particularly earthshaking, and we've been able to move along nicely. The next big pothole in the road will be filling the empty council seat in this November's special election. Marva Greeves is certain to run again so I'm getting ready to encourage Robert Brickley to give it a try. He's well qualified, and if he'll do it, I think he has a good chance of winning."

Strolling twenty paces behind Codd, Claudia said, "I suppose this sounds strange, but did you get the impression that fortuneteller was really a man dressed to look like a woman?"

"I guess it's possible. Meanwhile, I'd like to spy on Codd. Let's follow him and see what he does."

Skulking quietly behind Clement Codd, the cousins were surprised to bump into Hannah and Meggin.

"Mom! What are you doing? You look like you're trying to sneak up on someone."

Hannah's question was so close to the truth, Joyce and Claudia giggled over their silly spying.

Joyce said with a straight face, "I'm just rehearsing for tonight's pageant. Where's Steffie?"

"She took off with Mike McAvenue."

"Where?"

Hannah shook her head and looked to Meggin, who didn't know, either.

Claudia saw the expression on Joyce's face and remembered the prediction. "Don't panic, Joyce. They're around here somewhere. We'll find them." She asked Hannah and Meggin to start looking for Steffie. "Joyce and I will cover the fair from here to North Park Avenue if you two will look around from here to the schools on the south. Okay?"

Hannah remembered, "Mike rode over to the fair on his bike. He doesn't live far from here, and his mom and dad are sure to be listed in the phone book, if that helps."

"It might."

After fifteen minutes of frantic searching without sighting Steffie, Joyce stopped at the Animal Rescue booth to tell Donovon their daughter might be missing.

"I don't think so." Donovon explained Steffie stopped to tell him she was going to Mike McAvenue's house to look at his cat's new litter of kittens.

Joyce was incredulous. "Kittens! You believed that? Oh, Donovon!" She wanted to scream. Instead, she asked quietly, "Did you bother to ask Steffie any questions about this kid, Mike?" She took a deep breath. "Did you forget there's an axe murderer at large in Early?"

Donovon didn't know what to say until he saw Brady and Alice walk past the booth.

"Hey, Brady! Over here!" Donovon waved and, when Brady and Alice were close, told them, "My daughter, Steffie, seems to have taken off, and we don't know exactly where. Would you two mind keeping an eye out for her?"

Brady knew Steffie and described her to Alice. Donovon added she'd be with a boy about the same age who might have his bike with him.

"Uh-oh." Alice remembered seeing two kids on a bike near Miss Powder's house. "They were acting funny, like they planned to sneak into her home when no one was around."

"That's our Steffie." Donovon wanted to laugh but knew better. He watched as Brady took off like a shot to pick up the loaner at the Erin and drive over to the Powder house while Alice remained at the fair to help search for the girl.

Donovon was ready to drive to the Powder house as well, but Joyce said, "No, don't. It's up to me. I should have warned Hannah that Steffie might pull something stupid. Do you want to come along, Claudia?"

Claudia chose to stay at the fair to keep searching with Meggin and Hannah. It was understood whoever learned anything about Steffie's whereabouts would instantly contact the others.

Joyce hurried away. Panic had returned, replacing the momentary anger she'd felt toward both her husband and younger daughter.

13

Saturday – 4:30 p.m.

Steffanie Fellmeyer liked hanging onto Mike McAvenue as she rode sidesaddle on the luggage carrier attached to the rear of his bike. After they'd run into each other at the fair, Mike mentioned he knew where the late Miss Powder lived. That was enough for Steffie to suggest they take a ride over and check the place out.

They'd circled Miss Powder's block until they spotted Newkirk leaving. When Brady and the lady officer drove away, Steffie told Mike, "Let's roll!"

With only one car in the driveway, Steffie hoped she and Mike could bluff their way inside. She'd come prepared, making Mike stop at his house long enough to pick up pads and pens as well as one of his father's hats. Steffie found a piece of white cardboard, printed *Press* on it and stuck it in the headband of the hat for Mike to wear. She'd seen press passes in movies and thought her work would fool anyone.

The front door wasn't locked, and the pair of thirteen-year-olds entered quietly.

"Remember," Steffie whispered, "try to look like you know what you're doing and let me do the talking."

The first computer downstairs was a magnet for Mike, who couldn't resist sitting down and scrolling through Miss Powder's files. Steffie amused herself strolling from living room to kitchen to garage and back. The extension ladder still propped against the house in the backyard was a curiosity, and with no hesitation, she went out to see why it was there. Deciding the ladder would lead to something interesting, she climbed up and tried to open the windows.

By that time the penetrating oil applied earlier had loosened the once-stuck bathroom window allowing Steffie to easily raise the window completely and enter.

Climbing through the bathroom window headfirst was not a good idea. Steffie tried to land on the floor with her hands but couldn't pull it off. Her momentum was too strong, her arms buckled and she landed on her head on the floor. A kaleidoscope of colors exploded in her brain until, as if peering through the wrong end of binoculars, she saw a pair of large running shoes dashing into the bathroom, then blue jeans kneeling next to her. She saw a cell phone and heard a deep voice asking 911 Emergency for an ambulance.

It was Ted, who'd been searching Miss Powder's computers in the adjoining room. He'd heard the thud and was shocked to find a teenage girl barely conscious on the bathroom floor. He had another jolt when a second teen, wearing an adult's felt hat that had fallen over his ears, rushed into the room screaming, "Steffie! Steffie! You're not dead, are you?"

Wondering if he'd been disconnected from reality, Ted asked, "Who are *you?* What are you doing here?"

Mike shrank a little and said in as deep a voice as he could muster, "We're with the junior press section of the *Early Eagle*. We're here to help investigate Miss Powder's death."

Ted didn't believe the kid. However, at the moment the injured girl was more important. "An ambulance is on the way. Do you know how to notify this girl's parents?"

"Her mom and dad are both at the fair. Her dad's Dr. Fellmeyer, the veterinarian, and her mom's on city council."

Mike knew Steffie was going to be really mad later that she hadn't had a chance to snoop around Miss Powder's house.

Paramedics arrived quickly and carefully loaded the partially conscious Steffie onto a stretcher. She'd obviously suffered a concussion and was whisked off to Early General's emergency room.

Reaching Alice at the fair with the news, Ted asked her to try not to alarm Steffanie's parents. "Let them know she's not in serious danger but has been taken to emergency as a precaution."

That accomplished, Ted's attention returned to Mike. He saw the kid was fascinated by Miss Powder's computers, reminding him of himself at that age. When Mike said he wanted to grow up and be a computer technician just like Ted, he softened. "Okay, kid, scram. I'm not going to call your folks or tell the police who you are. If the girl mentions your name . . . well, that's something I can't help. But for now, go home or back to the fair and stay out of trouble, will you?"

Mike didn't need further prodding to beat it out of that neighborhood as fast as he could pedal.

"Freaked out" was the only way Joyce could describe her feelings when Alice and Donovon caught up with her. Learning Steffie had regained full consciousness in the ambulance before reaching the hospital did nothing to reassure her. The fortune-teller's prediction had come true.

Arriving at the entrance to the emergency room, Joyce and Donovon dashed inside and ran into Brady, who'd just seen and talked with Steffie.

"She's fine, folks. She's in the second room and I'm sure you can walk right in."

The Fellmeyers were still visiting their daughter when young Mike McAvenue and his father walked into the emergency lobby. Brady had a notion this was the kid with the bicycle who'd accompanied Steffie to Miss Powder's house. He walked over and asked, "Mike? Are you the fellow who went to Miss Powder's house with Steffanie Fellmeyer?"

His father answered, "Yes, and Mike is my son. We're here to find out Steffanie's condition. Have you heard anything?" His voice was filled with dread.

Brady took pity on the worried father and son. "She's okay. I've already talked to her. She'll have a headache for a couple days and a big lump on top of her head, but there's no fracture."

Both McAvenues sighed with relief.

"Can we go in and see her?" young Mike asked.

"I doubt it. Her mom and dad are visiting Steffie at the moment and I don't think the hospital will allow anyone other than family into the room right now."

Mike's father asked, "Will she have to stay in the hospital?"

"The doctor I spoke with said she'll have to remain here at least overnight. Tomorrow they'll take more x-rays and re-evaluate her condition. The doctor seemed to think, with luck, Steffie will be home by Monday."

"I wish I could send her a message or something." Young Mike had an obvious crush on Steffie.

His father told him, "We'll send her flowers. How's that?"

"I think she'd like candy better."

Steve McAvenue and Brady smiled at each other, remembering their own first loves.

"Mr. Kincaid." Mike turned to Brady. "Before I forget, I don't know if Steffie told you that, while we were waiting around outside before we went into Miss Powder's house, we saw some man drive by three times real slow. Steffie said he looked funny, like he had makeup on. I saw him, too, and thought he was casing the joint to break in or something."

Brady overlooked the colorful language and took Mike's words seriously. They hadn't yet been able to establish a motive for Miss Powder's murder, but if someone wanted to get into the house, obviously something inside it held the key.

He asked Mike, "What do you remember about the man's appearance?"

"Not much. It was his car that I remember best. It was a great big long four-door white convertible. It was real old, too, and I guess it'd been restored. I think you'd call the car a classic."

"What about the make?"

"I'm sorry. I don't know. It was one of those cars with trumpet horns in front that sound like *I-you-ga*." Mike glanced toward the hall. "Oh, gee, Dad, there's Steffie's mom and dad coming out of her room." Mike backed up a few steps, hoping they wouldn't see him.

"No good, Mikey. You have to face them and might as well get it over." Steve McAvenue waved at the approaching Fellmeyers and lowered his voice. "Don't worry, son. They don't look mad."

Mike's father turned and asked, "How's your daughter, Doctor?"

Donovon swallowed and said softly, "We are very, very lucky. Steffie suffered only a mild concussion and her doctor doesn't think we have to worry. Just make certain she doesn't do anything strenuous for a week or so."

"Or anything stupid," Joyce added, eyeing Mike.

"Oh, Mrs. Fellmeyer, I'm so sorry Steffie got hurt. We never should have gone over to Miss Powder's house."

Joyce softened at the stricken look on Mike's face. He was a good-looking boy, and she understood why her daughter liked him. "Steffie told us that Mrs. Greeves had a conversation with you at the park today about visiting Miss Powder's house."

"Yes, ma'am. She'd just put on her fortuneteller's costume and was standing outside her tent when I rode by on my bike."

Joyce's eyes grew larger. "You're telling me that Marva Greeves is the fortuneteller at the fair?"

Mike nodded. Steve McAvenue asked how his son had recognized Mrs. Greeves. He'd seen the fortuneteller at the fair himself and hadn't known it was Marva.

"Mrs. Greeves is a volunteer teacher's assistant at school and we see her all the time. She's always around when we eat lunch or hang out in the hall between classes."

Things were adding up for Joyce, and she asked Mike, "When you spoke with Mrs. Greeves at the fair this morning, what exactly did she say?"

"Mrs. Greeves talked about Miss Powder's murder and said she thought it'd be a lot of fun for me and Steffie to go over to Miss Powder's house and look for clues."

Brady asked, "How were you supposed to get past the police?"

"Mrs. Greeves told me, if anyone asked, to say we were working for the *Eagle* as junior reporters."

That was enough for Joyce. No wonder she'd been warned her curious daughter would get in trouble. "Brady, I want you to be sure that Newkirk is aware of the nasty squabble between Marva Greeves and Miss Powder. Marva tried her best to be appointed to the Library Board, and Miss Powder said that would happen only over her dead body. Was that prophetic or what?"

Donovon and Mike's father had become outraged and were ready to return to the fair to deal with Marva in their own ways.

"Ride with me, Doctor. I think if we approach her together we can scare the living sausage right out of that miserable troll."

"I think we ought to do more than just scare her. I'd like to get her kicked off the board of the Downtown Merchants Association. The school board should know she's a danger to our children, as well."

"Dad, could we buy the candy first?"

"Sure, Mike. The gift shop will take care of that for us." He told Donovon it would only take a minute, adding, "Mike wants to send Steffie some candy to show how badly he feels."

Donovon smiled. "Steffie likes teddy bears, too."

"Could we, Dad? Could we buy a teddy bear along with the candy?"

"Of course, pal."

After Donovon and the McAvenues returned to the fair, Joyce thought of something else. "Brady, it just occurred to me that Miss Powder made an enemy of Clement Codd, director of the Downtown Merchants Association."

"You think he could be a suspect in the murder, too?"

"Hard to tell. He's a bit of a wuss who walks around like he has a poker up his backside and looks embarrassed about it."

Brady tried to picture such a condition.

Joyce continued, "When Marva Greeves campaigned for appointment to the Library Board, Miss Powder publicly stated her strong opposition in very unflattering terms. At the same time Miss Powder let loose on Codd for allowing Marva on the DMA Board. I believe she used words like *spineless jellyfish* and pointed out the DMA under Codd was mired in useless make-work projects because poor Codd lacked the imagination of a dead mackerel."

Brady observed the librarian liked comparing Codd to jellyfish and mackerel and wondered if his name was her inspiration.

Returning to Steffie's room with Brady, Joyce decided, no matter how optimistic the doctors were about Steffanie's condition, to remain by her daughter's bedside.

She asked Brady as he prepared to leave to try to locate Hannah, Meggin, and Claudia. "Please let them know Steffie is going to be all right and that I intend to stay with her as long as the hospital will allow."

"Gladly."

"And please tell Carolyn I probably won't be able to attend the dinner party for Holly LaFrance and her agent tonight. I hope she understands."

Carolyn wasn't surprised. The day had been a disaster from the beginning. "Brady, would you mind terribly attending this little dinner party?"

He sighed. Having dinner with the Brickleys, the author, and her agent sounded interesting, but he didn't look forward to sitting at the same table with Claudia.

He had an idea. "Would it be all right if I brought Alice Drinker along as my dinner partner?"

"Alice Drinker? That's a surprise. I thought you were all wrapped up with Joyce's cousin."

Brady cringed. How many people knew how he'd felt about Claudia? "No, not at all. I just work for Mrs. Packer at the college."

"Sure, Brady, whatever you say. Bring Miss Drinker along, by all means."

Something in Carolyn's voice bothered him. "I hope you don't believe all those stories about Alice and her reputation."

Carolyn laughed. "If I cared about another woman's reputation, I'd be the world's biggest hypocrite. It wasn't that long ago when Robert and I began our romance, I was nearly branded with the scarlet letter. But with time and some wonderful friends like Joyce, I've lived it down and have become a respectable member of the Early citizenry."

Brady agreed to show up at the Erin by nine and privately wondered if Alice Drinker would accept his invitation. Or would she simply turn her back on him and walk away without a word?

14

Saturday – 4:45 p.m.

The editor of the *Early Eagle* had his hands full. His news reporter assigned to cover the fair was missing, obviously on another binge. Sorry he'd ever hired Eldon Sonnet, an old friend down on his luck, Bob Oden also regretted being such a soft touch.

Another disappointment was the photographer, Zebner. As far as Bob could tell, Zebner had worked his photography booth and hadn't bothered to circulate throughout the fair for shots to be included in the *Eagle's* next edition.

Bob Oden was only forty-two, still had his mop of thick yellow hair, and managed to maintain his weight at one hundred-seventy pounds despite frequent donut breaks at the paper. He hadn't had to report from the field in awhile, and it was almost painful.

Concentrating on his map of the fairgrounds, Bob made a wrong turn and found himself in front of Carolyn Brickley's booth. *Oh-oh.* Carolyn caught sight of him and he knew he was in trouble. If Sonnet weren't such a total flop, Bob would have had time to edit Friday's paper. He would have discovered and deleted Chanuary's offensive critique of *Farewell, Fjords* before the paper was distributed on the eve of the author's personal appearance.

"*Mister Oden!*" Carolyn's voice rattled Bob's brains. When she caught up with him, she asked, "Why, Bob, why?"

"Carolyn, I can't tell you how sorry I am about the review slipping through. It's all my fault. If there's any way I can make it up to you, please tell me."

"For starters, you'll print an apology in next Tuesday's edition and run every glowing review *Farewell, Fjords* has already received."

"Happy to oblige." He hoped that was it and took a step to leave.

"Not so fast, Bobby-boy."

Oden knew he was in for it.

"You'll also run at least a half-page about my shop, you'll mention the thousands of books in stock, that I fill special orders, that I offer discounts, and my store hours. You'll do a nice piece on the shop's reading group and what an interesting time all members have at our once-a-month meetings. Recent photographs of the shop's interior and storefront will be featured and anything else I dream up between now and your Monday afternoon deadline."

"That's asking a lot, Carolyn."

"I think it's fair in light of all the advertising space I've bought in the *Eagle* over the years."

Bob nodded and began listing Carolyn's requests.

"There's one more thing, Bob."

"What's that?"

"You have to attend the dinner Robert and I are hosting for Holly LaFrance and her agent, Worthington Smitterly. It's at nine this evening at the Erin, and you'll feel at home because your old pal, Brady Kincaid, will be there."

"He will! Thanks, Carolyn, I'll be there." Bob looked forward to seeing his good friend again. Aware, too, that Brady was helping investigate the Powder homicide, Oden hoped he might pick up some news to print in the *Eagle*.

Donovon and Steve McAvenue caught up with Clement Codd at the fair's information booth. Codd knew from their scowls this wasn't a friendly visit.

"We just came from the fortuneteller's booth, and Mrs. Greeves is still doling out fortunes. Codd, didn't my wife tell you earlier that Marva's fortunes are not in keeping with the spirit of Founders Day?"

"Uh-huh." Clement Codd wondered if these men were about to thrash him.

"Do you know what else that troll has done?" McAvenue did not wait for an answer. "She knew full well that planting an interesting idea in a thirteen-year-old boy's head would be irresistible, especially if it involved the girl he's stuck on."

Codd was bewildered. "What's that got to do with me?"

"By allowing Marva Greeves to even attend this fair, you put two youngsters in harm's way. Her hint to my son resulted in a near-fatal accident to Steffanie Fellmeyer."

"*Oh, no!*" Codd was nearly in shock. "What happened? Which booth is involved? Has it been shut down?"

Obviously, his first concern was the fair itself, and Donovon and McAvenue were ready to throttle the absurd pantywaist. Instead, Donovon controlled himself and explained, "You can relax, Codd. Nothing happened on the fairgrounds."

Watching the pitiful man exhale in relief stirred Donovon's anger and he told McAvenue, "You better explain what happened. I'm going over to see Marva and tell her to pack up and leave before I file a complaint with the prosecutor's office charging her with mischievous actions leading to the injury of a minor."

As Donovon walked away, Codd asked, "Can he do that? Can Marva be arrested?"

"Listen and learn, chum." Steve McAvenue's icy stare and deliberate, measured words warned Codd he'd better find another job, and fast.

The short walk from the fair's information booth to the fortuneteller's tent wasn't long enough for Donovon to cool down. Instead, seeing a crowd of a dozen people at the counter watching Zebner taking pictures of Marva Greeves in costume with various visitors only angered him more.

"Okay, everybody, that's it. This booth is closed as of right now." Donovon started lowering tent flaps.

"Wait just a minute, you. What do you think you're doing?"

"Closing you down, Mrs. Greeves."

"By whose authority?"

"Clement Codd's, for one. He now knows the whole story of your irresistible suggestion to Mike McAvenue, along with your prediction to my wife that our daughter's curiosity would lead to an accident."

"Codd is too spineless to close me down. You'll have to do better than that, mister."

"It's *Doctor,* and if you're not out of here in the next ten minutes I'm going to the prosecutor and file reckless endangerment charges."

Zebner had followed the conversation closely and wondered if Dr. Fellmeyer could or would do that. Marva Greeves, on the other hand, didn't question Donovon's intent and began gathering her equipment while he watched and waited.

Marva's parting words were "You Fellmeyers will be sorry for this."

"Sorry for what?" Bob Oden had heard something was going on at the fortuneteller's booth and hurried over to see if there was anything to report.

"I'll fill you in later, Bob. Right now I want to check in with Joyce at the hospital to see how Steffie's doing."

Oden turned to Zebner and asked if he knew what had happened.

"I'm not certain. Dr. Fellmeyer charged up and accused the fortuneteller of saying something and that he was going to take it to the prosecutor." Zebner shook his head. "I was totally surprised. I was taking shots of people having their fortunes told when this went down."

Oden looked closely at Zebner. The temperature was mild, in the mid-seventies, yet the man was perspiring. He'd noticed perspiration on Zebner's brow several days earlier when he hired the photographer to freelance for the paper. It seemed unusual and Bob wondered if Zebner's problem was a disorder called *hyperhidrosis,* and if he'd sought medical attention to ease the condition that, at the very least, had to be inconvenient, if not annoying.

"Before I forget," Oden added, "there's a dinner party at the Erin for Holly LaFrance, and her agent, Worthington Smitterly. I'd like you to show up to take some pictures. It starts at nine tonight, and you should get good shots of guests mingling and having fun."

"That sounds like a great assignment. I'll be there in plenty of time. Thanks a lot."

Oden wondered if he should caution Zebner not to expect to be invited to dine.

Newkirk phoned Brady first, then Alice to meet him and Jeffrow at Miss Powder's house for an update from the county crime lab. Assembling them in the living room, he reconfirmed the sweat found on the axe and on Miss Powder's car window was a ten-point DNA match. This was as close to exact as they'd ever come across, and was conclusive proof the person handling the axe and brushing against Miss Powder's driver's side window were one and the same.

"Unfortunately," Newkirk conceded, "the DNA isn't in the system yet so we don't know who it belongs to."

He glanced toward the archway. "Come on in, Ted. Let's hear everything you've gathered."

"For starters, most of you already know Miss Powder was the book critic known as *Chanuary*. She went to extreme lengths to hide her identity, with one of her companies supplying another that fed another. She kept her computers and her ledgers under lock and key so no one could crack her secret. However . . ." Ted paused and glanced about the group ". . . one person seems to have penetrated her Great Wall and he or she uses the moniker *Invincible.*"

He handed around printouts. "Here are e-mail communications between *Invincible* and *Chanuary*. You'll read things like 'I know who you are, Penelope Powder, and sooner or later I'll get you.'"

Brady was shocked. "That's a real threat. She should have gone to the police."

"She'd never do that." Alice pointed out, "If she went to the police her whole *Chanuary* façade would collapse."

Ted agreed. "She wouldn't want that to happen. Miss Powder collected, conservatively, nearly a quarter-million dollars every year from her syndicated column."

"Where does that leave us?" Brady wondered.

"With theories, I guess." Newkirk turned the meeting over to Jeffrow.

"Right now, without being able to identify the DNA, I'm going to take another direction. Who had the most to lose from Miss Powder's malicious *On the Chopping Block* reviews?"

"Authors."

"Publishers" was another answer.

"How about booksellers?" Jeffrow knew Carolyn Brickley and her bookshop were popular in the community, but he plowed on. "On the eve of an important book-signing event, Chanuary's inflammatory review was published in the *Eagle* and probably cost Mrs. Brickley a lot of sales."

Brady defended Carolyn. "You don't know Carolyn Brickley like we do. She'd never pull a stunt like that. Besides she's not tall enough and probably not strong enough to land those deep blows to Miss Powder's skull. And don't suggest her husband. Robert is just not the type, either, and I doubt at his age he could swing an axe with the strength it took."

"I don't think either Brickley did the actual killing. If they're involved, they hired someone. But we're getting off-track. Let's look at the time line." Jeffrow handed a sheet of paper to each person and read aloud.

"5:30 p.m. Friday - Miss Powder leaves the library early. Her assistants check her appointment book and find she has a seven-thirty p.m. appointment with the notation *Pic at Z's Studio. Take coupon.* We know that means an appointment at Zebner's Studio, next to Brickley's Books, at seven-thirty, with a reminder to bring along a discount coupon.

"5:30 to 7:00 p.m. Friday - From the evidence we know Miss Powder went home, prepared a frozen chicken dinner in the microwave oven, and ate. She changed her clothing from the dark suit and white blouse she wore at the library to the two-piece pink summer dress she was wearing when we found her at the bookstore

Saturday morning.

"7:00 p.m. Friday - Miss Powder goes to Zebner's photo studio a half-hour early to tell him she wants to postpone her session. According to Zebner, she exited his back door, presumably to drive her car away from the alley where she'd parked it.

"7:10 p.m. to 7:20 p.m. Friday - We have to assume Miss Powder drove her Austin Healey back to the library parking lot on Bank Street. We assume she walked from the parking lot to Booth 22, the rose exhibit, and dropped off her rose entries before the eight p.m. deadline."

Jeffrow paused. "That's all we really have on Miss Powder. Now, here's what we know about Mrs. Brickley at her bookstore Friday night . . . "

"Wait a minute," Alice interrupted. "Miss Powder didn't drive her car away when she left Zebner's. A ticket was issued at eight forty-five for overtime parking in the alley, and her car was also seen in the alley by several persons as late as nine-thirty Friday night."

Brady added, "There's another hole to plug. We have to check the rose exhibit to find out exactly what time Miss Powder's entries were clocked in. Perhaps we'll also find out exactly how long she stayed at Booth 22. Did anyone talk with her and did anyone notice which direction she took when she left the rose exhibit?"

Alice volunteered to check.

After jotting new notes onto his report, Jeffrow continued. "Mrs. Brickley kept her bookstore open until a few minutes after nine o'clock Friday night. We also know she and Miss Powder were well acquainted through their involvement with books. It isn't that far-fetched to believe Mrs. Brickley found out Chanuary's real identity. She was enraged Miss Powder, also known as Chanuary, published her mean-spirited review on the eve of the personal appearance by the author of *Farewell, Fjords*."

Newkirk commented, "That book was released in February yet Chanuary waited this long to publish her review. It's no stretch to think Miss Powder was aware, well in advance, of the autograph session scheduled for Saturday, June twenty-fourth, at Brickley's."

Alice understood. "Powder could have waited until *after* today's book-signing to publish the review. It seems Miss Powder wrote the cruel review months earlier and purposely waited until now to release it."

"Exactly."

Jeffrow had a question. "Who was hurt more by the critical review? The author, Holly LaFrance, or Carolyn Brickley?"

Newkirk's opinion was that Carolyn was hurt more. "The author has written more than a dozen books and has thousands of fans. I doubt her fans will stop reading her work because of heckling from Chanuary. Whereas, this book-signing is a one-shot deal for Carolyn. She put a lot of time and effort into planning and publicity, not to mention ordering a ton of extra books."

Brady objected. "You're forgetting Carolyn found Miss Powder's body in her bookstore. If she engineered the murder, why would she have the body left there?"

"Backward logic. Who'd suspect the murderer would leave the victim in her own shop?"

"No, no." Brady wasn't convinced. "First, Ted, I want to know when that threatening e-mail was sent to Chanuary and from where."

"Got it right here. The first e-mail from *Invincible* was sent a year ago, and it came from a computer set up for general public use at a high tech convention in Las Vegas."

"So anyone could have used the computer and sent that e-mail."

"That's pretty much it," Ted agreed. He admitted the three e-mails that followed were of the same pattern—messages typed on public computers that could be used by anyone and impossible to trace back to the actual sender.

Brady was satisfied. "It appears we have a likely suspect. To clear the Brickleys, I think we should find out exactly where they were when those four e-mails were sent to Miss Powder and signed *Invincible.* Since both have businesses, their schedules ought to be easy to verify."

Alice asked, "Were those the only questionable e-mails you found, Ted?"

"No, there were hundreds. Many had been double-deleted. Those I raised, along with current incoming e-mail, ran about 75/25 telling

Chanuary she was full of prunes. Most e-mails said Chanuary was too hard on authors and ought to lighten up."

"Any idea who the e-mail senders were?"

"Most e-mail addresses appear to belong to ordinary people. Their Internet service providers are easy to contact, and we'll have no problem tracking down the individual sending a particular e-mail message if it comes to that."

"Except for messages sent from public computers." Brady turned to Ted. "How about listing the exact time and location every *Invincible* e-mail came from. That's important if we're going to clear the Brickleys."

"I'll get right on that." Ted excused himself to return to Miss Powder's computers upstairs.

The meeting was over, and Newkirk took Alice and Brady aside. "I heard from Mr. Yee and he's certain he's put together the ingredients of the fragrance from the bookshop. I'd like the two of you to go back to the mall and see what he's come up with. It sounds interesting because he seems to have duplicated an exclusive fragrance coincidentally named *Invincible!*"

15

Saturday – 5:15 p.m.

"You drive, Brady. It'll be nice to relax." Alice settled back into the luxury of the Cadillac loaner.

The ride to Triangle Plaza was silent. Alice had nothing to say, and Brady was busy trying to think of a way to ask her to attend the Brickley's dinner party. He admitted he wasn't his usual assured self about asking for this date. If she laughed or sneered at his invitation, that would put a real damper on any romantic hopes he'd had.

Walking single file through the noisy mall filled with exuberant shoppers, they reached Yee's Empress Perfumery kiosk, where a smiling Peter Yee emerged from his laboratory.

After shaking hands, Yee invited them to join him in his workshop. "I spoke with old friends and associates in Europe. No one would admit how close my formula is to an exclusive fragrance put together by a house in Grasse, but that's their way. I did learn my version mimics a scent named *Invincible.* "

The *Invincible* name on both the fragrance and the threatening e-mail messages to Miss Powder couldn't be a coincidence. There was no doubt Yee was on the right track.

"Have you been able to trace the purchaser?" Brady asked.

"Not yet. Apparently, the client asked for total anonymity, and even went so far as to pay for his purchase with Eurodollars. He left no credit card paper trail for us."

"How much did it cost?"

"The equivalent of over eighteen hundred US dollars for a six-ounce bottle with atomizer."

Alice remarked, "Atomizers are usually for women. Don't men splash their cologne?"

Brady saw her point but thought the name *Invincible* was masculine.

Settling the issue, Yee advised, "At that price per ounce, no one will splash an expensive fragrance around. If he did, he'd not only waste his money, but the fragrance would be overpowering and unpleasant to most people."

Brady asked, "You mentioned *exclusive fragrance.* What does that mean?"

"It means the fragrance can be sold to only one customer as long as he should live or until he gives or sells his rights to the fragrance. That's why it is so expensive. The perfumer has concocted a marvelous scent but is under contract to sell it to only one person who may or may not ever buy another ounce."

"What happens when a *nez* such as yourself figures out the recipe? You don't have to abide by a contract."

Yee smiled at Alice. "That happens all the time, and the market is flooded with knock-offs. That is why I am here doing business in this kiosk. I can copy any scent, bottle it, and sell it for about twenty percent of the original. In fact . . ." He turned to his worktable. " . . . here is my work for the day. My family, to honor the Early police, came up with the name *Valiant.* That's what we've named this copycat, and I'm proud to present you both with testers. Used sparingly, both men and women can use this wonderful fragrance."

Brady reached for his wallet. "How much do we owe you?"

"Nothing. It is our pleasure to help the Early police. Should anyone ask either of you where they might purchase this marvelous scent, you will please refer them to our humble shop."

Alice and Brady thanked Mr. Yee and were about to leave when Brady recalled "This afternoon a funny thing happened at Early's Founders Day Fair. This scent was obvious in the outdoor booth where the Brickley's were selling books."

Mr. Yee remembered the bookstore. "Ah, yes. Brickley's Books where the murdered lady was found and where this scent was so obvious." He tapped the tips of his fingers together. "Perhaps the strong fragrance permeated the merchandise and was carried from the bookstore to the fair booth. I remember seeing stacks of new books with the title, *Farewell, Fjords*, in the back room where the scent was strongest."

Brady didn't think that was much of a possibility but would check out Carolyn's unsold inventory to see how fragrant it was.

Alice was more talkative driving back to Early. "That was nice of you, offering to pay Yee for these perfume samples. Newkirk never would have offered."

"Aren't you a little tough on Newkirk? He's a decent guy and works hard."

She stared at him. "You're not a woman. You don't know what it's like. These guys either act like I'm an invader from Mars, or they're hitting on me for a date even though I haven't given any of them the slightest encouragement."

Nuts! Brady thought inviting Alice to attend the dinner party with him was out of the question now.

"I don't know what you've heard," she continued, "but I *never* shot a husband in the butt. I caught one in bed with some bimbo but I only shot the ceiling, not his ass."

Picturing the surprised husband hearing a shot fired made him laugh, and Alice joined in. "I'm glad you've got a sense of humor about it. Some guys think I was too rash. I should have just turned around and walked away."

"What'd your department give you for firing your gun off-duty?"

"A thirty-day suspension. If you're curious, my lame-prick of a husband didn't even get a reprimand. That's when I decided to pack up. When Chief Rygard interviewed me and heard my side of the story, his reaction was a lot like yours. He thought it was funny and that I showed restraint not putting a slug in the jerk's butt. After that meeting, I knew working in Early for Chief Rygard was the right place for me."

"You don't have to answer if you don't feel like it, but I'm told before you came to work in Early, you also worked for Dover PD, where you had a domestic problem with another husband."

"Don't say another word. I married that guy on the rebound. He was also a cop and a total turkey to boot. He thought he'd caught me in bed with some rookie. But it wasn't me—just someone with a slight resemblance and the mix-up was straightened out eventually. Meanwhile, he filed for divorce and I thanked him. He'd saved me the trouble of hiring a lawyer. End of story."

Everett Rygard was exhausted. He'd chased all over the country club's golf course trying to catch up with Judge Wagon.

He wanted Wagon to sign the warrant to open Penelope Powder's safe deposit box at the Bank of Early. It hadn't been easy. Wagon was using a golf cart while Rygard had hoofed nearly the entire eighteen holes.

Worse, Wagon asked why the city's attorney hadn't properly presented the request in chambers. Then he wanted time to study the idea of unlocking the box until it was established Miss Powder's next of kin could not be found.

Rygard's patience was gone; and he was close to shaking the petulant judge, who sensed the burly police chief could throttle his skinny neck with no effort.

"Here," he said, "I've signed the damn thing. Now get out of here and leave me alone."

Driving to the Bank of Early on Bank Street, Rygard wondered why he'd voted for the crotchety Wagon in the last election.

Bank President Jerry Jerome was waiting at the entrance and unlocked the door to admit the chief. He made small talk as they approached the vault.

"Darn shame about Penny Powder. Any idea who did it?"

"Not yet. I have three detectives working on it. The county's crime lab is pitching in, along with a city computer technician and a city auditor. That leaves me to take a peek into Penny's safe deposit box to see if it holds a secret or two that'll help solve the case."

They went through the ritual of fitting and turning keys into the metal box. When it was placed on the table in the middle of the vault room, Jerome turned to leave.

"Jerry, I wish you'd stay. I'd be a lot more comfortable going through Penny's stuff if I had a witness."

Jerome nodded and took a seat across the table. Neither man knew what to expect.

Miss Powder's safe deposit box was the largest available and held the originals of documents she'd locked up at home: the deed to her home, a cancelled mortgage, title to her automobile, her diploma from Bayside University as well as Early High School, insurance policies and annuities, stock and bond certificates, certificates of deposit, and savings passbooks.

The original certificates of incorporation for both corporations were filed separately and an expanding wallet held a copy of a manuscript entitled *Purity's Passion.* A Certificate of Registration from the U.S. Copyright Office was also enclosed.

Jerome commented, "I wonder if Penny wrote this. If she did, she used the pen name *April Daye.* The copyright symbol on the manuscript is dated nearly thirty years ago, the same as the copyright office certificate."

He leafed through the manuscript and started reading from *Purity's Passion.* "Listen to this, Everett. This is how the book starts. '*She was betrayed by the only man she'd ever loved. He'd taken her self-respect, her confidence, her love. But he hadn't gotten away with her weapon of revenge—her pen!*'"

Jerry looked up. "Looks like Penny wrote a book. I wonder if it was ever published. Chief, if you wouldn't mind . . ." He hesitated. " . . . I'd like to have my wife take a look at Penny's book and see what she thinks of it. Martha reads everything she can get her hands on, and she'll know how to find out if it was published. Is that out of line?"

"Beats me, Jerry. I'm no lawyer, and as far as I'm concerned, help yourself. I can't see any harm in it."

Rygard was disappointed they'd found nothing that pointed toward her killer. About to lock up and return the storage container to its space in the vault, he came upon an envelope taped to the lid. The envelope held a letter addressed *To Whom It May Concern. In the event of my death, my last will and testament was prepared by Jonathon*

Gainer, Esq. of Lansing, Michigan, who has been instructed to act as my administrator. When contact is made with Attorney Gainer, one must use the password, 'Rosebudder,' so he can be certain notification is legitimate.

"I've never heard of needing a password to notify an attorney of a client's death," Rygard commented. "Penny Powder's life and death seem to have been a series of complicated twists and turns and I'm growing more uncomfortable with this case by the minute."

"Don't look, Hannah, but that geeky photographer is headed our way."

"No problem. Here comes your mom. She'll keep that jerk off our backs."

Claudia found the girls near the picnic tables at the fair and hoped they wouldn't think she was trying to butt in while they trolled for boys. "I just heard from Joyce. Steffie is going to be fine."

"Thanks, Mom, and please don't run away."

"Please, Claudia, stay with us."

Claudia was surprised but wouldn't spoil their invitation by asking why they wanted her company. She understood when Randall Zebner sidled up.

"I heard your little sister got hurt over at Miss Powder's house. How's she doing?"

"Fine," Hannah answered.

When she offered no more, Zebner asked, "What was she doing at Miss Powder's house?"

"I don't know." Hannah's tone was unusually curt.

"I see." Zebner was out of questions and, mopping his forehead with a handkerchief, walked away.

Claudia was close to scolding Hannah for her near rudeness but held back when Meggin began to laugh.

"What's the joke?"

"That guy's been following us around since we found out Steffie was hurt at the librarian's house" Meggin replied. "We can't stand being around him. He's just an old geek who sweats bullets when he's excited or nervous."

"Especially when he's around girls. He's a sweating geek, that Dad would call a *sweek*."

Peels of laughter reminded Claudia of growing up with Joyce and what a wonderful time that had been.

"I hope it's not too late to catch Holly LaFrance at the fair." Alice asked Brady to drive a little faster. "She asked to borrow the manuscript I found at Miss Powder's house."

"You took something from the house?" Brady was surprised she would breach a rule like that.

"I wish I hadn't now, so please don't lecture me. That's why I want to put the manuscript back where I found it before anyone else notices."

Brady remembered bending a few rules in his time and stepped on the gas. When they reached the booth, they found only Carolyn Brickley, explaining to a customer that Holly LaFrance was gone but had signed extra books for her fans.

"Will Miss LaFrance be back?" Alice asked Carolyn when she was free.

"No, and in fact, she was kind enough to stay an extra hour beyond her schedule."

"I have to find her." Alice's voice reflected her anxiety.

"You will, Officer Drinker. You'll see Holly at tonight's dinner party."

"What dinner party?"

Carolyn stared at Brady, wondering if he still planned to invite Alice or if she'd accidentally put the kibosh on his plans.

Clearing his throat, Brady stammered, "I meant to mention this earlier, Alice. Carolyn and her husband are throwing a dinner party in Holly LaFrance's honor tonight at the Erin. If you don't have other plans, would you like to attend?"

"With you?" Her tone was not encouraging and Carolyn stepped back before Brady was thoroughly embarrassed.

"Well, yes, I guess so. I thought it'd be nice." Brady wanted to kick himself for handling this so awkwardly.

Alice turned to Carolyn. "Are you sure you won't mind if I come to your party after this morning's interview at the station?"

"All is forgotten."

Alice brightened. "What should I wear?"

"I'm wearing a blue cocktail suit, and I expect Holly will wear something frilly. However, I doubt Joyce Fellmeyer's cousin came prepared for a party like this, so she'll probably show up in something casual. I suggest you choose whatever you feel comfortable wearing."

Brady took Alice's question as a *Yes* and asked when and where he should pick her up.

After a long stare, she answered, "Since you're already staying at the Erin, I'll drive myself over around nine."

That settled, Alice asked Carolyn if she knew what Holly LaFrance had done with Miss Powder's manuscript.

"She put it in her bag, said she was going to visit our library, and she'd see me later at the Erin."

"Thanks." Alice said hurried good-byes and dashed off in the direction of the library.

Carolyn spoke first. "Brady, I'm sorry if I put you on the spot about tonight's dinner."

"Don't be. You did me a favor. I'd been hawing all afternoon trying to find an opening to ask Alice to go to the party. What you said did the trick."

"I'm glad something's turning out for someone. Are the police any closer to solving the murder?"

Her question reminded Brady of Mr. Yee's testers. "Carolyn, do you remember the strong fragrance in your bookshop this morning?"

She did.

"Could you take a whiff of this and tell me if you think it's the same?"

Carolyn closed her eyes as Brady gently wafted the tester back and forth under her nose.

She wasn't sure. "I'm not very good about perfumes. Remember, earlier today you noticed a scent in the booth you thought could be the same. You and Newkirk went through all the credit slips and copied all the first names Holly recalled. The truth is, I didn't notice the scent at all so I don't think I'm much help. The one who has a good nose for scents is Robert. He's at home resting now, but you can ask him at the party tonight."

Somewhat disappointed, Brady said, "That's all right. I'd appreciate if you didn't mention my asking you to identify a fragrance."

He turned in the direction Alice had gone, hoping she was still in sight. "Carolyn, did Holly LaFrance say why she wanted to visit the library?"

"No. She just took off. Why?"

"I don't know. I have this funny feeling. Do you happen to know where Holly was last night between seven and midnight?"

"Brady! You're not serious! You surely don't think Holly had anything to do with Miss Powder's murder."

"I didn't say that, and I don't know what I think. But isn't it strange she took Miss Powder's manuscript along with her to the library? Seems to me she might have left it with you to return to Alice."

He had a point, and Carolyn suggested, "Why don't you take a walk over to the library yourself? Perhaps you'll find Holly and answers to your questions at the same time."

16

Saturday – 5:40 p.m.

The librarian at the main desk recognized Brady and told him Alice was scouring the building looking for Holly LaFrance. "We told her Miss LaFrance had come and gone but the officer decided to search anyway."

That sounded like Alice. Spotting Tony, the intern, Brady asked, "Have you seen Officer Drinker scouting around?"

"She went this way." He led Brady to the bank of card catalog files, where Alice was busy thumbing through the *Ds.*

Tony asked if she'd found what she wanted.

"Not yet. I'm looking for an author named April Daye but there's no card for her."

Tony wasn't certain how the card catalog file worked. He'd been trained on the computer to find ISBNs and Library of Congress numbers but was still baffled by the Dewey Decimal System.

He offered, "I thought I heard them tell you the used bookstore at the Triangle Plaza has the listings of every book ever published whether it's still in print or not."

"I know, but I wanted to check whether Miss LaFrance found anything by April Daye while she was here."

Tony didn't know. "Miss LaFrance said the author she was looking for published only one book. Then she asked for directions how to find Encore Books at the mall in Solo."

Brady told Alice, "I think we ought to try Encore Books." He turned to Tony, "Does this store sell old books as well as new?"

"Encore Books sells only used books, and they must have a ton of them. What they don't have in their inventory, they'll order for you. If you like to read, it's a wonderful store."

"Thanks, Tony. See you later." Brady took Alice's elbow and steered her to the library's entrance.

"Oh-oh. See that guy getting out of the touring car?" Alice pointed. "I think he's Holly LaFrance's agent and he looks mad, doesn't he?"

She was right; however, it was the white touring car with trumpet horns that attracted Brady. Hadn't young Mike McAvenue mentioned a weird-looking man driving such a car past Miss Powder's house more than once?

"Do you think we ought to try to waylay him?" Alice asked.

"What for?"

"Because if Holly LaFrance wanted him in on whatever she's looking for, she'd have told him. His body language tells me he's trying to catch up with her before she finds it."

"Oh, please." Brady never bought what he called pop psychology. People were misinterpreted all the time because someone else thought they could read a person's mind but were completely off-base.

"I still want to stick around and check him out. I don't like his looks. I've been around jerks like him all my life and I always know when a guy's planning to haul off and hit someone. Besides this guy's too chiseled. Like he's had a face lift and his jaw line was pulled a couple inches too tight."

She saw Brady wasn't convinced and told him he could leave without her. "I'm going back inside the library and see if I can't head him off."

Brady waited for her, and in a few minutes, Alice joined him with a big smile. "I was able to give the librarian a high sign not to tell that bozo where Holly went. I heard her say Miss LaFrance had mentioned she was going to return to her hotel room to rest before the dinner party tonight."

"Did it work?"

"Let's find out. If he heads for their hotel in Dover instead of Solo and the used bookstore, we'll know he bought it."

✦ ✦ ✦

Twenty minutes later, convinced Worthington Smitterly was on his way to Dover, Brady and Alice reached Encore Books.

"You take that side and I'll look for Holly over here." Brady made his way through a maze of bookshelves and benches occupied by engrossed readers. He searched from the front to the rear of the store and forward again.

Alice found him. "Any luck?" He shook his head. "Me, neither. Let's ask that clerk if he saw Holly or anyone asking for a book by April Daye."

Her charm brought a sparkle to the young man's eyes, and he told Alice, "Yes, we recognized Miss LaFrance, and everyone wanted her autograph. We even found a half-dozen of her books in stock. They were used books, but she was super about signing them. She got a big kick when we told her we were going to run right out and buy all her brand-new books."

Alice was patient while the clerk rambled and when he took a breath asked, "Were you able to help Miss LaFrance find a book written by April Daye?"

"I'm not sure. Let me find the manager. I think she and Miss LaFrance are down in the sub-basement looking for a particular book, though I'm not certain of the author's name."

He hit two buttons on the store's intercom and a half-minute later, a voice said, "I'm busy right now. Can it wait?"

"There are a couple people here looking for Miss LaFrance."

After a pause, the manager said, "She wants to know who they are and what they want."

Brady took the phone. "Please don't alarm Miss LaFrance. We're detectives from the City of Early, and we'd like to speak with her for only a moment when it's convenient."

The manager paused then told Brady "We'll be up in a few minutes. I hope you're legit and not some nutty fan." She hung up.

Back on the selling floor, Holly smiled seeing Alice and Brady and told the manager, "It's all right. I know these fine officers."

When her book purchase had been completed and the manager

was out of hearing range, Holly asked, "What in the world are you two doing here at Encore Books?"

Alice said, "I think we're protecting you. Your agent went to the the library, mad as hell, looking for you. The librarian didn't tell him you were going to Encore Books, and we followed him for awhile to make certain he drove to Dover, not Solo."

"He was angry, was he?"

Alice nodded. "If you're in danger, we can make arrangements to give you protection."

Holly snorted. "I don't think I need protection from that poor old toothless tiger. But thank you anyway."

"If you're sure."

"I'm sure." Holly started to turn away, then remembered. "Here's the manuscript you showed me. I read it and found it most interesting. Thank you." She opened her handbag and handed Penny Powder's rolled-up manuscript over to Alice.

There was nothing more to do, and Brady said, "I guess we'll see you later at Carolyn's dinner party."

Holly smiled and walked away.

Alice asked if Brady had Mr. Yee's tester with him. "I'd like to put some cologne on and drop in at his kiosk to see his reaction."

Brady dug into a pocket and handed over the little bottle. Alice dabbed the fragrance behind both ears and on her wrists. She asked Brady, "Where do you want yours?"

"Nowhere. I'm fine."

"No, you're not." Alice Drinker grabbed Brady by the ear and slathered his neck with the cologne.

Aware passersby were watching Alice, Brady stood still and took it.

"Satisfied?" he asked.

She was and handed the tester back as Holly LaFrance hurried to rejoin the pair. "I'm glad I caught up with you. Alice, would you do me the favor of hanging onto this book along with the manuscript? I'll let you know when or if I want it back."

"Sure, I'll be glad to." Alice was alarmed at the frightened look on Holly's face. "What's wrong?"

"Nothing. I thought for a moment I saw my agent. My mistake. Well, see you both later."

Watching Holly walk quickly away, Brady asked, "What was that all about?"

"I'm not sure. Let's hurry. I want to see Mr. Yee before we go back to Early. His reaction when we walk in wearing his *Valiant* will be fun."

She turned to Brady. "I also want to invite him and Mrs. Yee to the party tonight. Do you think Mrs. Brickley will mind?"

"Not at all. I have the impression Carolyn wants a big crowd for Holly's party so inviting the Yees should be all right. But why do you want them to attend?"

"Mr. Yee's nose. If *Invincible* is on the scene wearing his special scent, Mr. Yee will pick it up immediately."

Yee knew Brady and Alice had arrived before he saw them. "Your essence announced your presence." He whispered to Brady, "Less scent makes more sense."

Tell that to Alice. But instead of explaining that Alice had purposely doused him with the cologne, Brady invited Yee and his wife to join them at Carolyn's dinner party.

Alice added, "We think both of you will enjoy the evening. Mrs. Brickley is hosting the party in honor of a famous author and hopes to have a nice crowd of people such as yourselves attend."

Mrs. Yee had joined her husband and nodded she'd be happy to go to the party.

"We accept the kind invitation." Mr. Yee breathed deeply. "Will you be wearing *Valiant* to the party?" Both nodded and he asked, "Is there a chance another person will be wearing the identical scent?"

Brady and Alice glanced at each other. They didn't have to say a word as Yee knew the answer, telling them, "You can rely on me to alert you, with discretion, should the identical scent be worn to this party."

✦ ✦ ✦

Alice studied her notes on the drive back to pick up her Jeep at Miss Powder's house. "There are two more angles to cover, and we ought to split up to save time. I want to re-interview Sally at the beauty shop to see if Miss Powder's car was in the alley when she left after ten o'clock Friday night. I'm also going to ask her how she was able to identify Marva Greeves running around in that dark alley."

"What do you want me to do?" Brady was impressed with the way she was following up leads.

"I think you should check exactly when Miss Powder clocked in her rose entries at Booth 22. That'll give us an exact time when she left the photo studio. If the people running the rose exhibit were the last to see Miss Powder alive, maybe they know where she went after she left their booth."

"You know, Alice, you're running this case like a pro."

"Thanks."

"I wonder how you'd feel if I took the job Chief Rygard keeps offering." He glanced over to gauge her reaction. She maintained a poker face and said nothing.

He continued. "The chief likes you and has high hopes you'll become a top-notch detective."

Still no reaction and Brady plowed ahead. "The long and short of it is that Bebout and Newkirk are okay with having me on the detective squad. But more important to me is how you feel about it because you and I would be partners."

She sighed and took a moment to respond. "I'm all right with it, Brady. But you have to keep your hands off me. Understand?"

Huh? Brady was stunned—she'd called him by his first name. But the keeping-his-hands-off part was embarrassing.

The model of innocence, he replied, "Of course. Our relationship is and will be strictly business."

"Can the road apples, Kincaid. I know you've been sizing me up all day. I'm used to that. But, if we're going to work closely together, those are my ground rules. Take it or leave it."

"No problem, Alice."

"So, does that mean you're definitely going to take the chief's offer?"

"It means after we've wrapped up this case, I'm going back to Ohio, take a week, and consider it very seriously."

"Whatever you decide is fine with me. Meanwhile, we both have interviews and I have to hurry. If I'm going to the dinner party tonight, I have some fixing up to do."

17

Saturday – 6:30 p.m.

Relieved to find Sally still on duty at the beauty salon, Alice approached the hair stylist's booth and said quietly, "I have another question or two when you have a free moment."

"Sure. Take a seat. I'll be with you as soon as I finish this comb-out."

A few minutes later Sally joined Alice. "It's good to sit down and rest these tired dogs. I've been on my feet since eight o'clock this morning. So, what'd you want to know?"

Alice pulled her notepad and pen from a pocket. "When you left the shop somewhat after ten o'clock last night, did you happen to see Miss Powder's cute little roadster parked in the alley?"

"Not then that I recall. I did notice her car when I took a break around eight. We're not allowed to smoke in the shop, so I duck into the alley now and then to grab a puff."

That established the Austin Healey was parked in the alley at eight p.m. and had been moved by ten p.m.

"Now, why are you certain it was Marva Greeves running down the alley in the dark after ten o'clock last night?"

"Because by the time you and I talked this morning, I'd already heard that Marva was seen pawing through the expired groceries carton at the corner market. The market can't sell meats, dairy, or produce after certain dates, so they pile the leftovers in a box outside. Around eleven o'clock every night, someone from Holy Trinity's Breakfast Club drives over and picks up the food to feed to the poor." Sally added, "You should know the food's still good even though it's past the expiration date."

Alice agreed. "It's wrong to let good food go to waste."

"Exactly. So, as I was saying, Marva Greeves is famous for pinching food whenever she can get away with it. She nearly got caught again last night and that's why she was running for dear life. The folks at the market promised they'd have her arrested the next time they caught her."

Alice was satisfied and stood ready to leave when the shop's owner hurried over. "Officer, I meant to tell you when you were here this morning that Miss Powder had her hair styled on her lunch hour yesterday."

Alice knew that.

"I forgot to mention she made a second appointment with me for seven-fifteen last night. She was going to have her picture taken at Zebner's at seven-thirty and wanted to stop here first in case her hair had gotten mussed during the afternoon and needed touching up."

Alice found her notepad again. "So, Miss Powder was here in the beauty shop at seven-fifteen last night."

"Not exactly. She didn't show up for her touch-up until almost seven forty-five and that wasn't like her. Miss Powder was always punctual to the minute. She told me she'd been held up at the rose exhibit and actually apologized for being late. If only more of my customers were as thoughtful as Penny Powder—I'm really going to miss that lady."

"Did you have to do anything to Miss Powder's hair?"

"Not much. I rearranged a little on top, gave it a spritz of hair-spray, and she was all set."

"What happened next?"

"She gathered up her books. She'd left them with me because she didn't want to carry them along with her roses to the exhibit booth. Miss Powder said the books were going to be used as props in the photographs Zebner was taking for a library publication. We talked for a little while about her roses. Miss Powder often drops off a bouquet of fresh flowers from her garden, and she always remembers the anniversary of the day I opened this shop with a huge arrangement of her prize roses."

"A thoughtful lady," Alice remarked. "What time did Miss Powder actually leave your shop to walk to Zebner's Studio?"

"She left just after the timer rang to remind me that my customer under the dryer was done. That was ten minutes before eight."

"Do you remember if Miss Powder left your shop through the front or the alley door?"

"She went out the front door and turned right toward Zebner's."

"One last detail. Sally mentioned Miss Powder's little roadster was parked behind the shop in the alley at eight o'clock. Does that mean she entered your shop through the back door when she showed up for her evening appointment a half-hour late?"

"Not exactly. We'd talked about where to park when she had her hair styled on her lunch hour. She had to figure out, because the streets around the park are blocked off for the fair, the most convenient place to park to deliver her three roses to the exhibit. I suggested she park in the alley, carry her roses through the shop and across the street to the exhibit. Then walk back for her seven-fifteen touchup here and her appointment at Zebner's. She came back to the shop through the front door after she dropped her roses off at the fair exhibit."

"Did you actually see Miss Powder carry flowers from her car over to the rose contest last evening?"

"Yes, we all did. Everyone wished her good luck."

"What time was that?"

"I'd just started trimming my seven o'clock's hair. She was on time, but I was a little backed up. I'm fairly certain it was nearly seven-fifteen. That's when Miss Powder left her four books with me until she got back."

Alice thanked her and walked to Sally's booth to say good-bye. "Have to dash. I was invited to a dinner party at the Erin at the last minute, and I have to check that my one and only cocktail dress is pressed."

"That's nice. Do you have a terrific date for the dinner?"

"He's okay. He's a guy from Ohio. He's not on the force but he's helping us out on Miss Powder's case."

"You don't mean Brady Kincaid, do you?"

Alice became wary. "Yeah. Do you know him?" She wondered how Sally knew him. Had she gone out with him?

"Everybody in town remembers Brady Kincaid from last winter when he helped in the investigation of the murders of a couple city officials. Here in the shop, we thought he was one luscious hunk—not exactly handsome, but very sexy. Right?"

"I only met him today, and we're going together because we're working on the same case and it's convenient."

Sally grinned. "Sure, sure. Meanwhile, sit down. You have long, beautiful hair and I'd like to twist it into an elegant roll pinned to the back of your head. It'll be perfect for your big evening out and will only take a minute to pull together."

"Look, Sally. I don't know how to tell you but I haven't a red cent on me. I couldn't pay you until Monday."

"Forget it. This one's on the house." Sally turned to the shop's owner. "Right?"

"Right. We're used to giving freebies to the folks in blue, aren't we, Sally?"

The hairdressers' eyes danced as they laughed together at their inside joke.

The tension was thick enough to grab when Brady arrived at Booth 22. Judging for the rose exhibit had been completed though the winners would not be announced until eight o'clock. He saw the judges seated together at a table quietly talking to each other, carefully not making eye contact with exhibitors. In contrast, exhibitors roamed restlessly through the tent checking their competition.

Brady approached a woman whose badge identified her as a proctor for the event.

"Excuse me. I'd like to speak to the person who signed in Miss Powder's rose entries Friday night."

She summoned the registrar for the event, a worried-looking gentleman, who asked, "Is there a problem?"

Brady introduced himself. "I'm helping out in the investigation into Miss Penelope Powder's death. We're trying to retrace her steps from the moment she left the library at five-thirty Friday night. We understand the deadline for entering roses for the exhibition was eight o'clock, and we want to verify the exact time Miss Powder checked in her entries, if it isn't too much bother."

"No, of course, not. We're all still in shock about dear Penny and can't believe she's really gone." He turned. "If you'll step this way, I'll show you the register. As you'll see, we have a strict rule about our eight o'clock deadline and enforce it by having entrants actually punch this time clock with their registration forms. It works out quite well."

Brady was shown Miss Powder's separate registrations for *Chili Powder, Gun Powder,* and *Powder Puff.* The first rose was clocked in at 7:28 p.m., the second at 7:29 p.m., and the last at 7:30 p.m.

He noted this information and asked, "Is it possible, after the prizes have been awarded, to have a copy of these three registrations made for the police department's investigation?"

"Yes, indeed. It's our pleasure to cooperate in any way we can."

"One more thing. Who would know where Miss Powder went after she dropped off her roses?"

The registrar signaled the proctor. "Didn't Penny Powder take a quick walk around the tent after she registered and then stop and talk to you?"

"That's right. She gave her competition a quick once-over. Of course, she didn't express an opinion about the other entries, and I didn't expect she would."

Brady waited until the registrar walked away. "I understand competition between rose exhibitors is very intense."

The proctor nodded. "All growers believe their rose is the finest. If they didn't, there'd be no point exhibiting."

"Had Miss Powder made a particular enemy among any of the rose growers?"

She took her time answering. "If you're trying to find out if I know or even suspect anyone here of killing Miss Powder, I don't. Even if I did suspect one person or another, I'd certainly be careful naming anyone before I said even one word."

Brady backed off that line of questioning. "What did you and Miss Powder talk about after she registered last night?"

"Penny wanted to tell me about a book she'd just finished reading that she thought I'd enjoy. I'm a fan of historical novels, and Penny was always on the lookout for me. She was so thoughtful that way. I'm truly going to miss her."

Brady nodded solemnly. "When Miss Powder left the booth, did she mention where she was going next?"

"Penny said she had to hurry because she was already late for an appointment at the beauty shop. I thought her hair looked fine, but she said she was having her picture taken at Zebner's Studio. She was going to stop at the beauty shop first to have the strands on top brushed back in place. You have to realize Penny Powder was a perfectionist about everything."

"What time was that?"

"That was twenty minutes before eight o'clock. I know because another exhibitor checked in and I heard the registrar remark the new entrant had twenty minutes to spare."

"Did Miss Powder mention where she'd left her car?"

"As a matter of fact, she did. She parked in the alley behind the beauty parlor and the photo studio. That way it would be handy when she left Zebner's."

Brady had wrapped up the interview and was near the exit when the proctor caught up with him. "Penny left her flower carrier here to take her roses home after the prizes were awarded. It's a custom-made basket and somewhat valuable. What should we do with it?"

"I believe it becomes part of Miss Powder's estate. When you learn the name of the attorney handling her affairs, I suggest you contact him to find out what to do with the carrier."

"Thank you. The fact is, besides the real value of the carrier, it has sentimental value, as well. You have to understand, Penny Powder was an institution in Early. Between the library, her perfect roses, and all the thoughtful things she did for so many of us, she will never be forgotten."

Brady agreed, thinking privately that Penny Powder would soon be remembered for her scathing *On the Chopping Block* book reviews as well.

✦ ✦ ✦

Chief Rygard spotted Brady entering the bullpen and motioned him to join Newkirk in the office.

"Where's Drinker?" was the chief's first question.

"Alice went back to the beauty shop with more questions. She called me with what she picked up." Brady turned to Newkirk. "Together with the information I just learned at the rose exhibit, we can fill in more details on your flow chart." He took a breath. "To answer your question, Chief, Alice is on her way home. She agreed to go with me to the Brickley's dinner party at the Erin tonight. She wanted some time to get ready."

"What's this party all about?" Rygard asked. "My wife phoned that we're invited to the Erin this evening and I should come home and get ready before nine o'clock."

"It's dinner with Holly LaFrance and her agent. It's Carolyn Brickley's way of thanking the author for autographing books all day." Brady sat down next to Newkirk and asked, "What's new? Have any good leads developed?"

Rygard nodded. "I was able to access Miss Powder's safe deposit box. First, the lady was, by my standards, wealthy. But her wealth was nothing a killer could lay hands on quickly. Her stocks and bonds would take at least a week to cash. She kept most of her ready cash in savings and money market accounts scattered throughout the country. Her personal checking account didn't carry large balances."

"If this was a robbery, there wasn't much a thief could spend right away."

"Exactly. So, we have to believe the motive for killing Miss Powder was personal and vindictive. Chopping away at her skull proves that."

"Interesting choice of words, Chief. Her column was called *On the Chopping Block*."

Newkirk said, "That's the point Chief and I reached. We believe the murder was revenge for one of her lousy book reviews."

Brady sighed. "Where would you begin? She must have written two hundred a year times—how long was Chanuary in business?"

"Twelve years."

"So figure a couple thousand angry authors and publishers."

Rygard said, "We did, and we sent an officer back to Miss Powder's house to comb her files all the way back to the beginning. He's looking for anything at all threatening besides the e-mails from *Invincible*, although that person remains our best prospect. We're lucky Powder threw nothing away and was as meticulous with her files as she was with the rest of her life."

"We have one other road to follow that might lead somewhere." Newkirk glanced at his notebook. "Remember the librarians mentioned Powder carried four books home with her? She was found at Brickley's with only three books, which have been checked into the evidence room. The fourth book, *Street Monkeys,* is missing. And since we now know Powder wrote only reviews of the books she considered deplorable, is it possible that someone expected her to do a hatchet job on *Street Monkeys*? They could have intercepted her with the book and an argument followed. We all know Miss Powder was obstinate and would tell anyone she was going to write what she pleased no matter who threatened her. I picture a struggle that got ugly and she was axed. If the book became covered with her blood, the killer would have disposed of it."

Brady didn't think so. "That supposes the author or whoever killed her was carrying an axe. How do you conceal an axe over two feet long? Up your sleeve?"

Rygard stepped in. "Don't forget there were at least two people involved and, personally, I think Newkirk has the right idea. We're trying to get in touch with the author of *Street Monkeys,* S. J. Rancid."

"*Rancid?*" Brady thought that was a terrible name.

"It's a pseudonym, and I have someone tracking down the author's real identity and where he or she can be found right now."

"I don't like to be negative, but what if the killer swiped that particular book to throw you off track? And, by the way, do we know what the book is about?"

"It's a story about urban kids going bad. This author has written two earlier books on the same subject."

"Did Miss Powder write reviews of those previous books in her *Chopping Block* column?"

"Matter of fact, she didn't." Rygard added, "Miss Powder had a precise cross-reference system. Every review was filed by title, author, by date, and by subject."

Newkirk clasped his hands on top of his head. "I hate this case. Thousands of people with a motive, a clue here and there, yet here we are—stuck in neutral."

"Maybe not." Brady told him, "Alice expects to write up a complete report of this afternoon's activities. Meantime, here's the condensed version, unless you'd rather speak to her directly."

Brady wasn't surprised Newkirk shook his head *no.* "I can wait for Drinker's written report with the details. I'd like to hear your account now."

"Holly LaFrance, the visiting author, read part of a manuscript Miss Powder had written." Brady quickly covered the trips to Early's library and the Triangle Plaza where Holly gave the unpublished manuscript and a used book she'd just purchased to Alice for safekeeping. "Before Alice and I drove to the mall, we saw Holly's agent enter the library. Alice had the feeling he was checking up on Holly and gave the librarian a high sign not to tell him where Holly had gone. The agent believed the librarian and drove back to their Dover hotel."

Brady explained they followed him to be certain he returned to Dover. "I got a good look at the guy's car and guess what? It matches the description the McAvenue boy gave of the automobile he and Steffie Fellmeyer saw circling Miss Powder's block. It's a classic white convertible touring car with trumpet horns in front and side-mounted spare tires with metal covers."

Newkirk wondered if Mike McAvenue would be able to identify the agent. Shuffling through his notes, he said, "The agent's name is Worthington Smitterly."

"Goodnight, Minerva!" The chief shook his head. "That's a made-up name if I ever heard one. Run a check on him, too." He turned to Brady. "Let's hear what you and Drinker gathered for Newkirk's timeline chart."

Brady cleared his throat. "From what Alice and I were told at the rose exhibit and at the beauty shop, I've assembled, in order of exact time Friday evening, the following:

"*7:15 p.m.* – Miss Powder parks her Austin Healey in the alley behind the beauty parlor at the suggestion of the shop's owner. Miss

Powder is witnessed by the shop's owner carrying three rose contest entries through the beauty shop over to the rose exhibit, Booth 22. Miss Powder leaves four library books with the shop's owner until she returns later for her second hair appointment.

"*7:28, 7:29, 7:30 p.m.* – Miss Powder officially clocks in her three rose contest entries at Booth 22.

"*7:40 p.m.* – Miss Powder leaves the rose exhibit, after chatting with one of the proctors, an acquaintance of hers.

"*7:45 p.m.* – Miss Powder returns to beauty parlor. She's a half-hour late for an appointment with the shop's owner to have her hair touched up for a photograph to be taken at Zebner's Studio, less than one hundred feet away from the beauty shop.

"*7:50 p.m.* – Miss Powder leaves the beauty parlor through the front door and is seen walking in the direction of Zebner's Studio. She is carrying four books that will be used as props for the photographs scheduled to appear in a library publication.

"*8:00 p.m.* – Hair stylist Sally takes a cigarette break in the alley and sees Miss Powder's Austin Healey parked there.

"*8:45 p.m.* – A ticket is written for overtime parking in the alley and stuck under the roadster's windshield wiper.

"*9:07 p.m.* – Carolyn Brickley activates the alarm system and leaves her shop through the alley. She notices Miss Powder's car parked across from the beauty shop's back door.

"*9:30 p.m.* – Two other beauty shop employees leave work through the back door and see Miss Powder's automobile still parked in the alley.

"*10:10 p.m.* – Sally leaves the beauty parlor through the back door. The Austin Healey is no longer parked in the alley."

Brady closed his notepad. "That's all the two of us have dug up for now."

The chief had followed the report with eyes closed, visualizing the events described. "That kicks Zebner's version of events into a cat's hat. Another thing I don't like is the agent with the phony name skulking around looking for the author."

Newkirk decided the next thing to do was to line up the officers already on duty at the fair. "I'll have them canvass all the booths adjacent to Zebner's asking exactly when or if Zebner set up Booth 18 on Friday night like he said he did."

Rygard nodded. "Good idea. If you want to get going, you're excused. I'd like a moment with Brady."

The door closed; the chief leaned forward and smiled. "Well, Brady, I won't beat around the bush. It's obvious we need someone like you. It seems to me you're wasting your talents at that little teacher's college down in Ohio. Now, I'm here to tell you that you can pick your cases, your hours, and even your salary. That's how badly we want you."

Brady didn't know what to say.

The chief added, "Don't be concerned about Newkirk's or Bebout's feelings. They want you around, too. As far as Drinker goes, it appears you and she are already working together like partners should. When she aces the detectives exam next month, and I know she will, she's going to need an experienced partner like you."

"I'm flattered and I know I'd like it here. Can you give me some time to think it over?"

"Definitely. Kincaid, I admire your approach to problems and people. This is a special opening for you only. I don't have a line of candidates waiting to fill this job." The chief reflected briefly then added, "This city is growing rapidly and I'm looking to build a crack team of four detectives. Adding you will make that happen, so I hope you'll join us. Meanwhile, take as long as you need to decide."

Brady and Rygard stood, shook hands over the desk, and Brady left to join Newkirk in the bullpen.

"I saw you and the chief shake hands. Does that mean you're going to join the force?" Newkirk was smiling.

"I told him I'd think it over. Are you certain you and Bebout will be okay with this?"

"Are you kidding? It was our suggestion way back in December when we met you."

That was gratifying, and the more Brady thought about it, the more appealing the idea of working in Early, Michigan, became. Especially partnering with the lovely Officer Alice Drinker.

18

Saturday – 7:15 p.m.

Visiting Steffie at the hospital had turned into a social event for Hannah, Meggin, and two football players from Early High, their laughter heard all the way to the lobby. Brady had returned with more questions and found Mike McAvenue trying to hang on to his spot standing at the head of Steffie's bed. It was a hard go for Mike, three years younger and fifty pounds lighter than the visiting athletes.

"Where's your mother?" Brady asked Steffie and learned Joyce had gone home. She'd become confident Steffie was recovering rapidly and had enough company that she could take part in the Founders Day pageant at seven and attend Carolyn's dinner party later. Hannah and Meggin were going to stay with Steffie until eight o'clock when they had plans to attend a party of their own; and Mike happily volunteered to remain until nine, when visiting hours were over and his father would pick him up.

Brady cleared his throat. "Hannah and Meggin, if you wouldn't mind, could you and your friends step outside for a moment. I have official police business to discuss with Steffie and Mike."

Alone with the pair, he asked, "Do either of you remember the classic white touring car you both saw circling around Miss Powder's block?"

They nodded.

"Would you be able to identify it if you saw it again?"

Steffie wasn't sure, but Mike said, "Absolutely. I told my dad about the car I'd seen and we found it on the Internet. It's a 1935 limited edition Lincoln estate car. The guy driving around today had the top up, but I know it's the same car, especially with the pair of trumpet horns in front."

"Good. Now, how about the driver? If either of you saw him again, but not driving the classic convertible, would you be able to identify him? Could you look at photographs of six different individuals and be able to pick him out?"

Steffie thought so. "What I remember best about the driver is that he looked like one of those characters in an old vampire movie."

Mike agreed. "He was so pale, I thought he looked kind of green."

Brady was pleased. "How old would you judge him to be?"

The teenagers looked at each other and guessed. "Pretty old. Even older than you, Mr. Kincaid."

Brady let that pass and learned the man had a mustache and hair "as black as tar," meaning it was probably dyed.

"Mr. Kincaid, there's something else." Steffie glanced at Mike before continuing. "I don't know if anyone told you about the man who took our pictures at the fair today. He started to walk into my room a little while ago. But when he saw Mike and the other guys, he left."

"Do you know why he came to see you?"

She shook her head.

"Okay, Steffie, I'll keep an eye out for him and ask him what he was doing at the hospital. Maybe he made a mistake and started to enter the wrong room."

Mike didn't agree. "When Hannah and her cousin saw him, they got upset. Like he was following them." He turned to Steffie. "What was it your sister called that guy?"

She giggled. "A *sweek*. It's a combination word—*sweaty* and *geek*."

Brady made more entries in his notepad and thanked the pair.

Leaving the hospital, he hoped he could catch Newkirk and tell him about the photographer, known as the *sweek*, trying to visit Steffie's hospital room. That had to be Randall Zebner. Was there a possibility of tying the *sweek* to *Hot Paws*?

He decided to get in touch with Carolyn Brickley, as well. He wanted to ask her to invite Newkirk and his girl friend to the dinner party. He hoped Carolyn would say yes without asking too many questions.

✦ ✦ ✦

The editor of the *Early Eagle* had given up on his reporter, the drunken Sonnet. A welcome surprise had been the photographs taken at the fair turned in by Randy Zebner. They weren't bad and could be used with the material Oden was putting together about the event.

However, the murder was the big story, and he was thankful the *Eagle* was published only twice a week and he had plenty of time before Tuesday's edition was distributed.

It seemed odd how anxious Zebner appeared about taking pictures of the interior of Penny Powder's house. He'd even volunteered to interview Steffie Fellmeyer about being injured there. Bob thanked him and said he'd let Zebner know about the photographs and the interview.

Entering police headquarters, a half-block from the *Eagle,* Oden hoped his old pal Everett Rygard would share whatever information was available on Miss Powder's homicide.

The chief was on the phone when Oden entered the office and said when he'd hung up, "That was Carolyn Brickley confirming our invitation to her dinner party tonight at the Erin. I wonder why my wife and I are invited."

"I've been invited, too. I guess Carolyn wants me to make up for the blunder of printing that stinky book review just in time for the autograph session. I'll be there to interview the author, Holly LaFrance, and write a glowing article about her and all her books."

Oden shook his head. "It's going to be tough. I've never read so much as one line of Holly LaFrance's work and don't expect to start now."

"At least the food will be good."

Oden nodded. "Thanks for seeing me, Chief. I'd appreciate whatever you can give me about the Powder homicide case." He noted Rygard's pursed lips and added, as he pocketed his pen and pad, "You know I won't print whatever you consider still confidential."

"Okay, Bob. Here's the skinny, and it's all strictly off the record until I tell you otherwise. Miss Penny Powder has turned out to be a sort of Jekyll and Hyde. Her house is a fortress, with all kinds of locked rooms and a thick safe that contains secret ledgers and bank accounts. She had five separate computers, each containing separate data. Penny Powder lived her public life as librarian on the first floor of her home. But the second floor was where she did her business; and, Bob," the chief lowered his voice, "I think when we add up all her holdings, Penny Powder will have liquid assets in the millions."

Oden could barely contain his personal shock and surprise and wished he could be taking notes.

Rygard continued. "We found a letter in her safe deposit box directing us to an attorney in Lansing who drew up her will. Here's the kicker. When I reached the attorney and told him Miss Powder was dead, his only question was 'Was she murdered?' Now, doesn't that sound peculiar? Why wouldn't he ask if she'd been ill or been involved in an accident?"

Oden had no answer. "What else did Penny's lawyer say?"

"Just that his instructions were to deliver a letter addressed to Early's Chief of Police upon notification of her death by natural causes or otherwise."

"Wow! Penny must have expected trouble. Do you know when the letter will be delivered?"

"As soon as her attorney goes to his office in downtown Lansing then drives here to my office. I expect he'll arrive in an hour or two."

"I don't suppose you'd like me to hang around while you read her letter."

"Nope."

Oden said, "Getting back to Penny's house, I wonder if something about all her secret computers and locked rooms has leaked. Zebner, the photographer who freelanced for the *Eagle* today at the fair, was very anxious to take pictures of the interior. He seemed to know all about the McAvenue boy and Steffie Fellmeyer getting inside."

Rygard stiffened. "I can't believe either one of those kids would spill anything. Both Newkirk and Brady sat down with them and explained how important it was to keep whatever they saw inside Miss

Powder's house a secret."

The editor assured his friend, "I don't think Zebner talked with either one. He probably heard about Steffie Fellmeyer's accident when Joyce and Donovon were paged and notified at the fair that Steffie had been taken to the hospital. It's now known that Marva Greeves planted the idea of scouting Miss Powder's house in the McAvenue boy's head, certain he'd take Steffie along."

Chief shook his head. "Why would Greeves pull a stunt like that? Those kids could have been seriously hurt."

"Best guess is getting even with Joyce for trouncing her so badly in the last city council election."

Oden took a breath. "There's another angle on Marva Greeves. Did you know she tried to be appointed to the Library Board but Penny wouldn't hear of it? Penny stated publicly to city council that she'd resign from the library if Marva Greeves was ever appointed to the board."

Aware of Marva's vindictive nature, Rygard wondered if she'd found someone to carry out the murder. Marva herself was too short to have axed Penny Powder unless she stood on a box. He also knew Miss Powder was too careful to ever turn her back on someone like Marva Greeves. He made a note to ask Newkirk if anyone had interviewed Mrs. Greeves concerning her whereabouts last night.

Aloud he asked Oden, "Who wrote the unkind review of the visiting author's book?"

"The review appeared in a syndicated column, *On the Chopping Block,* written by someone named *Chanuary.*"

Rygard smiled. "I thought so."

Returning to the *Eagle* office, Bob Oden passed Newkirk on High Street and stopped to chat. Thinking Rygard's remark *I thought so* was curious, Oden believed if he were careful he might get something from the detective.

"Chief Rygard brought me up-to-date on the Powder investigation, though most of it's confidential and can't be printed yet." Oden took the chance. "That *Chanuary* column was certainly incendiary, wasn't it?"

"They all were. I had absolutely no idea Miss Powder had so much venom in her, did you?"

Maintaining a poker face and breathing evenly, Bob replied, "None at all." Not wanting Newkirk to get away, he asked, "Do you have anything else I can't write?"

"Well, this is not definite and don't mention this to anyone, much less put it in the *Eagle*, but Chief officially asked Brady Kincaid to join the force. He let Brady know we want him badly enough he can write his own ticket."

"How do you and Bebout feel about Brady moving into your department?"

"We suggested it. And," Newkirk lowered his voice, "Brady would be partnered with Drinker, so neither Bebout or I would have to train her." His tone made it clear not having to train Alice Drinker was a benefit.

"Before I forget and while you're here, Newkirk, have you had a chance to interview Marva Greeves about Penny Powder's murder?"

"Briefly. She definitely had a good motive to kill Miss Powder but Marva has a near-perfect alibi. She spent most of Friday evening taking care of last-minute problems at the fair. We did find one chink in her story. Around ten o'clock last night both the market manager and one of the hair stylists saw Marva in the alley behind the bookstore. When I confronted her about that, she denied it at first. Then she suddenly remembered searching for her car in the alley because she had forgotten where she'd parked it."

"That's a lame excuse."

"Right, it is. But I have problems suspecting Marva Greeves. First, she's too short to take advantage of Miss Powder even holding an axe. Next, at ten o'clock when she was seen running around the alley behind the bookstore, Miss Powder had been dead nearly two hours. We plan to subpoena Marva's phone records on the chance she used her telephone to put a contract out to murder Miss Powder."

Oden didn't think Marva's telephone records would be of much value. The woman was too devious to have used her own phone to hire a hit man.

He thanked Newkirk for the information and asked if he expected to attend the Brickley dinner party.

"Matter of fact, I just got a message from Mrs. Brickley inviting me and a date to attend her party at the Erin tonight."

"Guess I'll see you there."

They agreed the party was certain to be interesting.

19

Saturday – 8:00 p.m.

Letting the shower's hot needles bounce off his head, Brady relaxed. He'd returned to Lincoln's condo to change clothes for the dinner party and was surprised how energized he felt in spite of only a few hours of sleep Friday night.

His second shave of the day was interrupted by a call from Newkirk with information from the officers who'd questioned everyone manning fair booths adjacent Zebner's. A couple demonstrating miracle-cleaning products in the booth next to Zebner were asked if they'd seen him at any time Friday evening. They echoed what everyone else in the vicinity said: No, Zebner did not appear Friday night. He brought his photo equipment and started setting up his booth at nine-thirty Saturday morning, barely a half-hour before the fair opened.

Brady concluded, "So much for Zebner's statement accounting for his whereabouts during the hours Miss Powder was being murdered."

"The problem is," Newkirk replied, "we're really not yet ready to haul Zebner into the station for questioning."

Positive Zebner had a hand in Miss Powder's death, neither detective thought he was bright enough to have masterminded the plot. There had to be an accomplice, and they agreed they had to be careful not to spook the second killer before they were ready to make an arrest.

Brady finished dressing and, checking himself in the mirror, was surprised how well the dark blue summer suit fit. Not expecting to wear anything other than casual clothes for fishing, the suit had been borrowed, along with a white shirt, tie, and black shoes, from one of the Erin's waiters. Brady had never been much concerned about clothes before, but tonight he wanted to look sharp at the dinner party in front of Alice.

His mind went back to the puzzle of the bookstore's front and alley doors. If the alarm company recorded the time Carolyn locked her doors Friday night, why hadn't an alarm sounded when Miss Powder's body was carried in and dumped? How did someone get in and out of the bookstore without the alarm sounding? Why were the thumbturns on the locks for both doors in the unlocked vertical position when Carolyn opened early Saturday morning?

Of course! Brady remembered examining the roof of the bookstore's building during his last trip to Early. He'd discovered the lock to the access hatch into the store had been broken, allowing a burglar to enter from the roof.

He phoned Newkirk. "I think Miss Powder's body might have been brought into the bookstore through the roof hatch. They probably had to lower her body down the cramped shaft and accidentally dropped her, explaining how her ankles were fractured. Can you rustle up an extension ladder so we can climb up to the roof to see if the lock to the access hatch has been broken?"

"Now? I'm already dressed for the dinner party and told Beth I'd pick her up in twenty minutes."

"I understand. Would you mind if I call Alice to ask her to look at the roof with me. Maybe she can dig up the ladder I need."

There was a long pause on Newkirk's end, and he finally said, "Sometimes you're a bastard, Brady."

"Is that any way to talk to a future brother cop?"

"Have you decided to say *yes*?" Newkirk sounded overjoyed.

"Not yet, but it's very, very tempting."

Newkirk was instantly cooperative. No way would he jeopardize the chance of Brady's accepting the chief's offer. "How about this idea? I'll have someone on duty scrounge up a ladder and have it delivered to the alley. I'll contact Beth, have her meet me at the Erin and I can change clothes at the hotel. That ought to work, don't you think?"

"Sure it will," Brady agreed. Then mulling it over, he decided, "On second thought, let's skip it for now and attend the dinner party as scheduled. You and I can check out the roof tomorrow when we have more time."

"Tell the truth. Are you certain tomorrow will be all right?"

"Positively." About to hang up Brady asked, "Newk, may I have Alice's home number? I want to be certain she wears *Valiant*, the cologne Mr. Yee put together, to the dinner party."

A minute later Alice Drinker answered her phone, and Brady reminded her to dab on the scent that mimicked *Invincible.*

"How'd you get my number, Kincaid? It's not listed."

Brady explained he'd run a new idea past Newkirk and at the same time asked for her number. He noted he was back to *Kincaid.*

"Since I'm working the case too, mind running the idea past me?"

"Not at all." Brady told her about his discovery when Carolyn's store had been broken into six months earlier. "All three stores in the middle building on North Park Avenue can be entered through access hatches on the roof. The hatches were installed for the convenience of heating and air conditioning contractors so they wouldn't have to climb up and down a ladder from the alley every time they reentered the store."

Alice understood. "You want to see if the padlock to the bookstore's hatch has been tampered with and if that's the way Miss Powder's body was delivered into the bookstore." She thought for a moment. "Why bother with an extension ladder from the alley? All you have to do is ask the Brickleys if you can pull the folding ladder down from its platform above their storeroom. Then you can climb up to the platform, up the hatchway, and check the hatch door from the inside to see if it's still padlocked."

Brady was dumbfounded he hadn't figured that out himself. Checking his watch he said, "Good thinking, Alice. In fact, there's enough time to contact the Brickleys. I'm sure they're already here at the Erin. I'm going downstairs now to see if I can borrow a key to get into the bookstore."

"While you're at it, Kincaid, you ought to ask where they keep the pole with a slip hook attached." Alice knew by Brady's silence he didn't understand what she was talking about. She explained, "The metal pull gizmo loops onto a catch that opens the ceiling panel door to the folding ladder. Once that panel door opens, the ladder slides down to the floor."

She had just saved Brady more time and embarrassment. He'd probably kick himself later but asked, "Do you want to join me at the bookstore?"

"Sure. I'll bring a couple strong flashlights. Can you think of anything else we'll need?" He couldn't, and Alice told him she'd be waiting in the alley behind the store after she'd changed back to her uniform.

Despite yellow crime scene tape stretched across the bookstore's entrance, Robert Brickley unlocked the front door. He and Brady simply ducked under the tape and entered the shop. Letting Alice in through the alley door, they turned their attention to the large wooden panel in the storeroom's ceiling.

After the folding ladder was lowered and locked in place, Brady removed his jacket, white shirt and tie, took a deep breath and climbed up to the dark platform where he'd once suffered a near panic attack. That time he'd been in total darkness without a flashlight; now, even with light, he didn't feel much better. Once he left the platform to climb the next six feet to the roof, he was going to find himself in a cramped chimney-like space full of soot and cobwebs.

Brady wasn't certain how much time he'd spent on the platform priming himself to enter the hatch and climb its ladder to the roof. He heard someone climbing the folding ladder from the storeroom. He saw a beam from a flashlight and felt the platform give as a body stepped on.

"Why are you fooling around, Kincaid?"

"I'm just getting my bearings."

"Sure you are." Alice stepped to the metal ladder attached to the building's back wall and mounted the first step into the tiny hatch.

"Whoa!" Brady nearly yelled. "What are you doing?"

"I'm going up to check the roof access door. It's supposed to be padlocked. If it isn't, we'll know this is how Miss Powder's body was brought into the bookstore."

"I ought to do that, Alice. Not you."

She felt sorry for Brady. If he were claustrophobic, the tiny cramped hatch would definitely spook him.

"Brady! Shine the beam up to the top of the hatch, please."

He did as asked, at the same time feeling a tingle of pleasure he was back to *Brady*.

"Thanks. I don't have to climb all the way up to see that no one came in through the roof. There are brand-new hinge plates attached on the inside of the hatch door with an eyebolt and a heavy-duty padlock. The lock on this side is snapped tight and shows no sign of tampering. Take a look for yourself."

Brady focused the beam and saw quite plainly bright new metal hardware screwed to the hatch door and adjoining inside masonry wall with a commercial-sized combination padlock clearly in the locked position.

Back on the platform twelve feet above the bookstore floor, Alice stepped close to Brady and sniffed. "How much more of Mr. Yee's cologne did you splash on?"

"I completely forgot about the cologne after I showered. I'm sorry. I know I asked you to wear some and then I didn't."

"Forget it. The reason I asked is that I got a very strong whiff of cologne when I joined you on the platform. I think it's coming from the photographer's studio."

Alice knew the platform to the access hatch was shared with the photo studio next door. She couldn't see Brady's face plainly in the dim light to read his reaction as she asked, "Could we take a peek into Zebner's studio? You know, just open the door up here a crack to see if the cologne is more pungent in Zebner's quarters."

They had no warrant and Brady wondered if Alice's hunch the scent of the killer's cologne came from Zebner's studio constituted a reasonable search. He decided if they only opened the door leading into the studio and didn't lower the folding staircase, there was no harm. Especially if he and Alice were the only persons aware of what they'd done.

The door to Zebner's wasn't locked, leading Brady to want to talk to Robert about the lack of security on the bridge platform between the two stores.

The moment the door opened, Alice stepped to the threshold and inhaled. She knew. "There it is. Can you smell it?"

He could, and she said, "Come on. Let's climb down and see what we can find."

Brady shook his head. "There's a better way and we won't get in trouble." He closed the door to Zebner's studio, crossed over the bridge, and led the way back down to Brickley's bookstore.

Learning the inside padlock at the top of the hatch had not been broken, Robert asked, "Does this mean Miss Powder could not possibly have been brought in by way of the roof hatch?"

Brady nodded. "It also rules out the theory the body was meant to be dumped in Zebner's Studio and was left here by mistake."

Alice piped up, "We have to get inside Zebner's before that sweet smell vanishes."

Brady had a flash, recalling Hannah and Meggin joking about the sweaty photographer and calling him the *sweek*. He also remembered something else. "Robert, are Carolyn and Joyce and their two friends still liable for the lease next door?"

He explained to Alice that Zebner's Studio was formerly occupied by an antiques shop. The storekeeper's will specified her shop, its contents, and goodwill were bequeathed to Carolyn and three friends. They also inherited the responsibility of timely rental payments for the space.

Robert nodded. "The lease for that space runs through to next March. The ladies are subletting the store to Zebner until then." He asked, "Why?"

"Because I'd like to check things out over there. I think the landlady has a right to enter the premises if she, or her agent, smells smoke."

Alice took up the cause. "I smelled smoke, too. Mr. Brickley, by chance does Mrs. Brickley keep a key for the Zebner's Studio handy?"

Robert sorted through the key ring. "Here's the one that'll open his alley door. I understand Zebner has forgotten his keys any number of times so Carolyn keeps a duplicate on hand to unlock his door for him."

He walked to Carolyn's office and found a note under her desk blotter. "Here's the combination we'll have to tap in so the alarm doesn't go off once we've opened the door."

Brady shook his head. "I don't think you should come with us, Robert. The truth is, entering Zebner's on the pretext of smelling smoke is questionable. I don't want you to get in trouble because I used bad judgment not waiting for a search warrant."

"Nonsense, Brady. I'm coming with you. The photographer's studio needs protection and I'm bringing the fire extinguisher."

Brady didn't like it but followed Robert into the alley as it appeared he and Alice were determined to enter and search Zebner's with or without him.

Alice whispered, "Don't worry, Kincaid. If we're caught, you can count on both Mr. Brickley and me to hang tough."

Carolyn checked her watch again. Robert had been gone more than half an hour. She didn't know if that was good or bad. It was good if Brady and Alice found something to solve Miss Powder's murder and bad if this was just another dead end.

Glancing about the Erin's private dining room, she was pleased so many couples had accepted her last-minute invitation to the dinner party. The day that started so badly was turning out quite well, and she'd managed to sell nearly three hundred-fifty copies of *Farewell, Fjords.*

The arrival of Worthington Smitterly, attired in glistening white from collar to toe, caused a stir among the guests. He was alone, and explained in his grand expansive manner that Holly was a little under the weather.

"She might be a tad late."

Thereupon Smitterly turned his full charm and attention to the dinner guests who'd already arrived. Carolyn couldn't complain. By taking over the duties of host, he covered Robert's absence nicely.

She observed the photographer, Zebner, sidling about here and there. It appeared he was eavesdropping on conversations, particularly between Chief Rygard and Bob Oden. When he popped up beside her, Carolyn jerked involuntarily.

"You shouldn't sneak up on people like that, Randall."

"Sorry." He found his handkerchief and wiped his brow. "I'm looking for the detectives, Mr. Kincaid and Officer Drinker. I understand they planned to attend, and I'd like to take an informal photograph of them. You know, out of uniform."

"They'll be along shortly. They're just checking something at the bookstore. Robert's with them, and he knows the dinner starts promptly at nine."

"What are they looking for?" Zebner's perspiration pumped.

Carolyn didn't like the man's reaction—he was suddenly far too nervous—and she became wary. "Nothing important. Brady is only taking one last look around."

He nodded and drifted away.

Across the room, Lincoln signaled Carolyn she had a phone call. Hoping it was Robert and he was ready to return to the party, she took the call in the lobby.

"Carolyn." It was Robert. "If anyone can see you talking to me, please smile and act natural."

"All right, I'm smiling. What's wrong?"

"Nothing. We want you to invite the photographer, Zebner, to stay for dinner as a guest. I'll explain later. Please ask him now before he leaves. We don't want him to get away."

20

Saturday – 8:40 p.m.

Robert assured Brady and Alice, "Carolyn will invite Zebner to stay for the dinner. I know she'll make a special effort to see that he doesn't leave before we get back to the Erin."

About to unlock Zebner's alley door, Alice handed around latex gloves from her Jeep, and Brady reminded his companions, "Don't forget we *thought* we smelled smoke and that's why we entered the studio."

Once inside, there was no doubt about the pungent odor of *Invincible* cologne.

Alice remarked, "Considering how expensive that exclusive cologne is—didn't Mr. Yee say something about *Invincible* costing over three hundred dollars an ounce—someone is sure splashing it around."

At that price, Robert had a hard time believing Zebner could afford such a luxury. "He has a terrible credit rating. He's nearly broke, and he's late with the rent every month."

"Why does your wife put up with him if he's such a lousy tenant?" Alice wondered.

"Because he was the only person who wanted to sublet the space. Of course, the ladies could have continued to pay the rent from their own pocketbooks. However, they agreed among themselves to let Zebner open his business and crossed their fingers he'd make it."

There wasn't much to see inside the studio—just a barren-looking lobby with two plastic chairs and a counter with a phone and an appointment book without entries. A portable gray fiberglass partition screened the camera and lighting equipment set-up from the lobby. Cardboard scenery propped against the wall and several stools in the portrait area completed the studio's tableau.

In the tiny room that served as an office, Alice combed through a plastic file cabinet while Robert opened and closed nearly empty desk drawers.

"This guy is either not keeping books or someone else is doing his accounting for him. The only sign of running a business is this checkbook." Robert became alarmed. "Brady, look at this. Yesterday Zebner made a five-thousand-dollar cash deposit at Bank of Early. Where in hell would he have gotten that kind of money?"

Copying the account number and time stamped on the receipt, Alice noted the deposit was made Friday afternoon at four-fifty-five. "My guess is Zebner took a contract to kill Miss Powder and five grand was either his fee or the down payment."

"Don't forget we know two people, probably both men, were involved. If Zebner's inducement was money, who hired him? Who engineered the plot and what was the second killer's real motive?" Looking for the answers, Brady opened the door to a tiny bathroom and found soiled hand towels in a hamper.

He was certain the soiled towels were solid evidence in the case. "We have to get a search warrant for this place. Once these towels are delivered and tested at the crime lab, I've a hunch they'll find a DNA match to the sweat on the axe handle and in Miss Powder's car."

"The crime lab boys won't like that," Alice told him. "This is Saturday night, and their office is supposed to be closed."

Brady thought Chief Rygard was the person who could light a fire under Jeffrow to produce results before Sunday brunch. The DNA evidence was crucial and test results from the towels could clinch the case.

In the back of his mind, Brady wondered how he was going to broach the subject of obtaining a search warrant with the chief without giving away the fact he already knew what evidence was available. In a trial, even a first year law student would have every piece of evidence thrown out if his illegal search came to light.

Robert cleared his throat and asked Brady to look at something else. "One of the back legs of this desk is shorter than the others. To keep it from wobbling, Zebner must have stuck this book under the leg." Robert held a squashed copy of *Street Monkeys*. "Look inside. It says *Property of Early Public Library*." Robert was stunned. "This is one of Miss Powder's books!"

"Indeed it is." Brady recalled Miss Powder had taken four books from the library. Only three were found with the victim. *Street Monkeys* was the missing book.

Zebner had lied about not seeing Miss Powder's books. Brady wondered how the photographer was going to explain Miss Powder's copy of *Street Monkeys* stuck under a desk leg or where five thousand dollars in cash came from.

Satisfied that the photo studio was the likely scene of the murder, and having put everything touched back in its exact place, they were ready to return to the bookstore, where Alice was going to use Carolyn's office to change into her cocktail dress.

The studio lights had been turned off but as the back door closed, Brady caught a glimpse of a tiny red glow from inside the storage room. Reopening the door and asking Robert to disengage the security system again, he turned off the overhead lights to locate the red glow he'd just seen.

Brady had a moment of deep concern. He'd bent rules in the past in the name of expediency, but this time he'd crossed the line. If Zebner had a surveillance camera and they were caught snooping around without a warrant, the whole case would blow up.

When the lights were turned back on, Alice walked across the room and found the red glow came from a white rechargeable flashlight plugged into a wall socket. "They must have used this to see in the dark while they toted Miss Powder from Zebner's to the bookstore. It probably took at least an hour to carry her up and down the folding ladders and over the platform between stores. If so, the flashlight's battery no doubt came close to giving out and now it's being recharged through the electric wall outlet."

She unplugged the flashlight and handed it to Brady. "Look at the hanger at the bottom of the flashlight. What do you see?"

Ha! Brady examined the little white plastic loop used to hang the flashlight on a hook. "It looks like a tiny spatter of blood. If we're lucky, this is Miss Powder's blood."

He handed the flashlight to Alice to plug back into the wall socket. Here was another great piece of evidence to add to the search warrant. For good measure, the copy of *Street Monkeys* should be included as well.

Aloud Brady said, "There's no doubt Miss Powder was killed in Zebner's Studio. However, I hope you're both aware we can never, ever admit we entered and found this evidence without a proper warrant."

Alice shook her head. "Have a little faith, Kincaid. We're not going to give this away and screw things up. Right, Mr. Brickley?"

Robert nodded. "At the risk of sounding corny, in words from *The Three Musketeers*, I say 'One for all and all for one.'" He grasped Alice's hand, then Brady's, and formed a three-way handshake.

"Yes, Mr. Brickley, that's pure poppin' corn." Alice smiled. "But that's okay because that's the way I like it. How about you?"

The three-way handshake became firmer.

Returning to the Erin, the trio entered a dining room filled with laughter and animated conversations, helped along by an open bar and freely circulating waiters bearing trays with one tempting appetizer after another.

The subject of Miss Powder's murder was on everyone's lips, as well as the sad moment at the fair when the rose exhibit winners were announced. Penny Powder's entries in the competition swept the blue ribbons in three separate categories, but no one was there to accept her prizes.

Carolyn rushed to Robert's side. "Holly's still not here. According to Worthington she's a little 'under the weather,' and I'm worried she's become terribly sick. Should we call her hotel to find out how she is?"

Robert nodded, left to use the courtesy phone in the lobby, and returned looking grave. "The hotel told me Holly had the doorman summon a cab to take her to Dover Emergency. Her face was battered and she was holding one arm."

Beckoning Brady, Robert told him what he'd just learned. "Carolyn wants me to call the hospital to inquire about Holly's condition. I suppose this sounds insensitive, but without a guest of honor, this could put a crimp in dinner. If the party's cut short, will you be able to keep an eye on Zebner?"

A backup plan was needed and, first, Brady suggested that Newkirk make the call to Dover's Emergency. "His credentials will get more information from the hospital about Holly's condition than an acquaintance's would."

Newkirk learned Holly LaFrance had, indeed, sought medical attention in the emergency ward for a broken arm and facial lacerations. The Brickleys were appalled, and Brady remembered the agent's rage at the library trying to locate Holly. He also recalled the unexplained look on her face at Triangle Plaza. She'd been frightened and Brady wondered if Smitterly was the person she was afraid of.

"Where is she now?" he asked.

"Emergency information said she left without a physician's authorization. The parking lot guard observed her getting into a cab, but he didn't know where she asked to be taken."

Robert asked Newkirk, "Did she say who'd beaten her?"

"Holly told the admitting desk she'd been mugged leaving the mall, but they didn't buy it. Her purse and jewelry hadn't been taken."

Lincoln approached. "Where's Alice? She has a phone call she can take in the lobby." He added quietly, "The lady didn't identify herself but asked me to be discreet when summoning Alice to the phone."

Brady found Alice. "Smile, if you can, so we don't arouse suspicion. You have a phone call from a woman and it might be Holly LaFrance. Her so-called illness was a beating that included a broken arm."

Alice put on her having-a-good-time face and walked hand-in-hand with Brady to the lobby phone.

"Hello. This is Alice Drinker." She listened intently for a minute, hung up, and said, "Gotta go. Holly had a cab drop her off in front of the bookstore. She says she's too scared to go back to the hotel in Dover, and she doesn't know many people in town. Holly asked if she could stay with me for a day or so until she feels better."

"Why you?" Newkirk asked.

"One, because I'm a cop who carries a gun. Two, because staying with the Brickleys is too obvious. Three, because she likes and trusts me. Okay?"

Alice didn't wait for an answer and left at once, driving full throttle around the barricades on North Park Avenue the half-block to Brickley's Books to pick up Holly LaFrance.

Disappointed Alice wouldn't return to the party, Brady wished he could have told her he thought she looked sensational wearing the silky aqua dress that fit her long, lean body like a sheath and aquamarine pendant earrings that matched the glow of her green eyes.

He could hardly believe how well they'd gotten along at the bookstore and wondered if she could ever have romantic feelings for him.

Guests were starting to line up at the overflowing buffet table where he noticed Claudia partnered with Worthington Smitterly. She looked as lovely as ever in a summer cocktail dress she'd borrowed from Joyce. He watched as she laughed and smiled up at the man.

Once that scene would have pierced his heart, but tonight Brady's thoughts centered around Alice Drinker. He knew if he wanted to pursue that relationship he'd have to resign from Lombardy Teachers College and accept Chief Rygard's offer. Alice's close-to-positive reaction when he broached the subject earlier was tilting the scales in favor of moving to Early.

Brady's thoughts were returned to the party by Peter Yee's quiet approach. "Mister Kincaid, may I have a private word with you?"

In a corner of the lobby, Yee said, "An hour ago I had a call from France from a noted perfumer, the very person who created *Invincible*."

"Was he upset you were able to duplicate his ingredients?"

"Perhaps, though he didn't show it. Instead, he warned me that the client for whom he'd concocted *Invincible* has a violent history."

"Were you given the client's name?"

"Yes, Willard Stout IV. But it is known the client changed his name after his last arrest. The man was born into a very wealthy family, and he's dabbled in literature and academia."

Brady asked, "What was the man charged with?"

"Brutality. He's a woman beater. It's known he battered a wife, a whore, and a female student. His family connections got the latest charges dropped provided he left France and never returned."

"Thanks, Mr. Yee. You've been very helpful."

"Two more items, sir. One, the client is described as boastful, egotistical, and bad-tempered; and, two, may well be the gentleman who arrived driving a classic white Lincoln convertible."

Brady reacted. "Why do you say that?"

"Because earlier this evening, when Mrs. Yee and I arrived, a gentleman was handing his beautiful automobile over to a valet. When the car door was opened and the gentleman stepped out, both my wife and I noticed a particular fragrance."

Yee smiled. "There was no mistaking the scent of *Invincible!*"

21

Saturday – 9:30 p.m.

Concealed in the shadows of the bookstore's recessed entrance, dressed in a housecoat and slippers, Holly dashed to the Jeep when Alice pulled up. Her face was still swollen from the battering she'd taken, and she could barely close the Jeep's door with her right arm in a sling.

"Good God, Holly, I hope you made a police report. No one deserves to be beaten like that."

By her silence, Alice knew a police report hadn't been made, but she wasn't the person to deliver a lecture. She'd received repeated bruises from her first husband without having him arrested. If she hadn't become a police officer, they might still be living together; and she would no doubt still be suffering his abuse on a regular schedule.

"This is very kind of you, leaving Carolyn's beautiful party and taking me in."

"Don't thank me yet. I'm just coming off my third divorce, and I have a fifteen-year-old daughter from my first marriage living with me. So, until I get on my feet, we're living in Carlyle Acres, which is a fancy name for a not-so-fancy trailer park."

"Oh, Alice, I'm sorry. I didn't mean to inconvenience you or your daughter. Isn't there some sort of motel south of Early? I think it's called the Early Bird."

"Listen, my trailer may not be the Ritz, but there's plenty of room and you'll be super safe. You'll see what I mean when we get to the front gate. Matter of fact, here we are."

Pulling up to the trailer park's entrance, Alice rolled her window down and tapped code numbers on an identification pad. The gate swung open, and she drove through to 472 Happy Hollow.

"No one can get through the gate into the park without punching in personal ID numbers. Visitors have to speak into a closed circuit television camera to identify themselves and whom they came to see. The message is relayed to the trailer to be visited, and the visitor is either allowed in or not depending on the occupant's response."

That information and learning the trailer park had surveillance cameras and round-the-clock guard service added to Holly's sense of security. She relaxed completely once inside the clean and attractively furnished mobile home.

"You'll have to double up with me in my bedroom, Holly. My daughter, the princess, has the other bedroom to herself."

"No problem. It's comfortable here and I already feel at home. I don't know about you but I'm finally unwinding and getting hungrier by the minute. Could we order in a pizza? My treat, of course."

Pizza was delivered and devoured; Holly changed into a pair of Alice's pajamas, then fell asleep before Alice could ask her any questions about the beating.

Smitterly's name hadn't come up, though Alice was certain he was to blame. She wondered if this was the first time he'd battered Holly. Regardless, their author/agent relationship had to be severed.

Brady missed Alice's presence at the dinner party but didn't have time to fret. He had to talk privately with Chief Rygard and Newkirk about Mr. Yee's true nose identifying Smitterly's *Invincible* brand cologne. It wasn't enough to justify a warrant for arrest but pointed them in the right direction.

"Have you been able to establish a link yet between Hot Paws and Smitterly?" Rygard was hooked on giving suspects colorful nicknames and announced, "From now on, Smitterly's code name is *Mister Goodscent.* Can you two remember that?"

They nodded, and Newkirk admitted, "So far there's no obvious connection between, ah. . ." He hesitated, trying to remember the latest code name. ". . . Mister Goodscent and Hot Paws."

"Then find it." Rygard returned to the party.

Brady and Newkirk looked at each other, wondering what to do next. "Come on, Newk, let's go back to the party, too. It'll look suspicious if we don't."

Newkirk agreed and thought he'd make a better decision where to go next in this investigation if he relaxed and rejoined Beth. Something about that special woman brought out the best in him.

Brady had similar thoughts about Alice and phoned her at home. "Hi, Alice. Are you and Holly okay?"

"Why wouldn't we be?"

Her tone bothered him. She was pissed off about something. "Just checking. Wanted you to know Mr. Yee dropped a bombshell on Smitterly. He identified Smitterly's cologne as *Invincible*. And before I forget, the chief wants everyone to call Smitterly *Mister Goodscent*."

"Oh, *cripes*. That's corny."

"Tell Chief that."

"Maybe I will."

Alice wasn't communicating the way she should, and Brady wondered what she was holding back. It had to be something to do with Holly. He told her, "I'm calling because I hope you or Holly can help us. We're trying to find the connection between Smitterly and Zebner."

Alice's cell phone crackled, and Brady knew she'd walked to a location out of Holly's hearing range. She whispered, "I'm certain Zebner killed Miss Powder under contract with Smitterly."

Brady agreed. "What we need now is Mister Goodscent Smitterly's motive for wanting Miss Powder dead and how and why he hooked up with Zebner."

"Holly knows something she's not aware she knows. She's sleeping right now so I don't think I'll find out what we need tonight. Sorry, Brady, looks like you'll have to wait until tomorrow. I'll talk to you then."

She hung up and Brady noted that whatever was bugging her earlier had evaporated.

Returning to the dining room he caught a signal from the chief to join him at the end of the buffet table. "Brady, did you say that Mr. Goodscent went to the library in a big huff looking for Holly LaFrance?"

He nodded. "Alice gave the librarian a look not to tell Smitterly any details of Holly's visit to the library. He must have been satisfied and drove back to the hotel in Dover."

"What was Holly LaFrance after at the library?"

"An old book, I think. But the library didn't have it and told her to check with a used bookstore at the Triangle Plaza that carries out-of-print books. She went there and found what she was looking for. When Alice and I caught up with her at the mall, something or someone spooked her and she handed Alice the old book and Miss Powder's manuscript. That was before she left the mall and had her so-called mugging."

"Did I tell you Penny Powder had a Certificate of Copyright in her safe deposit box? The copyrighted manuscript was also in the box. It's a story called *Purity's Passion*."

"You might have told Newkirk."

"Okay, Brady, get together with Newkirk and figure this out. Also, get in touch with Jerry Jerome from Bank of Early. He took Penny's original manuscript home with him. You're going to have to see whether Penny's book, *Purity's Passion*, had anything to do with her murder. Also, try to come up with why someone felt it necessary to hack her up so brutally."

Brady didn't get the connection. "I guess I'm missing something. Can you give me some direction?"

"You told me the agent is in a lather to find out what old book Holly LaFrance is looking for. He's led off the track, and she finds the book at the mall. She gets scared and leaves that old out-of-print book with Drinker. Next, Miss LaFrance goes to her hotel and gets the stuffing knocked out of her, presumably by Mr. Goodscent." Rygard paused. "Are you with me so far?"

Brady thought so. "You're saying there's an old once-published but now out-of-print book and there's an old copyrighted manuscript from Miss Powder's safe deposit box."

Rygard smiled. "It's time the twain should meet. Get Penny's copyrighted manuscript from Jerry Jerome and compare it with the out-of-print book Alice is holding."

"What am I looking for?"

Rygard said only, "You'll know when you find it."

Bob Oden had taken notes during the dinner party and wondered why he, the editor, owner, and publisher of the *Early Eagle,* a successful hometown newspaper, had to cover the event instead of attending as a relaxed guest. This was a job for a reporter, and he wished he had one. If the drunken, unreliable Sonnet ever showed up again, he was definitely fired.

Oden watched Randall Zebner weave through the crowd taking pictures of Carolyn's guests eating, drinking, and giving the photographer smiles as well as stares. It appeared he crossed the line taking a photo of the agent, Worthington Smitterly. Oden distinctly heard Smitterly snarl, "Scram, sweathog," and Zebner answer, "I'll scram when you fork over the rest."

What's that all about? Oden was curious but knew he didn't have the interviewing skill of an investigative reporter. His forte was editing and managing, and he hired others to dig into the interesting happenings around the City of Early. When he spotted Chief Rygard taking Brady aside following Officer Drinker's disappearance from the party, he was certain something was up.

Waiting for an opportunity, Oden quietly told Brady, "I overheard a troubling conversation, and I'd like to know what you think of it." Repeating the dialogue between Smitterly and Zebner, he observed Brady's reaction—a cross between joy and surprise.

In fact, Brady looked as if he were ready to hug Oden. "Thanks, Bob. Please keep this to yourself for awhile. I promise you'll be the first to know when arrests are made in the Powder case."

22

Saturday – 10:15 p.m.

Brady couldn't believe the luck of Bob Oden's overhearing such an incriminating conversation between the suspects, Smitterly and Zebner, and immediately reported his news to the chief and Newkirk.

Chief Rygard asked his wife to remain at the party; he'd send a car to take her home. From headquarters, he contacted the city's prosecutor to be ready to draw up arrest warrants for Randall Zebner and Worthington Smitterly on charges of murder in the first degree.

That accomplished, Rygard checked his voice mail and found a half dozen messages from Jerry Jerome. There was nothing subtle in Jerry's voice.

"Everett, call me as soon as you hear this. You're not going to believe what my wife discovered when she read Penny Powder's manuscript."

In a ninety-second return phone call, Rygard told Jerry that Brady Kincaid was on his way to look over Martha Jerome's discovery. Privately, the chief was confident the primary motive for Penny Powder's murder had been uncovered.

Newkirk gave Beth a twenty dollar bill to take a cab home. He asked her to try to act casual about his leaving the party and begged her to please forgive him.

"Something huge has turned up in the Powder homicide case."

From the station Newkirk contacted Alice at home. "Have either you or Holly LaFrance read Miss Powder's manuscript and did you find a connection between it and the paperback Holly bought at the mall?"

"Not exactly. Holly conked out right after we ate. We'd both read the first fifty pages of the manuscript earlier. The rest is at Miss Powder's house. I'll give the other book a read if you think I should."

"Never mind. We'll get to that later. By the way, Bob Oden overheard Zebner asking Smitterly for the rest of some money Smitterly owed him. It has to be the balance of the contract to murder Miss Powder."

Boogers! They're having all the fun while I'm here babysitting Holly LaFrance. Aloud she asked, "What can I do? Should I come in?"

"Not now. Chief is getting the arrest warrants ready. Just sit tight and keep an eye on Holly. If Smitterly gets wind of what we know, he could skip out and track her down."

Brady took Robert Brickley aside to ask him to pass along his apologies to Carolyn for ducking out. Something pressing had come up.

Robert asked, "Can I help in any way?"

Trusting his discretion, Brady replied, "Yes, as a matter of fact, I'd like you to keep track of Smitterly. Don't let him leave the party before I get back if you can help it."

Across the room Bob Oden had noticed both Chief Rygard and Newkirk leave the party and now observed Brady in serious conversation with Robert Brickley. Recalling his earlier chat with Brady when the word *arrests* was spoken, Bob's interest was piqued and he joined the pair.

"If something's going down, I hope you'll let me in on it."

Amused by Oden's cop jargon, Brady told him, "Two things. Stall Zebner if he tries to leave. Perhaps you could ask him to take more photos of the party for the *Eagle*. Second, I just asked Robert to try to delay Smitterly from leaving the party in the next hour or so. Could you interview Smitterly for the *Eagle* before he heads for the door?"

Oden nodded, and Brady suggested, "You could talk about the classic Lincoln Smitterly wheels around in."

Brickley volunteered. "I can help out, Bob. I'm kind of a classic car buff and can ask questions about the restoration and who did it."

They were certain Smitterly loved his classic automobile and wouldn't mind talking for hours on the subject.

Brady found Jerry and Martha Jerome waiting for him on their front porch. Once inside, Martha said, "Mr. Kincaid, you won't believe what we found. I hadn't read but forty pages of Penny's manuscript when I knew I'd read it before. Sure enough, I was right."

Her husband said, "You have to understand, Martha has read just about every novel ever published and has never thrown even one away."

Martha nodded. "I wasn't certain about the title or the author but I knew I'd read it about the time our first child was on the way and we'd just moved into this house. It didn't take long looking through a stack of my oldest books to come across *Love No Evil* by Winifred Smith. Here it is." She handed the book to Brady.

He glanced at the cover then at Martha. "What should I be looking for?"

"First, check the copyright date. You'll see it's two years after Penny's. Then, though the title, the names of characters, the university, even the location, from Michigan to Wisconsin, were changed, everything else is identical. You'll see what I mean if you'll follow along on Penny's *Purity's Passion* while I read the first page of *Love No Evil* out loud."

She was right; only the names were changed. Winifred Smith had stolen Penny Powder's book.

Brady thanked Martha for her effort but didn't know how this was going to help nail Zebner or Smitterly.

Sensing Brady's uncertainty what good this information would do, Jerry asked his wife, "Do you want to tell him who Winifred Smith is or shall I?"

"Oh, go ahead. I know you're bursting with it."

"Martha's familiar with a web site that lists authors' pseudonyms and their real names. Winifred Smith is in reality someone named Warren Sytes." He noted the blank look on Brady's face and added, "Warren Sytes. Initials *W. S.*, the same, coincidentally, as Worthington Smitterly, the pompous geezer that all the ladies who bought books from Carolyn Brickley today had to listen to."

Martha made a face at him. "That so-called pompous geezer was very charming and very interesting. I enjoyed every word he said." She shook her head. "Too bad he may have plagiarized Penny's work."

Brady smelled a motive. "What I don't understand is how Winifred Smith or Warren Sytes got a copyright on a work that the copyright office in Washington D.C. had already certified."

Martha explained, "*Love No Evil* was, no doubt, never formally copyrighted. The copyright symbol followed by the year and author's name doesn't necessarily mean the material has been registered with the copyright office."

Brady was perplexed but let it go, accepting Martha Jerome's explanation. Aloud he said, "I'd like to take your copy of *Love No Evil* with me. I promise I'll make certain it's returned to you when this case is resolved." Then, opening the door to leave, he asked, "Do either of you have a theory what the connection between Penny Powder and Warren Sytes or this Smitterly character might be other than his stealing her work?"

Martha replied, "I understand Smitterly, or whoever he is, taught English literature and creative writing at a number of colleges all over the country. That may be how he and Penny met. He's about the right age to have been Penny's professor when she attended Bayside University. After all, that's the crux of the story in both books—a romance between a student and her professor."

"Thanks." This was an angle to pursue immediately, and Holly LaFrance would be the one person who would know most about Smitterly's background.

✦ ✦ ✦

Planning his next move driving back to the Erin, Brady received a call from Chief Rygard. "What'd you come up with?"

Quickly covering his visit with the Jeromes, Brady offered, "Here's an idea how to keep Smitterly from disappearing."

Rygard loved Brady's scheme and gave an immediate go-ahead. The plan involved the Erin's parking attendants, hired because they were adept at breaking into cars—not for their contents but to help patrons or condo owners who'd locked their keys inside. Brady thought if he could get inside Smitterly's classic car, he could lift the hood and remove the spark plugs. That ought to hold the agent around for awhile.

Back at the Erin, Lincoln had a better idea. "Instead of removing spark plugs that any road service can quickly replace, we'll remove the doors. He won't be able to go anywhere. It's not only dangerous but it's a moving violation to drive around without a door."

Brady didn't know whether to be scared or impressed that it took Chop Shop Sammy, the salad chef and reformed car thief, less than five minutes to disassemble the doors. Slipping Sammy a twenty-dollar tip, Brady trusted the parolee would keep his mouth shut.

After phoning Rygard and assuring him that Smitterly could not possibly get away, Brady rejoined the dinner party as it was winding down. He saw only Zebner, busy taking pictures of the hostess with the Fellmeyers. Smitterly was nowhere in sight. How could that happen? The man's automobile had been decommissioned.

Thoroughly alarmed, he asked Robert Brickley, "Where's Smitterly? Did he leave?"

"You'll find him in the lobby. He latched onto Joyce Fellmeyer's cousin. I saw those two chatting and laughing like old friends."

Brady felt a moment of betrayal. He'd tried for two years to break down the barrier between him and Claudia. Smitterly seemed to have done it in less than an hour.

It was suddenly clear to Brady. Claudia was part of the collegiate world of refined, well-educated persons, whereas he knew he'd never be a member of that community. He'd gone only as far as high school then straight to the police academy with a couple community college courses on the side. Aside from both working at Lombardy Teachers College, he and Claudia had little in common.

On the other hand, there was Officer, soon to be Detective, Alice Drinker. Alice might be a complicated handful, but Brady thought she'd be a lot more fun pursuing, and they had the police world of rough-and-tumble in common. If he took the job Chief Rygard offered and moved to Early, he wondered if Claudia would care at all.

He turned to see Newkirk and two uniformed officers enter the hotel, walking quickly through the Erin's lobby. Newkirk approached Zebner in the dining room and requested he step into the hallway. There, he was quietly asked to accompany the officers to the station for questioning. As those few remaining at the dinner party watched in surprise, Randall Zebner was led to a patrol car to be delivered to police headquarters.

Newkirk asked Brady, "Do you want to share the fun of questioning Zebner?"

"I'll pass. I think we're going to have a real challenge keeping tabs on Smitterly until you're able to get Zebner to implicate him in Miss Powder's murder."

23

Saturday – 11:30 p.m.

Brady watched Oden and Robert Brickley engage Worthington Smitterly in conversation. It wasn't going well. Claudia had already excused herself to join Joyce and Donovon, while Smitterly glanced irritably around the room. He heard Smitterly's booming voice as he took his leave, thanking Robert for the wonderful evening.

"Where is your beautiful and gracious wife? You are a very lucky man, Brickley."

Keeping an eye on the lobby, where Carolyn was saying goodnight to guests, Brady observed Smitterly pause for a few more words with Claudia.

"Alas, fair lady, we must end this unforgettable evening. I look forward to the moment we meet again when I visit the fair hamlet of Lombardy."

Claudia sighed as he kissed her hand. Brady looked away.

Oden and Robert approached, alarmed they hadn't been able to delay Smitterly's departure. "What should we do?"

"Nothing," Brady told them. "Act normal. He won't get far." He was certain Smitterly would soon storm back into the Erin, enraged his car's doors were missing.

It didn't happen.

Instead, a parking attendant dashed inside to tell Lincoln, "The man went crazy when he saw his car. But he jumped inside anyway and peeled out of here."

Brady rushed to the attendant. "Which way did he go?"

"He turned left onto North Park. I heard him hit the barricades as he barreled through. Then I saw him turn right toward High Street, even though Municipal Place is a one-way street."

Brady immediately notified Newkirk, who was already aware of Smitterly's short trip. "The old goat was just taken into custody for four driving violations—crashing police barricades, driving the wrong way on a one-way street, and operating an unsafe vehicle."

"That's only three."

Newkirk convulsed with laughter. "A rookie on patrol gave chase after he observed Smitterly driving like a cuckoo bird from hell in a vehicle without doors. After the rookie turned on his siren and flashers, the old fool stepped on the gas. He was up to sixty miles an hour when he went skidding around a corner. Without doors, Smitterly flew right out of his car. I guess he hadn't bothered to buckle up. Another violation. "

"Was he hurt?"

"I'm told he has multiple fractures and his entire left side is badly bruised. But he'll live. He's at Early General under guard."

"How long can you hold him on traffic charges?"

"Doesn't matter. Miss Powder's attorney from Lansing arrived and delivered a packet for the chief. Brady, if you'll go back to Miss Powder's house and find the letters she tied together with black ribbon, I'm told we'll be able to nail Worthington Smitterly's butt to the jailhouse floor."

"By the way, what happened to Smitterly's car?"

"It coasted until it bumped into a curb. Some kids walking home from the fair saw the driverless, doorless car with the motor still running. They jumped in and that's the last it was seen."

Driving to Miss Powder's, Brady phoned Alice to tell her Smitterly was in custody and Holly was no longer in danger.

"I'm on the way to Miss Powder's house to pick up some old letters she'd stored in her safe."

He wasn't prepared for Alice's reaction.

"You so-and-so! Why didn't you tell me about the letters before? They're certain to reveal something about Miss Powder—maybe a love affair. Why else would she have kept them?"

"Did I mention they were tied with *black* ribbon? That doesn't sound like love letters to me."

What would you know? Aloud she said, "I'll meet you there. Don't leave before I get there. Understand?"

Brady watched Alice's Jeep pull into the driveway and saw two people get out—Alice in uniform, and Holly LaFrance, her arm in a sling under an oversized Michigan State sweatshirt and wearing a pair of Alice's jeans, the cuffs turned up to fit.

"I woke up and felt great," Holly explained. "The pain killers the hospital gave me kicked in, and I want to be in on whatever you find in Miss Powder's personal correspondence." Noting Brady's distressed look, she added, "I've already promised Alice no one will ever know I was here or read any letters."

Brady had serious misgivings about Holly entering Miss Powder's home, much less looking at what might turn out to be key evidence against Smitterly. *First Robert, now Holly. Who's next?*

"Lighten up, Kincaid. Holly knows my badge is on the line and she'll keep quiet about my bringing her along. I trust her and you should, too. So, let's go inside, sit down in the kitchen, and pass the letters around. I'll bet we find all kinds of interesting tidbits."

Alice led the way and without ceremony untied the black ribbon.

Holly shivered. "Black ribbon is often synonymous with death."

The letters were in their original envelopes, and handing gloves to Brady and Holly, Alice noted, "These letters are really old. Look at the ten-cent postage stamps. I hope they don't fall apart on us."

The kitchen was silent as they read and passed around the letters Miss Powder had received as a young woman still in college and later, when she returned to Early and began her career in the library. Alice and Holly felt an emotional tie to the young Penny Powder so in love and trustful of the man of her dreams.

Brady didn't. He scoffed at the stilted, flowery tone of the letters from Warren Sytes and took issue with the poetry. "Who uses words like *thou* and *ere long*?"

"Worthy was simply lifting the works of Keats and other poets. He never had an original bone in his body." Holly put aside the letter she'd been holding. "When I read the beginning of the original manuscript for *Purity's Passion*, I remembered Worthy's only book, *Love No Evil*, written under the pseudonym, Winifred Smith. I had to get my hands on his book to compare its copyright date with the date Miss Powder inserted on her manuscript."

Alice resisted blurting out she'd been under the impression the paperback from Encore Books was *Purity's Passion* and hadn't paid attention to the title. She now realized the book was *Love No Evil*, and she should have looked in the bag and caught it. If she wanted to become a first-rate detective, she could never take anything for granted. That's what Brady Kincaid would have told her.

A voice inside asked *What do I care what he'd say? Good night! Why am I thinking about Brady Kincaid?* Another voice answered *Because he's smart, he's cute, and, for a change, you've met a truly nice, considerate guy.*

Alice pushed her chair back. "The book and Miss Powder's manuscript are in my trailer. I'll drive over and pick them up."

"No need," Brady told her. "Another copy of *Love No Evil* has been located." He told the ladies how Martha Jerome, after reading only forty pages of Miss Powder's copyrighted manuscript, recognized the same plot from another book. "She had no trouble finding *Love No Evil* in her attic, compared it to Miss Powder's novel, saw Miss Powder's copyright preceded *Love No Evil,* and notified Chief Rygard."

Alice relaxed, then noticed and opened an envelope near the bottom of the stack that didn't match the others. "Good for Penny Powder! Here's a report from a private detective. He checked into Warren Sytes's past and found that Sytes was in reality Willard Stout IV. It says here Stout had a violent past that his wealthy family hushed up. According to the report, Sytes phonied up teaching credentials and presented himself to colleges and universities as a world-traveled professor in English literature and creative writing. Whenever confronted by college administrators about his counterfeit diplomas and certifications, he quickly moved on."

"And that's where Penny Powder entered the scene and fell in love with the charming, affable, scholarly professor." Holly was familiar with the scenario. "The same thing happened to me about ten years later. Another school, another name, but the same old tired line."

"There's a big difference, Holly." Alice knew, though Holly no longer had feelings for the man, these revelations about Smitterly were difficult for her to swallow. "You were able to write and take credit for your books. Old Smitterly couldn't steal your plots."

"No, only my royalties."

"What?" Both Brady and Alice were alarmed.

Holly told her new friends, "The year before last I started looking at monthly sales figures from my book distributor again. I re-read the contracts I'd signed with my publisher to refresh my memory of the royalty's clause. Sure enough, I was to receive fifteen percent of the retail sales price of my books. A little math on my pocket calculator told me that, even after deducting Worthy's agent's fees, my income from royalties was short, at that time, by at least two hundred thousand dollars."

"I'd have killed the bastard," Alice said, and Brady agreed.

"What are you going to do?"

"I've already hired an accountant to dig through records going back to the first book published for which Worthy was my agent."

"Who was your original agent?"

"Nobody. My first book was what they call an over-the-transom submission. That means I mailed my manuscript to a publisher unsolicited. By the strangest stroke of luck, an editor read it, liked it, and offered a contract. Before I knew it, my first book, *Jennifer's Journey*, was in print. It sold a respectable twenty thousand copies, and the publisher asked for more."

"Why did you ever hook up with Smitterly?"

"He and I had a thing going while I was still in college. After I graduated and my first book was published, I couldn't help gloating a little. I looked up my old mentor and confided my success. The first thing Worthy wanted to know was the terms of my next contract with the publisher. When he read it, he told me I was being cheated. He could do a far better job handling my finances, and I would be free to write."

"You bought it, huh?"

Holly nodded, studying the floor. "I've grown up a lot since then. Right now, my accountant has someone scouring the country to find where Worthy has hidden the money. When we're positive he's collectible, we'll charge embezzlement and try to retrieve every cent he's stolen from me, plus all the punitive damages a court will award."

Holly smiled. "I'm told I can look most innocent and pathetic when need be."

Brady asked, "Don't you wonder what triggered Miss Powder's hiring a private detective? The tone of the letters I've read from Smitterly, alias Sytes, seems loving and serene. I've seen nothing that should have upset her so much she'd start investigating the man."

Alice agreed. "There has to be something in a letter just prior to hiring the P.I. that bothered her. Let's see . . ." She sorted through the bottom of the pile, looking at postmarks.

Picking up the very last letter, Holly read to Alice and Brady, "'My pure little darling, I haven't heard from you in so long. I'm worried sick. Aren't you well? What is wrong? Please answer. Your Warren.'"

Brady pulled the next letter from the bottom. "This one's pretty much the same old line as the earlier letters."

"Ah-ha! Here's an earlier one that Miss Powder tore into little pieces; then taped back together. Look how brown the old tape has become." Alice had their attention and read aloud, "'You dear little, pure little duckling, Thank you for the privilege of reading your latest effort, *Purity's Passion*. I'm proud of the progress your writing has taken and I encourage you to keep trying. Always your Warren.'"

"That bugger!" Holly growled. "Penny Powder had put together a decent, saleable romance, and he pooh-poohed it by encouraging her to re-write it one more time."

Brady shook his head. "He's just a common thief. He changed the title, location and character's names. Then had it published as his own work a couple years later."

"Worthy had obviously lost contact with Miss Powder and didn't know *Purity's Passion* was copyrighted. Sadly, Miss Powder never found a publisher for her work, but Worthy did. His publisher was probably impressed with his title and credentials. I wonder how he convinced the publisher *his* work was copyrighted."

"Why wonder?" Alice asked. "The guy was a slick confidence operator."

The chagrined author agreed. "And don't I know it.

Alice had a question and knew it must be asked with tact. "Holly, you needn't answer if you don't want to, but it would help our case against Smitterly if you told us why he beat you."

"I'll give you the details, but have it understood, I am not going to press charges at this time. I want to nail the old fart on embezzlement, and my accountant and lawyer hope to catch him off-guard before he hides his assets."

Neither Alice nor Brady agreed with Holly's position but promised she wouldn't be forced to file a complaint.

"Worthy was waiting for me at the hotel when I returned from the mall. Thank goodness, I left the partial manuscript and copy of *Love No Evil* with you, Alice. He demanded to know where I'd been and why. I tried to bluff, but he had the notion I'd found out why he was so vehemently against my signing books in Early."

Brady understood. "Smitterly must have become very nervous when he found out you'd be autographing books in Early knowing Penny Powder still lived here."

Alice said, "What I don't get is why he bothered to show up here. You're a big girl, Holly. You could have come to town and signed books alone."

"Worthy must be in control at all times. The thought that I might learn he'd plagiarized Penny Powder's work terrified him. In turn, he tried to find out what I knew by beating it out of me. I managed to lock myself in the bathroom. After he left, I took a cab to the hospital." She added, "Before I forget, Worthy's alibi of being at a book fair in Muskegon Friday night won't hold up. I'll help you get confirmation of that little fact tomorrow."

Brady's cell phone rang. It was Chief Rygard.

"For crying in the bucket, where are you?"

"We're coming in. See you in ten."

24

Sunday, June 25th – 12:45 a.m.

Chief Rygard and the city's new prosecutor, Norman York, made room for Brady and Alice at the one-way viewing window to watch Newkirk interrogate Randall Zebner.

"Where's Zebner's shirt and jacket and why are all those towels on the floor?" Alice wondered. "They look wet."

"They *are* wet," Rygard told her. "Zebner hasn't stopped crying. First, he took off his jacket. Next his shirt got soaked from sweat and tears. Then he went through a pile of towels. Every time Newkirk asked a question, Zebner broke down again. At least he's stopped perspiring, though his tee shirt looks pretty grungy."

"How far has Newkirk gotten?" Brady asked. "Has Zebner implicated Smitterly yet?"

Both men shook their heads. The prosecutor said, "Until and unless Zebner can control himself long enough to make a statement, we have nothing."

"I'd like to have a go at it," Alice volunteered.

Rygard and York stared.

Brady nodded encouragement. "How would you approach the matter?"

"With a nurturing attitude. If he's too scared and confused to talk to Newkirk, maybe a motherly approach would calm him down long enough to get him to talk. I'd try to convince him that he'd help himself in the long run if he explained why he killed Miss Powder and tell us who else was involved."

Rygard tapped on the interrogation room's door signaling Newkirk he wanted a word.

"Newk," he said when the detective stepped out, "I'd like you to give it a rest for awhile. Drinker wants to try the soft, feminine approach. Maybe the guy will relax and open up."

Newkirk shrugged. "Okay by me."

She asked Brady, "Any advice before I go in?"

He nodded approval as she loosened the collar of her starched blue uniform shirt and rolled up her sleeves, certain to gain Zebner's confidence with the less-rigid police image.

Their eyes locked briefly and he hoped his look warned her *Be careful asking questions for which you already know the answers because of our little visit to Zebner's Studio.*

Alice stared back thinking *Kincaid, you worry too much. I want to nail this sorry sucker as much as you do and am not about to give our discoveries away with a careless question.*

Chief Rygard caught the look between Alice and Brady and loved it. He calculated if they were already sweet on each other, there was a good chance Brady would sign on with Early's detective squad.

Once inside the interrogation room, Alice sat next to Zebner, who'd laid his head on his arms on the table.

"Hello, Mr. Zebner. Do you remember me?" she asked in a soft voice.

He raised his head, his eyes still red. "Sure. You're the pretty officer in the fine green dress."

"Thank you, Randall. May I call you Randall?"

"That'd be nice for a change. Everyone else calls me Zebner. Not even *Mister* Zebner."

"Are you still certain, Randall, you don't want to have an attorney present while we talk with you about Miss Powder's death?"

"Do you think I should have one?"

Alice shrugged. "I can't answer for you. I know, if I were in your shoes, I'd clear my conscience and trust the police and prosecutor to recommend a lighter sentence to the judge in exchange for not having to go through a trial."

She wondered if she'd tripped an alarm in Zebner's brain and changed the subject. "I can't wait to see all your pictures from Mrs. Brickley's party. I understand you took them for the *Eagle*."

"That's right. Bob Oden told me to take pictures of folks having a good time. He wanted at least one shot of everyone who attended."

"Were you able to do that?"

Zebner shook his head and stared at his hands.

"Who didn't want his picture taken? Was it Mr. Smitterly? We heard him tell you to go away."

"You did?"

Alice nodded. "He didn't want to pay you the rest of the money he'd promised, did he?"

Zebner's face crumbled as he started to weep again. Alice took him in her arms, patting his back.

"It's all right, Randall. It sounded as though he only gave you part of what he owed you. Did he pay you in cash?"

Zebner nodded.

"What'd you do with the cash Smitterly gave you? If it were me, I'd be afraid to walk around with . . . ah . . . did you mention how much cash he gave you?

"He gave me five thousand dollars in cash as a down payment. I put it in my account at the Bank of Early on Friday afternoon before they closed."

"That was smart." Alice took her time. "When was he supposed to give you the rest of the money?"

"He promised the other half, five thousand dollars, when Miss Powder was dead. We killed her Friday night around eight o'clock. But here it is, Saturday night, and he still hasn't paid me the rest."

"Randall, are you telling me you murdered Miss Powder?"

He nodded, his eyes lowered.

Alice knew she must be careful. "I want you to know that by confessing to murder, Detective Newkirk will return and arrest you immediately. He'll read you your rights. That means you may contact an attorney or have one appointed for you. While he's doing that, someone else will be in front of a judge getting a search warrant for your studio to look for more evidence."

"Why do you need more evidence?"

Easy now. Don't spook him. "Just to tidy up this case. It will help us determine the extent of another person's role in the murder."

"*Oh*." Zebner looked pleased and added in a barely audible voice, "I get it. Okay, I'm ready. You can do what you have to do."

"Thank you, Randall. After you've been arrested and booked, how would you like to come back to this room? We have more questions to ask and we can have a snack sent over from Mrs. Brickley's party at the Erin."

"Could you? I haven't eaten since noon and I'm really hungry."

"So am I. I'll see you a little while later."

As Alice left the interrogation room, the audience of four, watching through the viewing window, slapped high-fives with each other.

Alice had cracked the nut.

"Good work, Drinker." Rygard told Alice outside the interrogation room. He was proud of Alice and the delicate way she'd handled the fragile suspect, and she'd reinforced his confidence that she was going to become an excellent homicide detective.

Leading the way to his office, Rygard instructed Newkirk to have an officer present while arresting Zebner and reciting his rights. Next he asked Brady and Alice to assist York in preparing a search warrant for a judge to sign.

York insisted there'd be no delay in presenting the warrant to Thomas Tackle, the night court judge whose chambers were only steps away from headquarters. "He's a reasonable judge and, with Zebner's confession, we'll have our search warrant in no time."

They agreed the first thing to look for in Zebner's Studio would be his checkbook and receipt for a five-thousand-dollar cash deposit at the Bank of Early.

Alice mentioned the missing copy of *Street Monkeys*. "That book is a bestseller and I'll bet Zebner kept it to read later."

Brady wanted to tell York a rechargeable flashlight should be added specifically to the warrant, but couldn't take the chance. Instead he said, "It seems obvious Zebner and Smitterly killed Miss Powder in the studio. This was an exceptionally gruesome murder, and no matter how well those two cleaned up, the crime scene crew are certain to find Miss Powder's blood somewhere."

York agreed. "If Zebner and Smitterly swung the axe themselves, Miss Powder's blood must have spattered all over their clothes and skin. I'm going to add 'towels' to the warrant along with your suggestions. Can you think of any other specific items? We need all the evidence we can find to solidify this case in the event Zebner recants and I have to hand this case over to the county's prosecutor for trial."

Brady said, "Once the crime scene investigators go to work, you're certain to have more than enough evidence against Zebner, whether he recants or not. Their investigation will quite likely prove Smitterly's role in the homicide as well."

"Good. I can't ask for more than that." He smiled and left to draw up the warrant; then to visit Judge Tackle in chambers.

That left Brady and Alice waiting for orders from the chief.

"Do you want me to accompany York to Zebner's Studio?" Brady asked.

"No. I don't want either one of you present during that search. This Zebner is an unstable guy and it's possible he'll find a lawyer who'll say you detectives planted evidence."

Brady and Alice exchanged guarded looks.

"Brady, what I wish you would do is contact the Erin and see if they have enough of that roast beef left to make sandwiches for everyone. Then have someone pick it up."

Rygard turned to Alice. "You have to get ready now to interview Zebner about the actual crime."

"If I get Zebner to implicate Smitterly, how far should I go?"

"Ask him how he and Smitterly met each other. Since it seems obvious Smitterly hired Zebner, ask if Zebner knows why the old guy wanted to murder Miss Powder."

Brady added, "From what I've seen and heard, Zebner doesn't fit the profile of a killer." He turned to Alice. "I'm curious why he got himself mixed up in this murder."

She agreed and began to feel hopeful that Brady would accept the chief's offer to join Early's detective squad. He made helpful suggestions, never treated her with condescension, he'd been a calm, dependable partner throughout the day, and there was an indefinable appeal about the guy that Alice couldn't ignore.

✦ ✦ ✦

Forty minutes later, Zebner had been formally arrested and booked, and York had phoned to report that the search of Zebner's Studio was underway. Zebner's checkbook, the bank deposit receipt, a copy of *Street Monkeys*, a flashlight with a drop of blood, and two soiled hand towels were on their way to the county crime laboratory. "Two technicians from the crime lab are going to remain at Zebner's until they've examined every inch of the studio for blood, hair, fingerprints, whatever."

He added, "You're on safe ground to question Zebner about the specific evidence we've found so far."

Allowing Zebner to eat his roast beef sandwich in peace, Alice then picked up the interrogation where she'd left off.

Zebner veered from weeping to composure and back during the questioning. He confided to Alice, "You're the first person in a long time that's treated me with respect. I can't help that I perspire a lot. The sweating disease runs in my family. It's called *perspirosis*."

"Who told you that?"

"The radio doctor. He sold me some pills to cure it."

"Did they do any good?"

"Not yet. The doctor said I had a stubborn case and should buy more pills. I will when I get some money. They're expensive."

Alice maintained a straight face and resumed her questioning.

"Did Detective Newkirk tell you how we knew you were involved in Miss Powder's homicide after making DNA tests of your perspiration?" She was bluffing but continued. "We found your sweat on the axe handle, inside and outside of Miss Powder's little roadster, and even on a hand towel in your studio's bathroom."

Zebner held his head in his hands as he wept and wailed.

"I'll ask you again, Randall, if you want to call in a lawyer."

He shook his head, and Alice asked, "How did you hook up with Smitterly?"

"The old bastard had been keeping tabs on me after he found out Miss LaFrance was going to sign books in Early. He had a copy of my credit report. Between not making a dime with the photo studio and somehow finding out about my gambling debts, Smitterly knew I was strapped. He said he had a way to help me out of my financial jam. All I had to do was lure the librarian to my studio for a photo session and he'd do the rest."

"Didn't he explain you'd have to kill Miss Powder?"

"Not until Friday just before he handed me the down payment, five thousand dollars cash. I wanted to back out but he blackmailed me, saying he'd tell my bookies where to find me."

"So you decided it was better to commit murder and spend the rest of your life in prison than to face your bookies?"

"You have to understand, Office Drinker, Smitterly had a plan. He said he'd figured out the perfect crime. Once Miss Powder sat down to have her picture taken, he was going to appear and distract her attention away from me. When she wasn't looking, I was supposed to pick up the axe and whack the back of her head." He took a deep, sobbing breath. "I hated killing that woman. She seemed like a nice, polite person. But I needed the money bad. I was sick of looking over my shoulder all the time wondering when the bookie's boys would catch up with me."

Alice changed the subject. "Whose idea was it to leave Miss Powder's body in the bookstore?"

"That was part of Smitterly's plan. After he learned Miss La-France was going to sign books in Early, he tapped into the *Eagle's* web site. He read an article about how someone broke into the bookstore from the roof when the burglar really meant to break into the antiques shop. The reporter described the roof hatch and the platform between the stores."

Zebner grabbed a tissue from the box Alice had brought along and wiped perspiration from his neck. "The burglary happened before I rented the antiques shop space so it was news to me about pull-down ladders and the platform over to the bookstore."

Zebner paused for a moment. "If I hadn't rented that store, I would never have met Smitterly or been involved in a murder. Smitterly only used me because of the platform between my studio into the bookstore where he could dump the body."

"Smitterly had it all figured out in advance, didn't he?"

"Pretty much. He said he would have liked to have dumped her in the library *'just for the irony, but the bookstore would have to do.'*"

Alice took a moment to reflect on the meaning of *irony* then said quietly, "I hope you've been truthful with me so far this evening,

Randall. You see, we caught the little lie you told us when we spoke with you at the fair."

"Which one? I mean . . . ah . . . what lie?"

"The one when you said you didn't see Miss Powder carrying books when she stopped at your studio Friday night. But guess what, Randall? The crime lab found one of her books, *Street Monkeys*, stuck under the back leg of your desk. How do you suppose it got there? Did Miss Powder shove it under the leg to stop your desk from wobbling or did you put it there yourself?" Alice's tone had changed to impatient.

"I'm sorry, Officer Drinker. I'll never lie to you again. Please don't tell Smitterly I kept the book. He'll kill me if he finds out."

Alice waited while Zebner mopped himself up again and then asked, "What'd you think of the adorable little roadster?"

"I loved it. If I'd been paid the second five grand, I might have taken off in it."

"You did an excellent job wiping away fingerprints inside and outside the car. Who drove it to the library parking lot?"

"I did. Smitterly picked me up a block away on Bank Street and we drove back to the studio."

"What time was that?"

"Nearly ten o'clock. Smitterly said we had to get Miss Powder's car out of the alley before anyone noticed how long it'd been parked there and started nosing around."

"By then Miss Powder had been dead about two hours. What'd the two of you do before you moved her car?"

"Not much while Mrs. Brickley was still in the bookstore. We had to keep quiet until she left."

"Randall, would you mind explaining how and why the bookstore's doors were left unlocked?"

"That was Smitterly's idea. He thought it would drive the police crazy trying to figure out why the alarm company hadn't gotten a blip on their screen when Miss Powder's body was left at Brickley's. It was scary hearing Smitterly crow that he was outwitting the police and the alarm company by twisting both doors' thumbturns to unlocked. With neither the front nor the alley door actually being opened, nothing would be detected by the security system."

"There's something else, Randall. Did you know both Miss Powder's ankles were fractured? How did that happen?"

"Oh, geez, I thought she was already dead when she dropped."

"She was. Did you drop her on purpose?"

"God, no! It was Smitterly's fault. He wrapped her up in a cheap blue plastic tarp and told me to carry her over my shoulder while I climbed the ladder to the platform. How was I to know she'd slide out and land feet first before I got to the top?"

"That must have made a mess on the floor."

"Not as bad as having her brains fly all over the place." Zebner retched remembering the sight.

"How'd you keep your studio so clean? I'm told not even a trace of Miss Powder's blood is visible on the floor or walls."

"Smitterly took care of that. He'd brought along a bunch of sheets and rolls of plastic. When it was over, he scraped some blood off the plastic and smeared it on the axe. He said decorum dictated leaving a bloody axe with the body."

Alice thought Zebner was about to vomit and quickly offered a glass of water.

"Thanks." He gulped the water and feeling better said, "Smitterly bundled the sheets and plastic up and took them away. I didn't ask where. I felt too sick."

"What did you do with your clothes? They must have been covered with Miss Powder's blood."

"That was something else Smitterly thought of. Besides the latex gloves, he brought along long yellow ponchos for us to wear over our shirts and pants. White cotton socks, too, to put on over our shoes. He rolled those up with the plastic sheets that he took away. We wore baseball caps to cover our hair but Miss Powder's blood splashed on our faces so we had to rinse off in the bathroom."

He paused to take another sip of water. "The old guy spent a long time in the bathroom and when he came out, his cologne was strong enough to revive the dead."

Zebner gasped. "Sorry. I mean no disrespect to Miss Powder."

Alice patted his arm. "Of course not, Randall." She paused a moment. "A rechargeable flashlight was found. Did that belong to you?"

"Yes ma'am, that's my flashlight. I bought it in case I ever had trouble paying the electric bill and power was shut off to the studio."

Alice understood. "We have the notion you two carried Miss Powder's body by way of the platform between your studio and Mrs. Brickley's store." Zebner nodded. "You must have had your hands full carrying Miss Powder over your shoulder up the ladder, over the dark platform to the bookstore then climbing down the ladder into the unlit bookstore. How could you see where you were going?"

"Smitterly was close behind me carrying the axe and books and holding the flashlight so the beam hit the floor in front of me."

"When did he hand back the flashlight? After you'd left Miss Powder's body in the bookstore and everything was cleaned up?"

Zebner thought for a moment. "He didn't hand it back to me. After we got back to the studio, he plugged the flashlight into the wall socket himself and said, 'I'm recharging the battery so no one will suspect the flashlight was used for more than an hour.'"

"What time was that?"

"About eleven o'clock. Maybe later."

Alice hoped those watching her interrogation from the other side of the window were satisfied she'd covered that aspect of the crime. She asked, "Did Smitterly ever mention why he wanted to kill Miss Powder? And why so brutally?"

"Uh-uh." Zebner didn't know. "I tried to find out but the old creep shot me a look that said *butt out or I'll have to kill you, too.* I'd seen his face while he chopped away on Miss Powder and knew he'd have no qualms bashing my brains out if he thought I was going to squeal on the mastermind." Zebner had a flash. "Oh, my God. I've just squealed. What's going to happen to me?"

"Nothing, Randall. You're perfectly safe as long as you're here with us in custody. He can't touch you."

The woeful Zebner accepted her words and, after Alice left, laid his head on his arms on the table and took a nap.

25

Sunday – 1:55 a.m.

Holly insisted she'd be a good girl if allowed to accompany Brady and Alice back to headquarters, in turn, saving Alice the bother of returning her to the trailer park. They'd left her with the desk sergeant during Zebner's interrogation and later found her in the bullpen laughing and having a grand time with the officers on night duty.

Breaking away, she said, "I've decided to change the course of my career. You two dear people, along with everyone else I've met connected with Early's police force, fill me with the courage to capture all the colorful ideas floating around this station. What would you think if I, Holly LaFrance, were to start writing a detective series?"

"I don't know." Alice looked at Brady, who shrugged. "What about the rest of your book tour?"

"*That!*" Holly scoffed. "I couldn't be happier if I didn't have to make another personal appearance for a year. Don't get me wrong. I adore the wonderful readers who show up for an autographed book. It's the in-between travel that's so tiresome. I've been on this tour for five months, ever since *Farewell, Fjords* was released. I'm ready for time off."

"Don't you have some sort of contractual obligation to finish your tour?"

"That's between Worthy and the booking agent. Worthy signed the contract, not me. I'm free to go where and when I want. Right now, I want to settle here in Early, gather my laptop, dictionary, thesaurus, and pick everyone's brains, starting with the two of you. I'm interested in every gory detail you're willing to share."

"Police work can become very gritty, Holly. You didn't witness Miss Powder's condition and her slaughter wasn't the exception. Detectives come across nasty, hideous scenes all the time." Brady wondered why a woman like Holly LaFrance who gave the impression of a delicate flower would want to wade into the cesspool of violent crime.

She smiled. "I think Harriet Lowe from Altoona, P. A., can handle it." She answered their curious looks. "That's who I was before Worthy glommed on and glamorized my image with a new name and background."

She sensed the pair weren't convinced. "You have to realize, a writer borrows an idea then weaves a story around it to suit herself. I fancy sticking around Early and consulting with detectives, beat cops, the coroner, criminologists, and whoever else will give me a little time for all the necessary technical details."

Her eyes sparkled describing her latest brainchild. "Using Alice as my model, I'm creating Ivy Shaddow, Private Investigator. Miss I. Shaddow's first case will be solving the murder of a small town high school teacher who'd written a tell-all book about her fellow teachers, friends, and neighbors." She turned to Brady and Alice. "What do you think?"

They made polite, encouraging sounds, though *I. Shaddow* was a bit hokey for their tastes and sounded like something the chief would dream up. Fortunately, Rygard could not read the detectives' thoughts as he approached the bullpen.

"Drinker. Kincaid. Will you step into my office?" Chief Rygard nodded to Holly. "Evening, ma'am. Are you comfortable? If you need anything, the desk sergeant will be happy to help you."

With that he led Alice and Brady to his office, where Newkirk and Prosecutor York were huddled.

Rygard told them, "We're discussing strategy how and when to question Smitterly. We're convinced, even with Zebner's confession and details implicating Smitterly, the man will simply deny everything. At trial, it would boil down to Smitterly's word against Zebner's. It doesn't take a genius to predict Zebner's total meltdown, leading any jury to acquit Smitterly on all charges."

He turned to Brady and Alice. "What'd you two find among the letters Powder tied with black ribbon?"

Brady reported, "Miss Powder was informed the man she knew as Warren Sytes was a fraud. But we don't know when she discovered he'd stolen her story, or how she found out Sytes had become Smitterly and took revenge with her *On the Chopping Block* reviews."

Alice added, "Her *Chopping Block* column probably started out criticizing anything linked to Smitterly. But I think, in time, because Miss Powder tolerated only what she considered to be good books, all the rest became fodder for the *Chopping Block*. Obviously, Miss Powder's original plan to embarrass Smitterly and his literary clients blossomed into a big time venture."

Rygard suggested, "She should have named her company *Revenge, Incorporated.*"

How true.

Returning to the business of prosecuting Smitterly, York said, "I'm aware of Smitterly's traffic violations. But we need hard, criminal charges with real evidence to put this scoundrel away." He glanced about. "Who wants to start?"

Alice volunteered. "Smitterly should be charged with assault and battery. You saw Holly LaFrance's bruised face and broken arm. Smitterly did that to her."

York took note.

"Holly and her accountants are also gathering evidence that Smitterly has been systematically stealing from her royalties account. You can add embezzlement to your list."

Newkirk offered, "Using the name *Invincible*, Smitterly sent threatening e-mails to Miss Powder. I don't know what statute that violates but there ought to be one."

York made more notes.

Brady and Alice wondered how credible testimony from Mr. Yee, the *vrai nez*, would be. By the time Smitterly went to trial, the scent he'd left behind in the bookstore and photo studio, the scene of Miss Powder's homicide, would have vanished, leaving no evidence behind.

Rygard asked, "Have any of you decided exactly why Smitterly killed Miss Powder and why he chopped her up so brutally?"

Brady offered, "If Smitterly thought Miss Powder found out he'd plagiarized her love story, he must have been terrified she'd go public. His past, whether as Stout or Sykes or Smitterly, would be revealed and his reputation would be ruined."

Alice chimed in, "He'd lose his cushy job as Holly's agent collecting and stealing her royalties."

York interrupted. "I'd like to play devil's advocate. If Miss Powder's book had been plagiarized, isn't it more logical that she would kill Smitterly than vice versa?"

Brady considered that idea. "I think the final decision to kill Miss Powder came after Smitterly discovered she was Chanuary, who wrote *On the Chopping Block*. He took action on Friday when he thought he had the perfect alibi of being a hundred miles away from Early at the time of the murder. Chopping Miss Powder so brutally had to be Smitterly's ironic payback. At the end of her review of *Farewell, Fjords*, Miss Powder gave it *five chops*, her lowest rating; although, you'll remember, her skull was given only *three*."

Newkirk partially agreed. "Except, Chanuary's abusive reviews have been published over the last dozen years. Holly LaFrance has fourteen published books to her credit. My point is, why didn't Smitterly strike earlier?"

"I don't think he knew who Chanuary was until a year ago. The initial e-mail from Invincible supports that idea."

The prosecutor spoke. "This is all interesting stuff and I can charge Smitterly with assault and battery along with embezzlement if Miss LaFrance has the evidence and is willing to go ahead. But neither will put him behind bars very long. There's the very real chance that when a violent guy, as he seems to be, is released from jail, he'll hunt down Miss LaFrance and everyone else he feels he owes."

Chief Rygard understood what York was saying. "What you need is concrete evidence—fingerprints or DNA or a videotape of the murder."

Brady and Alice gasped. Carefully repeating that Zebner stated blood had spattered their faces, she said, "He and Smitterly cleaned up in the bathroom and must have used the very towels the crime scene investigators took back to their lab for DNA testing. If we're lucky, Smitterly's DNA will show up on one of those towels."

The chief nodded. "Sounds like a long shot, but it's worth the effort."

York agreed and added, "We also have to prove Smitterly was in Early Friday night at the time of the murder. We cannot rely on Zebner's testimony alone."

Brady said, "The crime scene team found only two soiled hand towels at Zebner's. If we learn when clean towels were delivered to his studio, and if Smitterly's DNA turns up on one of the soiled towels, that could prove where Smitterly was on Friday night and when."

Rygard followed the logic. "If you find out when clean towels were delivered to Zebner's and how many, we could be in business. Another point is, if Zebner's memory is accurate and he didn't handle the flashlight, the blood on the flashlight loop could be our best hope for arresting Worthington Smitterly."

Rygard stood up and stretched. "That's enough. I think we have everything covered for tonight and everyone knows where to pick up tomorrow. Let's put a lid on it."

He thanked everyone as they filed out of his office and told them he expected to have progress by noon Sunday.

Brady watched Alice and Holly roar away in the Jeep. He was dog-tired. He hadn't had the right kind of sleep Friday night and looked forward to sacking out. Pulling into the Erin's parking lot he glanced up at Lincoln's second-floor corner condo. Lights were on in every room.

What's Lincoln up to? Brady hoped he wasn't drunk again. There was only so much sympathy left for the love-stricken giant.

At the door to the entry hall, Brady heard the murmur of two voices—a man's and a woman's that could only belong to Miss Geraldine Pozy.

What to do? He could stay overnight at the Early Bird Motel south of town but he wanted his stuff—he couldn't walk around in the borrowed suit any longer. Maybe the pantry door that opened into the hall was unlocked. Brady turned the knob quietly. It worked and he was inside the condo. If he tiptoed to the extra bedroom, he could pick up his luggage and sneak out the same way.

Packing his suitcase, Brady felt a warm presence behind him. It was Geraldine Pozy, all six feet of her, wearing a pair of Lincoln's pajamas, smiling and ready to hug him.

"You're back!" He acted surprised.

"I'm back!" Her smile told Brady how happy she was.

"For good or just a visit?"

Pozy glanced up at Lincoln, wearing pajamas as well. "It depends. If Lincoln will have me back and if Bob Oden can forgive me for waltzing out like I did."

"I'm under the impression Bob Oden will welcome you back with arms wide open. Your replacement is a boozer and poor Bob has had to take all the assignments himself."

"That's what Lincoln said."

"So, what happened to your great television job?" Brady knew part of the answer. The twenty-three-year-old Pozy looked prettier than ever but had gained back at least twenty pounds. Television cameras weren't kind to plump ladies.

"Oh, I missed Lincoln and the *Eagle* too much. So, here I am."

Brady kept packing, and Lincoln asked where he was going.

"I can't stay here. You two have catching up to do."

"Nonsense. We promise to be quiet and not embarrass you. By the way, where's Smitterly? I told Geraldine about removing the doors to his car."

"He's in the hospital. He went careening around a corner on two wheels and took a header out of his car where a door used to be."

Oops. Lincoln and Pozy laughed like two little kids.

"I'd like to stay up and talk all night, Geraldine. But I'm dead on my feet, and I want to be sharp for tomorrow."

"What's tomorrow?" She automatically transformed into Pozy, the *Eagle's* star reporter.

"Plenty, and I'll let you and Oden in on everything when I can. Meanwhile, good friends, goodnight."

26

Sunday morning – 7:15 a.m.

Tiptoeing into the extra bedroom, Pozy and Lincoln smiled as they watched their sleeping guest. Brady stirred and opened an eye.

"What are you two looking at?"

"Our best man!"

"What? Are you getting married? To each other?" Brady forgot he was wearing only boxers and tumbled out of bed to hug the happy couple.

Breakfast was waiting in the kitchen, and over juice and cereal, they told Brady of their wedding plans.

"The big question, Brady, is if you're willing to be Lincoln's best man who should I ask to be my maid of honor?" Pozy added, "Linc told me you've gotten over Mrs. Claudia and last night at the party couldn't keep your eyes off Alice Drinker. I hope you know she's a wildcat."

Lincoln smiled hopefully. "Word's out you're seriously considering taking Chief Rygard's offer to join Early's detective squad. How about it?"

Blast it! That has to mean the Fellmeyers know about the offer, and in turn, Claudia will find out before I've had a chance to talk with her. Aloud, Brady said, "Nothing's definite. I'd appreciate the less said the better until I've had a chance to either resign my job in Lombardy or decide to sign on for another year with the college."

Lincoln nodded as he answered the phone. "Good morning, Mrs. Fellmeyer. You're looking for Brady?" He interpreted Brady's wild hand signals and told Joyce, "He left early this morning. I think he's on his way to the station. Maybe you can catch him there."

Lincoln listened for a moment. "I heard that, too, but don't know if Brady is seriously considering moving to Early." After a few more words from Joyce he said, "I have a surprise for you, and I'll put her on to say *hello*."

Pozy took the phone, and Joyce's squeals of pleasure learning she was back in town to stay were plain to hear. When Pozy announced she and Lincoln were going to be married, the screams grew louder.

While Pozy was busy and out of earshot, Lincoln told Brady, "Geraldine doesn't know it, but I found out yesterday she was fired from her television job."

"Fired? Why?"

"She got into a brawl with her cameraman and bopped him while the camera was rolling. I'm told she'll never work for any television news organization again. Too bad, huh?" Lincoln's wide smile told how sorry he was about that.

Brady asked, "How come you didn't tell me she was coming back?"

"I didn't know if she'd want to see me and if she wanted to take up where we left off. And by the way, *ix-nay* telling Geraldine we know about the *iring-fay*."

Brady agreed and quickly finished his breakfast. "I have to roll. If you hear from Alice, tell her I'm at Zebner's Studio checking out the name of the towel service. I hope I can get in touch with someone on Sunday. Hate to lose a day."

The barricades around Pride Park had been taken away and most signs of the Founders Day Fair—tents, picnic tables, and portable toilets—had been removed. Only litter strewn about the park that hadn't yet been picked up remained.

Brady found Robert Brickley had already unlocked the studio door for Alice. She'd discovered the phone number for the towel service on a label pasted to the dispenser and had gotten in touch with the manager.

"The manager is willing to go to his office and check the delivery log. That'll tell us exactly when soiled towels were picked up and how many fresh hand towels were delivered. He thought he could call me back in another ten or fifteen minutes."

"Where's Holly?"

"I took her to her hotel to pick up her luggage and check out. She thinks she can drive with one arm in a sling and is keeping the rental car to get around. Meanwhile, she's decided to bunk with me while my trailer park manager cleans up an empty unit for her to move into."

"You're kidding." Brady looked at Robert, who only shook his head. Neither man could picture Holly LaFrance living in a trailer park.

"Hey, guys, Carlyle Acres isn't that bad. There's plenty of green space between each home, it's clean, it's well protected, and troublemakers are given the boot immediately. Besides, it's only temporary until Holly finds a permanent place here in Early."

As she spoke, Newkirk entered the studio with fresh coffee and glazed donuts for everyone. "Morning, all. Anything new? How are you coming on the towel service?"

"I've contacted the manager regarding delivery." Alice updated Newkirk and added, "He thinks he'll be able to call back with the information we want within the next fifteen minutes."

Brady asked, "How about you, Newk? Have you heard from the crime lab yet about testing the hand towels for DNA?"

"Not yet. I hate to call too early. I want to stay on Jeffrow's good side for the sake of future cases."

"I don't think you need worry on that score. My impression, after meeting him yesterday, was that he loved helping solve crimes. I'm certain you can phone him now."

"Hope you're right, Brady."

With misgivings, Newkirk placed the call to Jeffrow.

The criminologist answered and said, "I was wondering when you'd call. Your report is done, and there was too much cross-contamination on the towels for a DNA test."

Jeffrow knew Newkirk was disappointed and quickly added, "We did come up with several items you *can* hang your hat on. First, the blood spatter on the flashlight's plastic holder ring matches Miss

Powder's blood perfectly. Next and possibly more helpful, we came across a fair amount of substances used in anti-wrinkle creams and concealers on one of the towels."

"Would that have come from Miss Powder?"

"That was our first thought and we hustled to the morgue, then checked Miss Powder's cosmetics at home, to see if her makeup matched. It didn't. Miss Powder wore a foundation with a delicate pink tint. The cosmetics we found on the towel from the photographer's studio have very little hue. They're close to snow white."

Newkirk tried to remember anyone who purposely wanted to appear pale. "What about lipstick?"

"Not a trace. This might not have come from a woman. There are men who wear moisturizers and makeup to minimize lines and wrinkles, though most prefer to appear tan and healthy and would have chosen a shade of beige, not white. "

Newkirk was confident a person wearing white make-up would be easy to spot. He knew it wasn't Zebner, who always appeared flushed and sweaty. But it could well be the second killer.

Jeffrow said, "You should also know these particular cosmetics are not brand name products. They are custom-blended to one individual's specific needs."

Newkirk thanked him excited this new information from the crime lab would sew this investigation up quickly and neatly. Repeating Jeffrow's findings to Brady and Alice, it was immediately concluded that anyone using custom-blended facial creams had to be the same individual wearing expensive one-of-a-kind cologne. There was absolutely no doubt that the person wearing extra-pale, special-order make-up was Worthington Smitterly.

Newkirk phoned York to order another search warrant. It was time to look through Smitterly's personal belongings in his hotel room in Dover, as well as the hospital room where Smitterly was recuperating from his accident.

In the midst of the detectives' jubilation that they might soon have evidence proving Smitterly took part in Miss Powder's murder, Holly LaFrance entered the studio with her usual exuberant flourish.

She announced, "Everyone! I just had the most amazing phone

conversation with the person in charge of the book fair held Friday in Muskegon. She double-checked the registration book and guess what? She could not find his name because Worthy never showed up!"

Holly waited for a reaction and without one asked, "Don't you get it? Being in Muskegon, clear across Michigan at least a hundred miles away, would have meant Worthy could not have been in Early on Friday evening. But he wasn't in Muskegon at all and has no alibi for Friday evening, the time of the crime."

Where was he? Brady and Alice smiled at each other amused that Worthington Smitterly was going to have to come up with another alibi—one that would fall apart as well.

Donovon wondered why he was the one who had to confront Brady. It was obvious Brady didn't want to go on their fishing trip if Claudia and her daughter, Meggin, were along. Too bad. He'd looked forward to Brady's company for the week. However, he saw Brady's point of view and couldn't blame him. He thought Joyce should understand, as well.

Parking in front of Zebner's, where he'd tracked Brady down, it seemed to Donovon word about Brady taking a job with the Early police had gotten around very quickly. The idea something was going on between Brady and Alice Drinker was flying about, too. He wondered if there was any truth to either rumor.

Brady caught sight of Donovon and told Alice, "No matter what I tell Donovon, do not, I repeat, do not contradict me. Understand?"

"Understood, sir." She didn't salute.

He asked Holly, "Can I count on the same from you?" She nodded. Brady knew he didn't have to ask Robert Brickley, who'd already quietly assured Brady he had no intention of ever telling Carolyn about entering Zebner's studio Saturday night.

Donovon and Brady gave each other hearty hellos; then Donovon asked if he could speak to Brady privately. Outside on the sidewalk, he apologized. "Look, Brady, I didn't see the need to come down here to talk but Joyce made me."

Brady remembered what being a husband could be like.

"Anyway, we're packed, and as soon as Joyce brings Steffie home from the hospital, we're ready to head north to the lodge. We don't want to leave without you if you still want to go fishing."

Brady shook his head. "I hope you understand but I don't see how I can break away right now. We're close to pinning the second person involved in Miss Powder's murder. It'd be hard on the entire squad if one of us wasn't there to help close every little rat-hole the varmint might try to crawl through."

"Okay, I'll tell Joyce. She's going to be disappointed but she'll get over it. Especially if the rumor you're going to start working here in Early is true." Donovon's raised eyebrows asked for a reply.

"You know better than to trust gossip."

About to climb back into his van, Donovon turned and asked, "Would the varmint be Worthington Smitterly?"

Brady's smile was his answer.

Robert met Brady at the front door and asked quietly, "Did Donovon say he'd heard he was mentioned in Miss Powder's will?"

"No! Was he?"

"I could get Dyanne Dove in a world of trouble by telling you this so you must keep it confidential. Dyanne agreed to work with Penny Powder's attorney from Lansing, and she's going to file Penny's will in probate court tomorrow."

Brady guessed. "Dyanne took a peek at the will."

"Dyanne phoned Carolyn to tell her Penny left all her books, probably ten thousand, to Carolyn to dispose of as she wishes."

"Wow! I bet Carolyn was surprised."

"Yes, and even more surprised learning that Penny left five million dollars to Early's public library general fund, and enough money to set up an endowment to award annual scholarships in the literary arts at Bayside University."

"You said Donovon was mentioned in the will."

"Penny left another five million dollars to the Animal Rescue Society to be administered by Dr. Donovon Fellmeyer, DVM."

Robert reflected for a moment. "Penny Powder was a meticulous woman. She left explicit instructions for her funeral. She'd picked out her casket, the funeral home, the cemetery, even her headstone. She thought of everything."

"Did her will say what would happen to her newspaper column?

"What are you talking about?"

"I'm talking about *On the Chopping Block* by Chanuary."

"Did Penny Powder have something to do with those terrible book reviews?"

Brady's silence answered the question.

"Dear Lord!" Robert shook his head. "Carolyn will not take this news well at all."

That was an understatement, and Brady hoped he wouldn't be around when Carolyn Brickley learned Penny Powder was the real *Chanuary*.

Alice was ecstatic. She'd learned the delivery driver was late making his rounds Friday. Twenty-four clean cloth hand towels had been delivered to Zebner's Studio at seven-fifteen Friday evening and twenty-four soiled hand towels were picked up and taken back to be laundered. The two towels delivered to the crime lab had to have been soiled after seven-fifteen Friday evening.

With traffic re-routed around Pride Park because of the fair, the towels had been carried in through the alley door. While Zebner signed for the delivery, the driver saw another person lurking about in the front area of the studio. That person was described as "an old guy with black hair and spooky white skin that looked as if it had been floured."

Alice rejoiced, "We've cornered the old boy, haven't we? As soon as the crime lab matches Smitterly's special-order cosmetics to those found on one of the hand towels, he's just another drowned rat." She asked Brady, "Do you think I can be in on the arrest? I've never worked a case like this before, and I'd like to see it through to the end."

"Why not? You've earned it."

27

Sunday evening – 8:00 p.m.

Everett Rygard couldn't remember the last time he'd felt this overjoyed. Yes, he could. When he'd gotten married. When each of his three children had been born, and when he'd been promoted to chief. But this was different.

The break in the Powder murder case came Sunday afternoon with the discovery the facial cosmetics on the hand towel were a perfect match with the one-of-a-kind personalized anti-wrinkle and concealer creams found in Smitterly's hotel room.

Wearing only an inelegant hospital gown, Worthington Smitterly was arrested and charged with first-degree murder.

Wrapping up Miss Powder's homicide in less than thirty-six hours was fantastic, and the chief was ready to celebrate with a backyard barbecue. Originally planned for the officers and detectives who'd worked the Powder case, the picnic quickly grew to more than fifty people. The chief didn't panic. He simply ordered another forty pounds of prime tenderloin and porterhouse from the butcher across the street from headquarters, who happily accommodated the chief with a Sunday home delivery.

Lincoln and Pozy's arrival at the picnic caused a stir among those not already aware she was back in town, that she'd rejoined the *Eagle* staff, and had taken on the assignment of writing the Penny Powder murder story. Greeting old friends and acquaintances, Pozy caught sight of Holly LaFrance. The opportunity was too tempting to pass up, and in no time, she had the author deep in conversation about "poor old Worthy," his past, and his future.

Recognizing their common bond, the writers immediately trusted each other. Though one wrote fiction and the other reported facts, by collaborating in researching Miss Powder's background, interviewing acquaintances, delving into her web site, and reading the complete text of *Purity's Passion,* both would profit. Pozy would have sufficient material to fill an entire page in the *Eagle* to honor the librarian, and Holly was certain the ideas she'd pick up would add texture to the murder mystery already rattling around in her imagination.

They agreed learning when and how Miss Powder discovered Smitterly had plagiarized *Purity's Passion* was their number-one goal. The jackpot would be finding a diary.

The better Holly became acquainted with Geraldine Pozy, the more she realized Pozy, with her investigative skill and curiosity, was the perfect intellectual model for her character, I. Shaddow. Between Pozy's brains and Drinker's beauty and personality, Holly believed she was about to create the perfect female P.I. and could hardly wait to get started.

While Pozy and Holly became friends, Lincoln joined Brady who was watching every arrival at the barbecue waiting for Alice. When she appeared, looking spectacular in white shorts and low-cut peach-colored shirt, Brady was ready to make his move.

"Slow down, pal," Lincoln cautioned. "You mustn't crowd her, and I promise, Alice will keep. I have a strong hunch she'll make the next move. Be patient."

His advice was right, and when Brady found a place to sit down and eat, Alice carried her steak dinner to his table and asked, "Is there room for me?"

Later, he didn't remember what they talked about. He knew it had nothing to do with police work. He recalled saying he was going home on Monday, and she'd looked disappointed and asked, "Why?"

"I have a lot of deciding to do."

"You mean like whether you're going to take the chief's offer?"

He nodded.

Alice said softly, "I hope you do, Brady. It's been wonderful working and becoming acquainted with you. I'm going to miss you while you're gone."

She said no more and excused herself to join Holly.

Monday morning, June 26th

Brady was ready to board his bus for Detroit, where he'd transfer to another bus to Toledo. His good pal, Mary Canova, was going to pick him up there and drive him home to Lombardy, about seventy miles south.

Lincoln didn't like the arrangement and argued he would gladly drive Brady all the way home. "It sounds like a big inconvenience for Mary."

"Maybe so, but she offered before I asked. Mary and I are in the same boat, trying to decide whether to stay at LTC or move on."

"Won't Claudia be at a big loss if both of you leave?"

"The truth? She'll survive. She's landed the job she always wanted. At least for the time being. I'm certain she'll set her sights on the college president's job next. She has a handsome, successful husband, a good-looking son away in college, and a very bright fourteen-year-old daughter. She'll replace me in a heartbeat."

That said, Brady Kincaid boarded the bus and waved so long to his friend. He wondered if he'd sounded bitter. Perhaps. He reminded himself he'd had a couple of very good years with Lombardy Teachers College. But maybe it was time to move on.

While the bus rolled along, Brady weighed the pros and cons of changing jobs. He wondered how he'd feel becoming a citizen of Michigan after a lifetime of being a proud and loyal Buckeye from Ohio. Could he root for University of Michigan when they played Ohio State?

He'd miss the old house he'd rented in Lombardy, with its big sunny rooms. He'd miss Mary Canova, too, and realized, aside from Claudia, Mary was the only real friend he had in Lombardy. Whereas, he'd made at least a dozen good and close friends in Early. That had to count along with a huge increase in salary if he took the job there.

Closing the Powder homicide case so quickly had been a great satisfaction. Brady wondered if they'd ever find out how and when Miss Powder discovered Smitterly's plagiarism.

Another unanswered question was why Miss Powder maintained the *On the Chopping Block* column for so many years. Brady guessed she started it because she couldn't forgive the professor who broke her heart and stole her only novel. The widespread popularity of the *Chopping Block*, along with the prosperity it brought, must have been good reasons to continue to write the hundreds of stinging reviews of books she didn't like.

Miss Powder's indomitable, complex personality had to have caused the supreme egotist, Worthington Smitterly, to crack. Brady concluded it was unlikely Smitterly would ever explain exactly what finally spurred him to develop his detailed plan to brutally murder Penelope Powder at that particular time and place.

Brady reflected on the thrill of the hunt in a homicide case and the satisfaction of bagging the quarry. To him that was what being a homicide detective was all about. He wondered if he was really ready to get back in the game.

Then there was Alice Drinker to consider. They'd both been around the block more than once. Would traveling that bumpy road together be the exciting trip he imagined?

Watching the towns and cities fly by as his bus neared Detroit, Brady decided he'd see how he felt tomorrow after a long night's sleep.